# The Marks You Made

## Amy Fillion

*For Heather and Kristen*

# Also by Amy Fillion

## Adult books

Broken and Breaking Free

Little Things

Secrets of Spaulding Lane: Nancy

Secrets of Spaulding Lane: Marni

Secrets of Spaulding Lane: Rose

Grace and Ally

Surprise Me (Grace and Ally book 2)

One Day (Grace and Ally book 3)

## Children's Books

The Room of Reveries Series:

Fairville

FenneGig

Esmerelda and the Courageous Knight

Wonderwell

SkyTopia

The Ancient Curse

A Magical Farewell

# Prologue

I t was a Thursday evening in early November when the police came for her son.

Her Ring alarm system chimed on her phone, indicating that there was a presence in her driveway. She paid it no mind; it was probably the mail carrier or a delivery truck. Then, after the lapse of a few moments, another chime sounded, followed almost immediately by the ringing of the doorbell.

She pulled her hands from the sudsy water of the kitchen sink and wiped them on a towel; she'd return to the dishes after she learned who had unexpectedly shown up at her house.

She smoothed her hands down her T-shirt, wiped the last suds and lingering water droplets from her hands, turned the knob, and opened the solid wooden door. A cool fall breeze swept into the house.

And there, looking directly at her, were two local officers, imposing in their uniforms and stoic, inscrutable expressions.

1

She tilted her head and creased her brows. "Can I help you?"

"Are you the parent or guardian of Jace Weatherbee?" It was a man that spoke, tall and thin. He didn't look much older than her sixteen-year-old son, his face still reminiscent of an adolescent's with its rounded contours and wide eyes.

"I am." Her voice belied her confusion. Why were two officers on her doorstep, and how did they know Jace? "I'm Brooke, Jace's mom. But what—"

"There's been a formal complaint made against your son. We need to talk to him."

"A formal… a formal complaint? I don't understand." Her fingers clutched the edge of the thick front door, bracing legs that suddenly felt heavy and weak. "Who would complain? Why?" And then, lacking a more succinct response, she repeated, "I don't understand."

"There are allegations against your son," the officer continued. The fact that he had made no introduction upon arrival eluded her, nor had she thought of checking either his badge or the small tag on to the chest of his uniform that supplied that information for her. She couldn't think and lacked the ability to comprehend what was transpiring right in front of her.

And then the officer said a word that sent her crashing, a statement that altered the course of both her and her son's lives from that very moment onward, though she didn't yet know how severe that alteration would be.

"Your son has been accused of rape." No sugarcoating, no softening of the eyes to ease any discomfort she might have felt at the sound of the abhorrent word from the lips of the young officer.

"Wh—what?" She pressed her eyelids together and embraced the blackness that enveloped her. When she opened them, it was to the still-stoic face of the officer before her. His partner stood erect at his side, hands behind his back, feet splayed.

"Rape," he repeated. "Your son has been accused of rape. And we need to speak with him."

"Rape?" Her voice was a whisper, her vision blurry.

A few moments passed, and then she felt it. A hand on her shoulder, a presence behind her.

"Mom?" It was the voice of her son, her Jace. "What's goin' on?"

"Are you Jace Weatherbee?" the officer asked.

"Yeah."

"We need to talk to you. Down at the station. Mrs. Weatherbee, you'll take him. Can't talk to him without you."

Her head was swimming, dizzy, dizzy. She took a step back then two. Jace grabbed her under her shoulders, helped to guide her to the bottom stair, where she sat and spread her palm on the wall. Her fingers slid, down, down. Her arm was limp, and she lost control of it, her hand smacking the stair next to her thigh.

"I don't get it," Jace said.

She could hear her son, but even though he stood right in front of her, she couldn't see him. Her vision swam; it was all she could do to sit upright.

"Why do you want to talk to me?"

"There's been an accusation made against you."

"What?"

She heard the confusion behind her son's voice, deep, where, only a few years ago, it had still been the high-pitched cadence of her little boy.

"You've been accused of rape, and we want to talk to you," the officer announced, a bit more forcefully.

Rape. Again, there was that detestable word.

"What?" Jace's voice rose. "That's bullshit!"

"Jace." She meant to admonish him; how could he use such language in front of the officers, especially in light of the fact that he had just been accused of assaulting someone? Surely, these men already had their preconceived notions about her son; why make them worse, help those notions to further settle in? But instead of a stern voice, her son's name came out weakly through her lips. She looked up. She could see him now: narrow face, prominent nose. His blond hair hung over one blue eye. His high cheekbones were tinged with red, and his lips were pursed. Clearly, he was furious.

"Who the hell said I raped them?"

"We'll talk down at the station," the officer replied.

"No," Jace said, his voice firm. He exuded strength, a protective mechanism that had arisen after his father left. He hadn't taken his father's betrayal well—at the time, Jace hadn't yet turned fourteen, after all—but he had packed up the pieces of their shattered familial existence and moved forward.

Her boy. She was supposed to protect him, to shelter him from such heartache, but she had failed so miserably.

And now this.

How had it come to *this*?

"I want to know who the hell said I raped them." Jace had lowered his voice. He was seething. She could see the clenched fist at his thigh, his rigid posture.

"We'll tell you at the station."

"I want to know now. If you want my mom to take me to talk to you, I want to know."

Brooke watched as the officer looked at Jace, his brows

furrowed, the lone indication of emotion. What was he thinking?

Eventually, he released the slightest of sighs. And then a name, spoken slowly, the officer still scrutinizing her son with narrowed eyes. "Madison Crawford."

Jace made no reply, but she could see her son was clearly confused, hurt. The angst this name elicited was evident on his face.

"Di—Did you just say 'Madison Crawford'?" Brooke asked.

The officer nodded.

Brooke grasped at her pants, scrunching them in her fists. She clenched her jaw and closed her eyes. Nausea roiled, a sudden explosion within. Her heart beat, *thump, thump.* She could hear it in her ears, feel it in her chest.

And then she leaped from the bottom stair and passed her son in a flurry to the bathroom. She held her palm over her mouth as she used her free hand to lift the toilet seat. She fell to her knees on the hard tile floor, leaned over the bowl, heaved, and vomited, her body shaking, her mind reeling.

Madison Crawford.

The daughter of her best friend.

# Chapter 1

## *Six years earlier*

"Happy birthday, Jace!"

It was early October, and the family was in the large backyard of their new home in a new town in a new state. Jace's father had acquired a job that necessitated this move, and in an effort to support her husband's happiness —he had been miserable in his last position, after all— Brooke gave her notice at the hospital at which she worked and applied for a nursing position in southern New Hampshire. She had been hired and would start work on Monday. Boxes lined the halls and were piled throughout rooms, and the family was living out of suitcases. They had moved into this new home just yesterday. But they needed the money, so she had agreed to start work as soon as possible. Forget finding new doctors, dentists, grocery stores, and the like— she'd have to make calls when she had a free moment and then get all their personal information transferred over, which she knew might be time-consuming.

But today was Saturday and her son's tenth birthday.

She'd devote this day to her family. Offices weren't open, and although they desperately needed to unpack those plentiful boxes and sort through their belongings, she'd make the time later. Surely, a free block would present itself.

"How does it feel to be in the double digits now?"

Jace smiled up at his mother, his lips spread wide, his crooked teeth poking out from behind. He'd need braces for sure. The dentist in their old town had said as much. But not now, thankfully.

"Fine," Jace replied.

"Just fine?" She ruffled his hair, still bleached blond from the strong summer sun. If the past was any indicator, his hair would darken a bit before too long, but for now, she'd bask in the sight of hair that seemed to glow, a halo around her young son's head. She loved it when it was this light.

Jace was still smiling, and as Brooke looked at his raised cheekbones, she surmised they'd aid a handsome visage when he was older. Even at ten years old, she could tell. She was looking into the future, she knew. She should embrace this time she had with her son now, hold on to the little boy that sat before her, but she could see him, this teenage son of hers. She could sense the young man he'd become. And it filled her with pride.

"Yep."

"What's this 'yep'?" Brooke asked. "Yep," she repeated playfully.

Jace laughed.

"Big deal, bud," her husband said. "Ten."

"Okay," Jace replied with a shrug of his shoulders.

"Your dad's right," Brooke said. "You'll never be in the single digits again. That's in the past. You're getting to be so big now. It is kind of a huge deal. Definitely something to celebrate."

"Okay," Jace repeated.

Brooke smiled. "Okay" seemed to be the word Jace used for everything these days. How are you feeling? Okay. How did you sleep? Okay. Don't you think you should eat more healthy foods? Okay. Can I have a hug? Okay.

"Sorry we couldn't celebrate in a bigger way," Brooke told her son. "It would have been so nice to have a party with friends, wouldn't it? We should have had a party before we moved, but we were just so busy, Jace, packing and sorting through things and buying this house and selling our old one. Phew. It's a lot."

"Okay," Jace said.

Brooke looked at her son. The movers had placed their outdoor table and chairs on the deck, and that was where they sat now, the autumn day, thankfully, gorgeous. Their backyard was surrounded by trees, and the vibrancy of the leaves here in New Hampshire at this time of the year was breathtaking. She felt blessed to have found this home. And in researching school systems, she'd found that this town appeared to place emphasis on the education of its children. She desperately hoped her son would have an easy transition to this new school, especially as he'd be starting late; his classmates had begun their year together at the end of August. He'd be the new kid in school. Would he be readily accepted? Would he make new friends? Or would he be labeled the outsider, sit alone at the lunch table, sit on a swing with his chin on his chest at recess, with no one to play with? She didn't want to think about that scenario.

"I hope we're not interrupting anything."

Hearing the chipper voice behind her, Brooke turned.

9

Walking toward her were a man, a woman, and two children—a boy and a younger girl.

"Oh," Brooke said, a bit startled at their presence. "There's no interruption."

"Good to hear." The woman was beaming. The man beside her wore a smile, though it was minute in comparison to the woman's. The boy was shuffling his feet along the cobbled walkway, clearly wanting to be anywhere but at the Weatherbees' house, and the little girl walked with one arm laced beneath the woman's.

The woman and girl approached the table first, the man arriving moments later, while the boy lingered behind, his gaze set on the ground.

"We're your neighbors," the woman said by way of introduction. "Well, not technically, I guess. But we live down the street, close enough to walk on over. And it's such a beautiful day, isn't it? I mean, to walk over, that is. Actually, it's a beautiful day even if you're not walking. I mean—"

The man cleared his throat, glancing under his lashes at the woman beside him.

"Yeah, yeah, I get it," the woman said to the man before looking back at Brooke. "Gus is always telling me that I talk too much. 'Get to the point,' he says. Actually, I don't think I talk too much. I think I have so much more to say, and you'd be surprised at how much I shut my mouth when I really don't want to. I kind of force myself to, though." Her smile hadn't faltered the entire time she was speaking, and as the woman extended her hand toward Brooke, Brooke found that a smile had broken out on her own face as well.

"I'm Jenny Crawford. This guy right here"—she thrust

her unoccupied thumb to the side as her extended hand found Brooke's, her fingers limp—"is my husband, Gus, but I guess you already guessed that. This peanut here is our daughter, Madison—she goes by Maddy—and Mr. Gloom over there is our son, Michael, who's upset because we won't let him go to his friend's house today. I told him we'd already made plans as a family, but that's a teenager for you, I suppose. Kids, why don't you say hello to Mr. and Mrs.—oh, I don't even know your name. I'm sorry!"

Brooke's eyes had gone wide, but her smile remained. Brooke wasn't much of a talker herself, but she prided herself on the fact that she was a good listener. She surmised, even in the few minutes that Jenny had stood in her backyard, that she and this neighbor of hers might have an easy time striking up a friendship, and for that, she was truly thankful, as she didn't yet know anyone in this new town of hers that she was now obliged to call home. And for Jenny and Gus to gather up their children, walk over to Brooke's house, and introduce themselves—surely, that spoke of their natural cordiality.

"I'm Brooke Weatherbee. This is Dan. And this is our son, Jace."

Jenny took a step back and nudged her son.

"Hi," Michael grumbled.

Jenny flung her hand in the air dismissively and rolled her eyes in response to her son's lack of civility.

"Nice to meet you." Maddy unlaced her arm from her mother's and extended her hand toward Brooke first, who shook it, then to Brooke's husband, who was looking at the petite girl with an amused expression. Maddy smiled coyly at Jace, which caused Brooke's brows to raise in a bit of beguiled surprise.

"How old are you, Maddy?" Brooke asked the little girl. If she had had to guess, she'd have deduced perhaps eight.

"Nine," Maddy readily responded.

"Ah, I see," Brooke said, concluding that Madison most certainly was not naturally shy or inhibited. She looked at the little girl more closely then, at her wide gray-blue eyes and at long lashes that Brooke herself lacked but would have loved to possess. Maddy's hair flowed thickly down to the middle of her back. Dark brown, the same dark brown, Brooke noticed now, as her brother's, though strands of a lighter shade were interwoven throughout Maddy's tresses. Brooke wondered if, like Jace's, Madison's hair had been lightened by the summer sun and if, now that October had arrived, she would lose those eye-catching highlights. She was slight of stature, which was why Brooke had surmised her to be a year younger than she actually was.

"Jace's birthday is today, and he's ten years old." Brooke lifted her chin toward her son across the table. She turned back to the little girl. "When is your birthday?"

"April," Madison replied.

"I think that means that you and Jace are in the same year in school. Is that right? If Jace had been born just a week earlier, he'd be in the next grade up. I think he might be one of the oldest kids in your class."

Madison shrugged her narrow shoulders.

"What grade are you in?" Jenny asked Jace.

"Fourth."

"Oh, look at that, Maddy," Jenny said. "You're in the same grade as Jace. Isn't that wonderful?"

Maddy merely smiled up at her mother then looked at Jace.

"Who's your teacher, Jace?" Jenny asked.

"Mrs. Blackthorn."

"Oh," Jenny replied. "That's not who Maddy has. What a bummer. But you're still in the same grade. That's just serendipitous," Jenny said. "Isn't that a great word, 'serendipitous'? We find out we have new neighbors and they have a son just your age, Maddy. Well, almost your age, but in the same grade, anyway. You have a new friend, Maddy, isn't that so? You'll have to introduce Jace to everyone at school, won't you? Make him feel welcome. I just—"

Gus interjected, his voice raised in an attempt to drown out his wife's. "The women are dominating the conversation," he said to Brooke's husband. "I'm Gus Crawford. Number 19 up the road."

Brooke watched as her husband rose from his chair and offered Gus his hand. "Dan Weatherbee," he said. "Good to meet you." She looked back at Jenny but had one ear tuned to her husband's conversation while Jenny continued to speak.

"And you. What brings you to town?" Gus Crawford asked.

"New job," Dan replied. "Moved up from Maryland. Don't know the area at all, but happy to be here. Thanks for stopping by."

"Not a problem," Dan said. "Got a poker club. We meet once a week, alternate houses. You should join us."

"Haven't played poker in a while," Dan replied, "but I bet it'll come back to me. When are you meeting next?"

"Monday," Gus said. "Seven o'clock. Usually meet on Mondays. Seemed to be the night most guys could get together. It's at my house this week. Would love to have you."

"Very nice of you, Gus," Dan remarked. "I'll be there."

"I'm sorry, Jenny, hold on just a moment," Brooke said.

"Dan, we both start work on Monday, and Jace will start at his new school. Don't you think it would be a good idea for us all to be home Monday evening? That way, we can enjoy dinner together and talk about our days."

Dan lifted one shoulder. "Suppose," he said. "But then again, we've got all week for family dinners."

"Not a problem," Gus chimed in. "You can always join us next week instead."

Dan pursed his lips then gave a slight shake of his head. "Think I'll be there on Monday. Brooke, we'll get pizzas on Tuesday, make up for my absence."

"Oh," Jenny interposed, flinging her hands exuberantly into the air. "There's the best pizza place in town. And they deliver. Brooke, what's your phone number? I'll save it and text you the information. Plus, we're neighbors now, we'll need each other's numbers, right? And oh, have you thought about joining the PTA? I'm on the PTA for the elementary school, have been since Michael started there. And now I've joined the PTA for the high school, too, since that's where he's at. It's a great group of parents, really. We have meetings once a month, but we keep in touch a lot even when we're not meeting. There are so many responsibilities, you know? We do fundraisers throughout the year and different fun events for the kids. The PTA is so important. I don't think a whole lot of people really know that. They don't know how much we do. But it's such a good way of giving back to the school, right? To help them and to help the teachers. What do you say?"

Amused, Brooke thought it surprising that Jenny had paused for Brooke to reciprocate with words of her own. "I…" She shook her head. "Oh, I don't really know about that," she said. "I'm not much of a PTA person, honestly. I'm willing to help the school out, but… no. I don't think the PTA is for me, especially because I work full-time. I'd like to be home for Jace."

"Oh, you'll be home," Jenny assured her. "You don't have to take on a whole lot, you know? Just as much as you'd like. And we can do things together. Wouldn't that be wonderful?"

"I guess…" Brooke's voice trailed off, unsure how to effectively let Jenny down when the two women had only just met.

Jenny's expression brightened. "I'll convince you," she said. "Just you wait and see."

"Leave the woman alone, Jenny," Gus said, though his voice was playful. "They just moved here. Let her breathe."

Jenny swatted her husband's arm. "I am letting her breathe," she insisted. "I'm just being neighborly, you know. This is what neighbors do. They say hello. They introduce themselves. And they invite their new neighbors to be a part of the community. See? I'm being neighborly." She grinned at her husband with an upturned corner of her lips.

"Jace, would you like to come over for a playdate tomorrow? You and Maddy can get to know each other more. Maybe I can invite a few more kids to the house so you can get to know them too. That is, if it's okay with your parents."

Brooke looked at her son, searched his face for any sign of hesitancy. When she found none, she asked, "Would you like to go to the Crawfords' house tomorrow?" She had been hoping for a family day before the start of school, but she supposed it would be beneficial for her son to meet some of the children that lived in this new town of theirs. Perhaps one of those children would be in the classroom he had been assigned to.

"Okay," Jace said. There was that word again. But

Brooke took it as affirmation that her son did, in fact, want to attend this outing at the Crawfords' house.

"That's settled, then," Jenny said, clasping her hands in front of her chest. "It's a date! How about noon? I'll give the kids some lunch. I'm sure others will be able to join us, even on such short notice. I can walk down with Maddy and pick Jace up. Does that work?"

"I can walk him to your house," Brooke suggested.

"No, that's okay," Jenny said. "I can't sit still, so the walk will do this body good."

"She's not kidding there," Gus said. "About not sitting still. She's always on the move. Drives me nuts sometimes, but she gets stuff done."

"Well, all right, then," Brooke agreed. "I'll have Jace ready before twelve o'clock. Thank you so much for the invitation. And thank you for coming over today."

"Oh, no problem," Jenny said. "I was so happy to see that we had new neighbors. The house wasn't on the market for long, you must have snagged it up pretty quickly. It is a really nice house, though, isn't that right? I would have snagged it up, too, if I didn't already have the house we have now. I mean—"

"Jenny," Gus said, "let's leave the Weatherbees alone. They probably want to go about their Saturday. They did say it was Jace's birthday. And... look at the cupcakes. I think we interrupted."

"Oh," Jenny said. "I suppose we did. Well... we'll see you tomorrow, anyway. So good to meet you all!"

"Nice to meet you as well. Thank you for stopping by. It was very kind of you to welcome us to the neighborhood," Brooke said.

"I'm so glad you're here, Brooke. And Gus and Jace. See you tomorrow!" She clasped Maddy's hand, turned on a heel, and the Crawford family walked down the cobble-stone walkway and out of view.

"I guess we just met some new neighbors," Dan said with a deep chuckle.

Brooke laughed. "Yes," she agreed. "I suppose we have."

# Chapter 2

## *Six Years Earlier*

Piper was going to Maddy's house today, and she was thrilled. She loved Maddy's house. Loved it! Maddy's mom always made them snacks and gave them drinks that she claimed were healthy but that tasted so, so good. Drinks and snacks that Piper's mom never made, so it was always special for Piper. And she loved Maddy. She and Maddy had been friends since kindergarten, so a long time now. In fact, Maddy was her best friend. She hoped they'd be best friends forever. She had even begged her mom to buy her a charm bracelet set. She wanted to give one of the bracelets to Maddy to prove how much she loved her. Each bracelet held half of a heart, and when those hearts fit together, they made a whole.

Just like how she felt when she was with Maddy: whole.

Her mom hadn't bought the set, but that was okay, Piper supposed. Maddy was still her best friend, even if they didn't have matching bracelets.

Maddy wasn't in her class this year, so Piper had to try her best to see her friend whenever she could. They sat together at lunch and played together at recess. And Maddy had Piper over to her house a lot, thank goodness. Piper's mom allowed Maddy to come to her house, too, but Maddy didn't usually want to come to Piper's house, instead preferring that Piper go to hers. Piper didn't mind, and she didn't think much about it, really. She was just happy to be with her friend.

Piper was a lot shyer than Maddy. Maddy was outgoing and had a lot of friends. If Maddy hadn't been Piper's best friend and Piper Maddy's, then Piper might have been seriously jealous of the other girls Maddy hung out with. Piper didn't have many other friends herself, but that was okay. She was happy with Maddy. She didn't need many other friends.

Apparently, there was a new boy on Maddy's street, and he was going to be at the playdate today. Piper didn't much enjoy the company of boys, but that was okay too. She understood that Maddy and her mom were trying to help this new boy, trying to get him to meet others, and she thought this was mighty good of them. Maybe he wouldn't be super annoying like so many boys in her class. Maybe he'd be cool.

Princess was going to be there too. Yes, another girl she and Maddy hung out with was named Princess. No joke. Piper's mom said that Princess's mom was batshit crazy— those were the words she used. Her mom didn't often hold much back, even to Piper, who was only nine years old. She pretty much said what was on her mind, so Piper had heard a whole bunch of stuff about people that she knew and even people that she didn't know, especially people that her mom worked with at the restaurant, where she was a waitress. She said a lot of them were batshit crazy too. Piper didn't know; she had never met them. Plus she didn't entirely know what it meant to be batshit crazy. Was *she* batshit crazy? She didn't think so. Anyway, her mom would have told her, right? What she did know was that her mom's face scrunched up when she said those words, so batshit crazy probably wasn't something good to be.

By the time her mom dropped her off at Maddy's house, the boy was already there. Princess wasn't, though. Piper figured she'd show up soon. If her mom remembered.

"Hi, Pipes!" Maddy exclaimed when Piper walked through the large front door and into the foyer of her friend's spacious home, so much bigger than Piper's own. She beamed as Maddy threw her arms around her neck and gave her a great big hug.

"Hi, Maddy," Piper said.

"I'm glad you came over. Mom made cookies. Can you smell them?"

"Yeah," Piper said. "It smells like chocolate chip."

Maddy smiled. "That's because they are chocolate chip. And she made these weird little things, kind of like mini sandwiches, which, yuck—but these ones have cream cheese on them. Isn't that cool? Cream cheese on a sand-wich? Mom said the cream cheese was mixed with some sort of spice or something, but whatever. I don't care. They look pretty good, though. But chocolate chip cookies? Yay!" She swept her long hair off her shoulder and flicked it onto her back.

"Your mom is always so cool," Piper remarked.

"Yeah, I guess."

And then she saw him, the boy who had just moved in down the street from Maddy. He was tall. Like really tall for a ten-year-old. And he *was* ten, right? Hadn't Maddy said that over the phone last night when she invited Piper over? Maddy had her own phone. She was so lucky. Piper's mom was constantly telling Piper that there was no way a nine-year-old girl needed a phone, and nothing could be so important that it couldn't be said or done by using the phone that her mother owned. Piper disagreed. If Maddy had a phone, why couldn't she?

Maddy must have heard him approach, because she turned to look behind her. She had to look up in order to see the boy's face. It almost made Piper want to laugh, though she didn't know why she found it so funny.

"This is Jace," Maddy said, turning back to Piper. "He moved in down the street. He's the boy I was telling you about."

Jace furrowed his brow at Maddy's back but then looked at Piper and said hello.

"Hi," Piper replied.

"So, want to go to my room?" Maddy suggested.

"Sure," Piper agreed. She took a step forward and followed Maddy up the winding staircase. Halfway to the second landing, she turned to look back. She hadn't heard Jace following them. When she looked at the main-floor landing, she saw him standing at the bottom, looking her way. "You coming?" she asked.

Jace didn't reply, but Piper watched his face transform with a small smile as Maddy rushed down the steps, grabbed his hand, and yanked him forward. "Come on, silly," she said.

In Maddy's room, Maddy, Piper, and Jace made themselves comfortable on the queen-sized bed, and then Maddy touched the screen of her phone, tapped with her fingers, and before long, music began to play. Piper recognized the song; she and Maddy listened to it often.

"Know this one?" Maddy asked Jace.

"Yeah," he replied.

21

Maddy narrowed her brow and then said, "Really?"

"Yeah," Jace confirmed. "I listen to it sometimes."

"Oh yeah?"

"Yeah."

Maddy paused, looked at Jace through squinted eyes, then leaned back against her pillow. She crossed her arms and smiled. "Cool," she said. "You might be all right, Jace Weatherbee."

Jace sniggered in response.

Maddy frowned. "What was that for?"

"I might be all right?" Jace asked, his voice lined with apathy as if he didn't care one lick what Madison Crawford thought.

Maddy scrutinized Jace once again. Eventually, she uncrossed her arms, leaned forward, and laughed. She extended a fist to Jace. "I like you," she said decisively.

This time, it was Jace's turn to laugh. He fisted his fingers and bumped Maddy's knuckles with his own. "I think I like you too," he said. He swiped a tendril of blond hair from his eye.

As Piper watched the exchange, a new feeling overcame her, and she wasn't sure what to make of it. She hadn't really felt this way before, but the look Maddy gave Jace and the look Jace gave back to Maddy...

"Hey, guys," Piper said, breaking up the pair. When both Maddy and Jace glanced her way, Piper asked Jace, "What teacher did you get?"

"Mrs. Blackthorn," Jace replied.

"Oh, wow," Piper said. "That's who I have. Maddy doesn't have her, though. She has someone else. We're not in the same class."

"Yeah," Jace said. "I know."

"Oh," Piper said a bit forlornly. She would have liked to

impart some news to this new boy. "But you'll like Mrs. Blackthorn," Piper continued. "She's really great."

"Yeah?" Jace asked.

"Yeah," Piper confirmed.

"Jace," Maddy said, "you should sit with us at lunch. There are a couple of other boys, too, so you don't have to worry about being the only boy, you know."

"That wouldn't worry me."

"Well, anyway…" Maddy shrugged a shoulder. "I think you'll really like everyone."

"Okay," Jace said.

The doorbell chimed, interrupting their conversation.

"Oh!" Maddy exclaimed, bouncing onto her knees and tumbling awkwardly to the floor, which set her into a fit of giggles. "That's Princess. Come on, you guys!"

Piper and Jace followed Maddy out of the bedroom and down the stairs, where Maddy proceeded to open the large front door wide and usher her friend into the house. Piper smiled when she caught sight of Princess. Although nobody was as cool as Maddy in Piper's book, Princess came in a close second. Piper liked her very much, and the three girls made quite the team, she thought. Princess was smiling brightly as she stepped over the threshold and into the foyer, her round cheeks lifted, creasing the skin around her dark-brown eyes. She tucked a tendril of hair, so dark that it almost appeared black, behind an ear. Piper loved Princesses' hair. It wasn't long like Maddy's, only chin length, but it was super straight and really shiny. Sometimes, when Piper wasn't feeling like it was too weird, she'd ask her friend if she could run her fingers down her hair. That was what that shine did: made her want to touch it. Thank goodness, this seemed to amuse Princess instead of making her think Piper was nuts.

"You're Jace," Princess said as she caught sight of the new boy behind Maddy and Piper. That was another thing about Princess: like Maddy and unlike Piper, she wasn't shy in the least. She often said what she was thinking, but she wasn't unkind. Just blunt.

"Yeah." Piper turned her head at the sound of Jace's voice and saw him smirking, one tendril of bright-blond hair obstructing part of an eye.

"You'll like it here," Princess offered. "Are you doing any clubs or sports?" Another thing about Princess: she cut right to the chase.

Jace shrugged. "Don't know," he said. "Just moved here yesterday. I don't know what clubs or sports there are."

"Oh," Princess said, moving farther into the hallway. "They've got some." She held up a hand and counted them off on her fingers, one by one. "It's fall, so track, soccer, football for sports. Not a lot for sports, I guess. The elementary school sucks like that, and you don't even do sports there. You have to join a club through the town. The middle school doesn't have a lot, either. But there are tons more in high school. And you can do art club at school right now if you're into that. There's a book club, but no thank you." Princess rolled her eyes.

This was one area where she and Piper differed. Piper really loved to read, though her friends didn't know how much. Piper kept this information to herself, mostly because of how much Princess said she didn't like to read, and because Piper knew that Maddy didn't really like to read, either. She felt a little embarrassed about this particular passion of hers.

"I played soccer before I left my old school," Jace said. "And I ran track. I like to run cross country."

Princess eyed Jace. "Then do it here. I bet you can sign up late because you're new."

"Yeah," Maddy chimed in.

Piper wasn't surprised. She knew that her best friend often felt left out if she couldn't interject herself into conversations. Piper preferred to remain on the outskirts, listening.

"They'll let you run. Running is kind of boring, though, isn't it?" Maddy continued.

"I don't think so," Jace remarked. "Me and my friends did it together. And I'm good."

Princess scrutinized Jace with her hands on her hips. "Are you?"

"Yeah."

"That's really cool," Maddy said. "Running isn't something a lot of kids do, though. Most boys like football here."

"I'm not most boys," Jace said.

Piper found she was smiling. She was liking this new boy more and more.

"No..." Maddy's voice trailed off as she looked at Jace. And then she said, "I guess you're not."

"Hey, kids!" Maddy's mom called from the kitchen. "Come in here. I've got a little surprise."

"Come on!" Maddy grabbed Piper's arm, and with the fingers of her free hand, she snagged Princess's shirt. She tugged her friends forward. Once she'd passed Jace, she looked back and repeated, "Come on!"

The friends approached the sizeable kitchen, open to both the dining area and the living room. On the granite countertop sat a crystal cake stand, and on top of the stand rested a circular chocolate-frosted cake with ten sparkling candles.

Piper halted and immediately looked over at Jace. His

surprise was clear in his slightly abashed smile and the pink tinge to his sun-kissed cheeks.

Piper grinned. She loved this about Maddy's mom, just loved it. Yeah, Piper's mom was pretty cool in her own right, but she never did anything like Maddy's mom did. Whenever Piper was over at Maddy's house—and it was often—Jenny made treats: cookies, pastries, muffins, you name it. And she'd make platters filled with various fruits for the girls to partake of. And she always, always kept tubes of squeezable yogurt in the freezer because she knew these were Piper's favorite. Her own mother didn't bake, like, ever. If she volunteered to bring something to a bake sale at school or to provide a snack for one of Piper's classroom parties, she always stopped at the supermarket. Piper knew her mom was super busy, and she understood this, but just once, it would have been nice if her mother made a home-made treat like Maddy's mom did.

Gosh, Jenny Crawford was just so cool!

"Happy birthday, Jace!" Jenny announced enthusiastically. "I hope you like chocolate. It's chocolate cake with chocolate frosting. I didn't know what you liked because we just met each other, but I said to myself, I said, 'Jenny, what kid doesn't like chocolate?' you know? Maddy loves chocolate, so I thought I was pretty safe with the choice. I thought this would be a nice little surprise to further welcome you to the neighborhood. Happy tenth, Jace!"

"Thank you, Mrs. Crawford."

"None of this 'Mrs. Crawford.' You can call me Jenny. All the kids do."

"Okay," Jace said.

Piper wondered if he would. It had taken Piper a little while to get used to the idea herself back when she had first started coming over to Maddy's. Piper's mom always said it was rude to call an adult by their first name, that Piper should always use Mrs. or Mr. as a mark of respect. But it had been what Jenny wanted, so Piper obliged. And now she didn't give it a second thought.

"Mom," Maddy demanded with a smirk, "why didn't I smell you baking cake? I thought you just made cookies."

"I did make cookies," her mother replied. "I know you love your chocolate chip. Those can be for later, or... whenever. I made the cake when you were in bed last night."

"You're sneaky," Maddy said.

Her mother winked. "I can be," she remarked. And then, turning to Jace, she said, "Well, these candles won't blow themselves out. They're dripping! Come here, Jace, and we'll sing to you."

"Oh," Jace said. "You don't have to sing to me."

"Nonsense." Jenny flung a hand in the air. "It's your birthday. Well, yesterday was your birthday, but"—she smiled widely—"it wouldn't be the same without singing to you. We won't embarrass you, will we?"

Jace shook his head.

"Well, then. Come on over here, birthday boy."

Jace stepped forward, and Jenny began to sing, "Happy birthday to you..."

Piper chimed in once she heard both Maddy and Princess's voices ring out, theirs loud and clear, hers more restrained.

"Make a wish!" Jenny instructed, looking directly at Jace with an enormous grin.

Jace took a deep breath in, closed his eyes, and—leaning over the counter—circled his lips and blew at the flames. Each one flickered and, in just an instant, was extinguished, black smoke wafting in spirals toward the ceiling.

Jenny clapped exuberantly, while Princess clapped with

a bit less enthusiasm and Maddy stood with her hands on her hips but a smile on her face. Piper laced her fingers behind her back and watched as Jenny cut into the cake with a large silver-bladed knife. "A huge slice for the birthday boy," she announced, plonking a giant slab onto a small white plate. She stuck a fork into it and handed it off to Jace.

"Thanks, Mrs. Cr—ah, Jenny."

"You are so very welcome. I like to bake. You'll learn that about me in time if you come over more often, and"— she looked at her daughter with a smile—"I think you will be."

"Okay," Jace said, clutching his plate close to his chest.

"You can take that right over to the table," Jenny instructed.

While Jace made his way to the glass-plated dining table—Maddy's house just seemed to sparkle, from the chandelier in the foyer to the off-white walls, large windows surrounded by white wooden molding, light-colored tiled kitchen floor, off-white-and-gray bathroom cabinetry, and light-gray living room furniture—Jenny continued to cut into the cake and offer a slice to each girl. Piper happily and perhaps a bit greedily accepted hers, her mouth watering slightly at the sight of the moist chocolate sponginess with its brown frosting center and swirling sugary border. She had devoured Maddy's mom's cakes before and remembered just how incredible they had tasted on her tongue. Cake *and* cookies? What a playdate!

She made her way to the table and sat beside Jace, who had already begun to eat his cake, a small smattering of frosting lining the corner of his mouth as he chewed.

"Good, isn't it?" Piper asked.

Jace turned to look at her and nodded, his brows raised. He was clearly enjoying his treat.

"Jenny's the best baker," Piper announced.

"That's right," Maddy said, as she plonked down in a chair, scooted herself in, and forked up a piece of cake. "My mom's the best."

"Mmm-mmm," Princess said, lips shut tight, as she chewed her first bite.

Maddy sat up straighter with pride as she brought her forkful to her lips.

The friends continued to eat, and just as Piper was scraping the last bits of cake and frosting from her plate with the edge of her fork, Mr. Crawford entered the room. "Where've you been, Daddy?" Maddy asked. While Maddy called Jenny Mom, it was always Daddy when she addressed her father, and Piper noticed, too, that Maddy's voice often rose an octave when she spoke to him.

Mr. Crawford ruffled his daughter's hair. "I told you, I have to work."

"Oh, yeah," Maddy said, a slight pout on her lips. "I forgot. But... it's the weekend."

"Work doesn't wait," Mr. Crawford replied. "Even on the weekends."

"Your father works too much," Jenny told her daughter. She sidled up next to her husband and placed her head on his shoulder momentarily before lifting it off and looking him in the eye. "But that's one of the reasons we love him so much, isn't it? He's such a hard worker."

"I guess," Maddy said, though the tone of her voice didn't convince Piper one bit that she was being truthful.

"Cake, huh?" Mr. Crawford asked as he looked down at his daughter's plate, her slice half finished.

"Yep," Maddy confirmed. "Mom made it for Jace."

"Ah, yes," Mr. Crawford said, turning his gaze to their new guest. "Your birthday was yesterday, wasn't it, young man?

"Yes," Jace said.

"Leave it to Jenny," Mr. Crawford said. "Always thinking of other people."

Jenny grinned and looked appreciatively at her husband.

"I'm done," Maddy announced a few minutes later. She pushed her chair back, left her plate on the table, and addressed her friends. "Want to go back to my room?"

"How about you go outside?" Mr. Crawford suggested. "Beautiful day out there. Fresh air will do you kids some good."

"No, Daddy," Maddy said. "We want to go to my room." She turned to look first at Princess, then at Jace, and, lastly, at Piper, her gaze lingering. "Right, guys?"

Piper nodded, Jace made no move to confirm his wishes one way or the other, and Princess verbally responded with a "Sure do."

"Well, all right, then," Mr. Crawford said. "Don't understand you kids these days, wanting to stay inside when you've got the whole wide world at your fingertips."

"Oh, leave them alone, Gus," Jenny said playfully. "Maddy, go on up. You all have fun, now. I'll bring up more snacks in a bit. We've got the finger sandwiches—they taste fantastic if I do say so myself—and the cookies."

"Thanks, Mom," Maddy said. She made for the hallway, raised her hand, and called, "Bye, Daddy."

Piper immediately followed.

Time passed quickly in Maddy's bedroom. All four friends sat on her queen-sized bed. Maddy's bed always made Piper jealous. Although Piper fit on her own bed just fine, hers was a twin and paled in comparison to Maddy's. Piper often had to admit most things did. She didn't mind: Maddy never rubbed it in her face, never made her feel bad about anything. Any feelings elicited from Maddy's worldly possessions were Piper's own doing, perhaps stemming from her sense of inferiority.

The friends chatted and laughed. They snacked and drank an orange-hued juice. Jace seemed to fit into their circle rather well. Piper noticed that he didn't appear to be uncomfortable at all. He added to their conversation and even made the girls giggle quite a bit. Maddy's brother Michael, Piper had learned, wasn't home, and even if he had been, he wouldn't have bothered them. Michael kept to himself when Piper was over at the Crawfords' house.

Eventually, Jenny knocked on her daughter's closed door. "Come in," Maddy called.

Jenny opened the door a bit and poked her head through the slit. "It's time for Jace to head home," she said. "I promised his mom that we'd walk him back."

"We can do it," Maddy offered, already bouncing off her bed. "You don't have to come."

"All right, then," Jenny said. "I suppose that's just fine. I'll text Brooke to let her know."

After Jace thanked Jenny—Maddy's father had gone back to work—Maddy led the way out the front door and onto the walkway. They sauntered happily down the driveway and onto the narrow, paved road. While Piper often found she felt most comfortable on the left side of the road, where her mother had taught her to be, Maddy preferred to walk in its center. Her road wasn't well traveled, so this was typically okay to do. Plus when a car came, Maddy slowly retreated to the side, which placed Piper at ease.

The friends soon found themselves in Jace's driveway. The garage was open, and a woman poked her head outside. At first glance, Piper assumed this was Jace's mother. She and Jace had similar facial features, but while Jace's hair was bleached blond and his eyes blue, this woman's hair was light brown, and her eyes, Piper could clearly see even from this distance, were brown.

"Oh, hello there," the woman said with a smile. She walked forward and met Jace in the driveway. She gently touched his shoulder and then looked at the girls. "Hello, Maddy."

"Hi," Maddy replied.

"Thanks so much for having Jace over today."

"You're welcome."

"I bet you had a great time," Mrs. Weatherbee said to her son.

Jace nodded.

"I'm Brooke Weatherbee," Jace's mom said as she looked at Piper and then turned her gaze to Princess, a smile still on her lips.

Piper got good vibes from Mrs. Weatherbee. There was something there that she couldn't quite decipher, but the woman had immediately made her feel comfortable somehow.

"I'm Piper."

"Nice to meet you, Piper."

"Princess," Princess said by way of introduction.

"Princess?" Mrs. Weatherbee wore a confused expression.

"Yeah. That's my name."

Mrs. Weatherbee's brows rose. "Oh, she said. "Well, it's nice to meet you, Princess."

Princess nodded.

"Well, thanks for walking Jace home," Mrs. Weatherbee said to the girls. "That was very nice of you. And thanks again, Maddy, for having him over. I told your mom I'd like him home at this time because I want to have a family dinner tonight before he starts at his new school tomorrow. It's very helpful that he knows you girls now; that way, he'll have some new friends to look out for when he walks through those doors."

"We're in the same class," Piper announced.

"Are you? That's just great!" Brooke looked at Jace. "Now you'll definitely have a good first day at school."

"Okay," Jace said.

They said their goodbyes. Maddy and Princess turned and started walking down the driveway. Piper waited a moment and watched as Jace was led by his mother into the garage, his mom's arm slung over his shoulder and an enormous smile on her face. Just before Piper turned to run and catch up with her friends, she saw Mrs. Weatherbee gently place a kiss on the top of Jace's head.

And as Piper reached Maddy and Princess, she found she was already looking forward to school tomorrow.

Because tomorrow, she'd see Jace again.

---

Jenny sat with her husband on their living room couch later that evening after she had tucked Maddy into bed. Michael had been sound asleep an hour later after a long day at a friend's house. Her son often complained about his bedtime, saying his friends' parents allowed their kids to remain awake until ungodly hours of the night, but Jenny wasn't a conformist, and therefore, to bed he went.

The afternoon's entertainment had been a success. She

had harbored no doubt that it would be on her part; she knew she provided a safe and amiable environment for her daughter and her daughter's friends and prided herself on her culinary ambitions. If anything was to give her pause, it would have been her daughter. Maddy could prove unreliable at times when it came to her social circle and the information she relayed back to her mother. Jenny knew that her daughter was wont to regard a particular peer affectionately one day and the next, for whatever reason, unfavorably. Jenny often paid no heed, as she considered such circumstances with apathy. She had been a little girl once and knew that nine-and ten-year-old children often changed their minds. They were exploring who they were, their likes and dislikes. They were meeting other children, feeling out what they had in common with each other. Jenny was always telling her children that it was okay not to like someone, but that was no cause for disrespect. You could dislike another human being—heck, you could like someone well enough but not want to expend the energy on constructing a closer-knit relationship because of lack of commonalities —but you were to always, always treat them well.

So when it had come to her daughter and Jace, Jenny had been unsure how the afternoon would play out. Would Maddy take a liking to the boy, this new neighbor of theirs? Or would she be hasty in her assumptions and want to spend her time with Piper and Princess, thus ignoring Jace, instead? You could talk until you were blue in the face, try your darndest to instill particular traits in your children, but at the end of the day, they were who they were.

Thankfully, Jenny had intuited by the look on her daughter's face shortly after Jace's arrival that the boy would fit right in, and thank goodness for that. Although she wouldn't have minded in the least if her daughter didn't get along with a random child at school, the fact of the matter was, Jace was a new neighbor, and their close proximity would elicit particular complications if Maddy didn't take a liking to the boy. The last thing Jenny wanted was to begin her relationship with her new neighbors on strained terms, wearily waving as she passed them by, with the knowledge that their son had probably informed them that no, he and Maddy had not hit it off.

She was relieved. She liked Brooke, had liked the softness of her smile when the two women had met each other just yesterday. She liked the way Brooke had held herself as she sat at the table on the deck in her new backyard. Jenny could sense that she was a woman of character: confident but not cocky.

Yes, she had a feeling she and Brooke Weatherbee were going to become very good friends indeed.

Jenny had a knack for intuiting these things, after all.

A new friend for her, a new friend for her daughter, and a possible new friend for her husband as well.

How wonderful!

# Chapter 3

## *Two Years Earlier*

A car horn sounded from her driveway. Brooke peeked out her front window, a habit only, for she knew who it was behind the wheel.

Nearly four years had passed since her family's move to town, and Jace's eighth-grade school year had begun, the last he'd spend in middle school, which, when Brooke thought about it, filled her with both pride and trepidation. That her only son was going to be in high school next year escaped her comprehension. Time seemed to be passing so swiftly that she often felt pieces of herself had lifted and been surreptitiously carried off in a gentle breeze to linger behind, just past her reach. She could grasp, lean, leap, but they would still be in the distance, floating away, farther and farther, until they were but memories.

For Brooke, the transition from elementary school to middle school two years prior had proven emotionally difficult. Jace, however, had been thrilled when the day had come. Maddy, Piper, and Princess had been an integral part of her son's incorporation into their new town, and Brooke thanked her lucky stars every day that Jace had been fortunate enough to have met those girls. It had only taken a few days for Jace to come home, plonk his backpack on the mudroom floor, and start chatting about several boys he had met in school through Maddy, in particular. Of these new friends, Dustin had been spoken of most enthusiastically, and it was Dustin that was still close with Jace today. They had a lot in common. They both ran cross country and were into music. Dustin was at the house often, and Brooke didn't mind one bit. He was the type of boy she wanted her son to associate with: kind, respectful. And he never appeared to pressure Jace into being who he was not, as far as Brooke was aware.

In the past nearly four years since moving to town, Brooke and Jenny had become quite friendly. Brooke didn't relay to the other woman all the circumstances of her life, past and present, but Jenny was the best friend Brooke had in town. Even with the passing of time, their relationship hadn't progressed to the level of divulging intimate details, but it was by no means due to any lack of overtures on Jenny's part. Brooke was convinced they'd get there in time, but while Jenny didn't work, either in the home or out, Brooke did. She was exhausted by the time she arrived home, and she preferred to spend her evenings with her family when they were all available, asking Jace to regale her with clippings from his day at school or his time at cross country and attempting to coax her husband into speaking to his family as well. It had gotten to the point that she didn't entirely care what Dan chose to speak about; just to get him to talk at all was a feat in itself. The job that had uprooted them and moved them to this town and to this home in the first place had proven unsuccessful, both financially, when Dan hadn't been offered the monetary bonus he had been verbally promised, and also with his emotional contentment. In short, Dan didn't like his job, and it hadn't been long after they'd purchased their new home and Jace had started in his new school that Dan had begun actively seeking different employment.

It had stressed Brooke to no end. She felt that she had made myriad sacrifices in both her career and her personal life to ensure her husband's professional happiness, and that expectation hadn't come to fruition. Would he now seek employment in a different state than New Hampshire, uproot his family once again, and leave Brooke to seek out another doctor's office or hospital? While she did believe that it was integral to one's mental well-being to find contentment in the job one possessed, that went for her as well. Not just her husband. They had spoken at length about their situation, and Brooke had been left frustrated and feeling put-upon, her emotions disregarded. And those were just *her* feelings. What about their son's? This ten-year-old boy who they had removed from his hometown, who had had to say goodbye to the only friends he had ever known. What about Jace? How would another move—and so soon—affect *him*?

Their relationship had taken a turn after that conversation. Brooke was sure that was the point at which it had. Though perhaps she simply hadn't been paying close enough attention. Were there other examples, other things she could put her finger on, to explain why her husband didn't speak with her much anymore? Why their relationship had become distant and detached?

She gave him credit: he had come home most nights to eat dinner with her and Jace in those earlier days. But as the days passed and Jace had become more serious about cross country, their son would, upon occasion, be with his team at dinnertime, leaving Brooke and Dan alone. And Dan, instead of wanting to eat with his wife, preferred to take his plate to the living room, click the power button on the television set, lean back, and rest. Without her.

And after a time, Brooke began to refrain from complaint, often sitting at the table alone, looking out the window and into the backyard and eating her meal with the sound of the television blaring in the adjacent room. And now, at present, she had come to expect the distance between them. She even found herself welcoming his absence on the days he didn't make it home for dinner.

She had tried speaking with Dan, had tried several times after he had initially declared his discontent with his new job and begun searching for another, the time she presumed had marked the beginning of their relationship's demise. Yes, she had tried. So many times, in fact, that she had lost count. But her efforts had proven futile. Dan brushed her misgivings off, said that no, there was nothing wrong beyond his grievances with his job. And "No, Brooke, it's not you. Yes, I'm sure. I should know my own mind."

And now, at present, Brooke felt alone. Sure, Dan inhabited the same home she did, but he had moved himself comfortably into a spare room, and there he remained, leaving Brooke to slumber at night, partnerless, in their king-sized bed.

Besides the fact that he wasn't entirely present in their marriage, Dan had also neglected many of his parental duties. Despite Brooke also working full-time, she carted Jace here and there: to after-school activities, cross country matches, friends' houses. Jace had even wanted to attend a celebration at the end of his seventh-grade year at school with a handful of close friends, and Brooke had been thrilled. She had taken him to purchase a new outfit and treated him to dinner out, just the two of them. And while she cherished that time spent with Jace, she also lamented the absence of his father. It was one thing for Dan to ignore her and an entirely different matter for him to ignore their son.

The car horn beeped again from the driveway.

"Jace," Brooke called up the stairs, "you're going to be late."

Although school had only been in session for two weeks, Maddy had declared her distaste for the bus and had implored her mother to drive her to school. Jenny had happily agreed, and since Jace lived just down the street, Jenny had asked Jace if he'd like her to pick him up as well. Apparently, Maddy had been enthusiastic about the idea, and Jace, not particularly enjoying the bus ride himself, had accepted.

Brooke heard her son's footsteps on the stairs before she caught sight of him. At the last stair, he flung his hefty backpack over a shoulder, stepped to the floor below, and leaned over to give his mother a quick, light kiss on the cheek. "Bye, Mom."

"Bye, babe," Brooke said. "Have a good day at school. I'll pick you up from practice."

"Okay."

Brooke smiled softly to herself. Even after all this time, her son still used the word "okay" as if it was the sole word in his vocabulary. Just last night, she had asked if he had completed his homework, to which he had replied, "Okay."

"I asked a question," Brooke had said. "You don't answer that type of question with 'okay.'"

Jace had looked at her sheepishly, which had made her grin even more widely before she tousled his hair—blond as it ever had been after a sun-soaked summer.

"Mom," Jace had protested, smoothing the tendrils back into place, the braces adhered to the fronts of his teeth on full display behind his grimace.

Brooke had merely smiled with adoration at the son of hers who was growing up and seeking more autonomy.

"See you later," Brooke said to Jace as he rushed out the front door and into the sun of the cool September morning.

Jace raised a hand, miming a wave. Brooke leaned out the doorway and watched his retreating figure then shouted a thank-you to Jenny, which she knew her friend would clearly hear through her open car windows.

"You're welcome," Jenny called back. "Don't forget about those balloons and the decorations."

"I won't forget." Although Jenny had tried on several occasions to get Brooke to join the PTA, Brooke had respectfully declined. She had, however, promised to offer aid if Jenny was ever in need. The school would soon be hosting an open-house evening for students and their care-givers, and Brooke had agreed to help decorate for the occasion.

As soon as Brooke watched Jenny's car reverse down the driveway, she hurried into the mudroom, grabbed her purse, and walked into the garage, where she climbed behind the wheel of her vehicle and set off for work. Although her current job—the job she had acquired when she and her family were looking to move to this town—didn't provide her with the fulfillment that her previous job had, it was still steady employment, and she had to admit, she liked it well enough. Plus, when Dan had been looking for a new job shortly after their move, he had, thankfully,

41

found one only twenty minutes from their home, which had enabled Brooke to remain where she was. She had been relieved that they'd be staying in town.

Brooke made it to work just on time, and her day began. It progressed as any normal day would, but she was glad when it was time to leave. She'd have the opportunity to stop off at home, change her clothes, and have a snack before setting out again to grab Jace from practice.

She knew Dan wasn't due home anytime soon. He had texted to let her know that he'd be late tonight. No, Dan didn't often spend time with his family, and he was aloof when he was at home, but at least he texted updates. Because of Dan's absence, Brooke thought that maybe she'd surprise Jace with a night out as well. Perhaps, if he was feeling up to it, he'd like to get a burger or a sandwich with her, a break away from the monotony of dinners at home.

She waited for Jace in the parking lot of the middle school with her engine off and her windows down. Only a few minutes after her arrival, she saw some members of the cross country team round a bend behind the brick facade of the building and make their way toward the lot. Jace and Dustin were both at the front of the line. They met their coach at the main doors of the middle school, where they had left their backpacks, and waited for the other members of their team to join them. The coach said some parting words, and Brooke watched her son walk toward her car, Dustin at his side, both boys grinning widely, their shoulders relaxed even with the weight of their backpacks to contend with. Brooke smiled as she watched them move, her son a full head taller than his best friend, a tendril of sweaty hair plastered to his temple.

Jace made his way to the back seat of the car, opened

the door, and shoved his backpack inside. When he closed the door, he laughed at something Dustin had just said, some inside joke, perhaps, since Brooke hadn't found it humorous herself. Jace walked around the back of the car and slid himself into the passenger seat.

Dustin leaned over Jace's open window, elbows resting on the sill. "Hi, Mrs. Weatherbee."

Brooke smiled. "Hi, Dustin." She watched him swipe at a droplet of sweat that ran down his forehead and to the bridge of his nose.

"Jace here's got some news."

Brooke looked at her son, who was grinning with unbridled pleasure. "Does he now?" she asked.

Jace looked her way and his brows rose, his grin spreading.

Dustin pushed his shoulder. "Tell her," he coaxed.

"Coach said I might make states."

"What?" Brooke asked, her eyes widening.

"That's right!" Dustin said enthusiastically. "My boy's goin' to states!"

"I thought that wasn't something a lot of kids got to do." Brooke's gaze was set intently on her son.

Jace shook his head, so slightly that the sweat-streaked tendril of hair that covered a portion of his eye didn't budge. "They don't."

"But *you* are?" Brooke's voice rose as the significance of the apparent opportunity fully dawned.

"Coach said yes."

Brooke was delighted, and her countenance clearly expressed her pleasure. "But what does this mean?"

"Don't know," Jace said. "Not much yet. Coach told me a bit, said only a handful of kids get chosen from the whole state to compete, and he thinks I'll make it."

"Jace," Brooke said breathily, "that's amazing!"

Dustin bellowed a laugh. "Sure is!" he exclaimed.

"And what about you, Dustin?" Brooke asked.

"Nah." Dustin waved a dismissive hand in the air. "I'm no Jace Weatherbee. Jace said it was bull, thought I should make it too—"

"You *should* make it," Jace interjected. "You're as good as me."

Dustin scoffed, though it was playful. His eyes still gleamed. "You're deluded, man."

Jace rolled his eyes in response.

"Jace, I just… this is amazing. I can't believe it," Brooke said.

Dustin patted his best friend on the shoulder. "Gotta go. I see my mom. Later." Dustin retreated, jogging toward a car in the distance.

Brooke turned back to her son. "I still can't believe this, Jace. States? Only a handful of people? That's incredible!"

"Calm down, Mom. It's not that big a deal."

But Brooke saw the smile her son was attempting to mask. It shone through, brightened, radiated outward, even reached his eyes.

"I'm so proud of you!" Brooke leaned over the center console of the car and kissed her son on his gleaming forehead. He wiped her affections away with a swipe of a finger, but she didn't mind. These days, Jace tended to do this move by rote. At least she was still able to plant a kiss without him moving away with a grimace, evading her entirely.

She'd take what she could get.

"Well," Brooke said, "that makes my idea all the more special, I think."

"What do you mean?" Jace asked.

"I was going to see if you wanted to have dinner out. Maybe sandwiches or burgers and fries. Whatever you like. Now, we can make it a celebration dinner. If you'd like to head out, that is. We can still have dinner at home if you'd prefer that instead."

"No," Jace said. "Out would be good. Burgers. Extra cheese. Fries. Extra—"

"Ketchup," Brooke said with him. When Jace looked at her with a lopsided grin, Brooke laughed. "All right, Mr. Cross Country Star. Let's go get you that burger."

Brooke set off and out of the middle school parking lot, following a few other parents and caregivers who had also picked up their children. It only took ten minutes for them to arrive at their destination, Jace's favorite local burger place. When they walked indoors, they were second in line at the counter, and once their turn arrived, Jace was decisive with his order. He always got the same cheeseburger, same toppings. Same fries that he loaded with an immense amount of ketchup and extra salt.

"Make that two," Brooke told the young employee.

"Anything to drink?" the attendant asked.

"No, I'm good." She turned to Jace. "You?"

"Can I?"

"Of course."

Jace looked at the young man in front of him. "Large fountain drink."

"That it?" the attendant asked.

Brooke raised a brow questioningly to her son, and when Jace shook his head, Brooke turned back to the young man and said, "Yeah. That's it."

After Brooke paid for their food, the attendant slid a large cup across the counter and gazed over Brooke's shoulder, ready to help the next customers in line. Jace grabbed the cup.

"I'll find a seat," Brooke told her son. "You get your drink and meet me?"

"Okay."

They parted ways, and Brooke surveyed the area. It wasn't large, but there was a vacant seat in the center of the room. Brooke also spied a couple of empty tables outdoors on the patio. She headed outside and sat down in a metal chair, squinting as her eyes attempted to adjust to the sun's rays.

A minute later, Jace joined her, already sipping from his plastic straw. "Let me guess," Brooke said. "You mixed all the sodas they had?"

Jace grinned, which was all the confirmation Brooke needed.

"Yuck. I still don't get why you do that."

"It's good," Jace claimed.

Brooke furrowed her brow, but she wore a grin. "If you say so."

"I do say so."

"Well then," Brooke said. "There we have it."

Jace took another large sip from his straw, swallowed, leaned back in his metal chair, and sighed dramatically before smacking his lips together.

Brooke shook her head. "You're a goof."

Jace smirked and, with slow exaggeration, brought the tip of the straw to his lips. He sipped, his cheeks concave. Brooke laughed.

They chatted for a few minutes before Brooke excused herself to go check on the status of their burgers. This place wasn't a sit-down restaurant with waitstaff. Instead, one ordered at the counter and picked their food up there as well. To her son's great satisfaction—he wasn't a patient boy by any means—the food didn't take long to prepare.

With tray in hand, Brooke approached a small counter, where she squirted a great deal of ketchup into several thumb-sized paper cups and grabbed a few packets of salt. She walked toward the patio door, pushed it open with her hip, and made her way toward her son.

When Jace spotted her, he grinned. "Yeah!" he said enthusiastically.

Brooke plonked the tray onto the table, and Jace immediately reached for a burger. He removed the top bun and deposited several cups' worth of ketchup on the patty. He repositioned his bun and pressed down, some of the ketchup oozing out the side and dripping onto his fingers. He brought the burger to his mouth, took a large bite, and chewed.

Brooke chuckled. "Bummer you don't like it," she teased.

Jace wriggled his brows, swallowed, and immediately took another large bite of burger.

"So," Brooke said as she lifted her cheeseburger from the plate on the tray. "I know how practice went, Mr. Going to States and all, but how was school? It's been a couple of weeks now that school's been in session. Going well? Liking your classes?"

Jace nodded. "Yeah," he said through a mouthful of food. "They're okay." He tore open a couple of the salt packets and poured their contents over the remaining cups of ketchup.

Brooke gave her son a sideways glance. "Just okay?" she asked before taking a small bite of her cheeseburger. No ketchup, no relish, no mustard. Just the meat, bun, and cheese for her.

Jace shrugged. "Yeah," he said. "Just okay."

"How about your teachers?"

"Okay," Jace replied.

"You've got nothing else for me?" Brooke asked with a grin. "Nothing else to say?"

Jace merely shrugged again before lifting several fries out of their box, dipping them in a cup of ketchup, and stuffing them into his mouth. Table manners were not one of Jace's strong suits despite years of insistent reminders from his mother.

"All right, then," Brooke ventured. "Then tell me about... let's see... tell me about your first-period class this morning. What was that?"

"Math."

"Math? And?"

"And what?" Jace asked.

"And what did you do? What are you learning? Do you have any homework? Any friends in class with you?"

"Kid in my class was acting up for the first half of the period," Jace said. He pushed some more fries into his mouth. "Teacher made him leave after that, but we didn't get much done. Yes to homework, and yes to friends."

"That's great," Brooke remarked. "About having friends in class, I mean. Not about the kid being a nuisance."

"Okay," Jace replied.

"Who?"

"Who what?"

"What friends do you have in your class?"

"Couple kids you don't know," Jace said. "And Dustin and Piper."

"Hey," Brooke declared with a large grin. "Dustin and Piper. That was very lucky."

"Okay," Jace said after a fresh bite of his half-eaten burger.

"It makes me think of study groups."

"Wha?" Jace asked, his lips curled.

"Why do you do that?" Brooke asked her son with a smile. "There's a T at the end of that word, you know."

Jace rolled his eyes. "Okay, Mom."

"Study groups," Brooke said, elaborating on her previous statement. "I see kids getting together in movies sometimes, a group of older teens, usually. Kids your age, too. They'll go over to one friend's house and study for a test, maybe. I never did that, and honestly, I don't remember my classmates having study groups, either. At times, I'd see kids in the library at school, and it looked like they were studying together, but that's about it. And you haven't had any study groups that I'm aware of. But for some reason, thinking about Dustin and Piper in class with you made me think of study groups."

"Okay," Jace said. "Weird."

Brooke laughed. "It's not weird," she replied. "Or are you calling *me* weird? If you're calling me weird, then yeah, maybe."

Jace lifted a brow then popped the last of his cheeseburger into his mouth.

"And…" Brooke let the word linger in the air as she searched her son's face, eager to notice any alteration in expression that her next statement might elicit. "Some kids tell their parents they're going to study at a friend's house, but really, it's just an excuse to get together with a crush. Close the door, be alone… you know."

"Okay," Jace said.

Brooke paused, then asked, "How about you? Do you have a crush on anyone?" She attempted to make her voice light, nonchalant. But she was aching to know. Recently, she had detected a change in her son. She had first noticed it when she had taken him out for ice cream. They were sitting at an indoor table—she with her cherry-dipped vanilla soft serve and Jace with his waffle cone stuffed with mint chocolate chip—when Brooke saw her son's eyes surreptitiously follow a girl who appeared to be about his age. When Jace had quickly looked back at his mother, Brooke had averted her gaze to her ice cream, pretending to snag a piece of the cherry dip so that her son wasn't cognizant of the fact that she had seen what had just transpired: her son was noticing girls.

Jace lifted a fry, while he shook his head and diverted his eyes from his mother. "Why do you want to know?"

"Because I'm your mom and I love you, and I want to be a part of your life. You don't have to tell me who. I'm just curious if you do have a crush, that's all."

Jace shook his head again, still averting his gaze.

"Okay, then," Brooke said. "But… do you notice girls? Or is it boys? Or maybe both?"

"Oh my God, Mom!" Jace lifted his eyes and looked at Brooke across the table.

Brooke laughed and lifted her hand, palm facing out. "All right, all right," she said, her smile wide. "But you know—"

"Girls, okay?" Jace said.

"Of course that's okay," Brooke teased.

"Ugh. That's not what I meant."

"I know it's not," Brooke said. "But whoever you're attracted to, Jace, you know that's—"

"I know, Mom!"

Brooke found herself chuckling again, gleaning entirely

too much pleasure from the conversation and Jace's reaction. She loved these moments with her son.

"I'd like to get serious for a minute, though, Jace."

"Okay." He popped another fry into his mouth, a glob of ketchup grazing his lower lip, which he quickly licked off with the tip of his tongue. She could see the braces lining his two top teeth.

"When things do happen with a girl, I just… be careful, okay?"

"I know. You tell me this all the time."

"Not all the time; that's an exaggeration. But yeah, we've talked about it before. And this won't be the last time. It's important, you know. To be careful. To be respectful. We've talked a lot about personal boundaries and asking permission and—"

"Ugh! Mom! I know."

Brooke offered a soft smile. "I know you know," she said. "But it's important to touch on the subject every once in a while, right? True, I know we've talked about this before, Jace, but it's really important."

"I know."

Brooke looked at her son. He was taller than she was now; had been for a while and, while sitting, his torso extended beyond hers, so her gaze was set slightly upward in order to look him in the eye. She was pleased that his blond hair hadn't darkened. Neither she nor Dan had blond hair, nor did anyone in their extended family, which made her love it all the more. It made Jace Jace. It lent him originality.

Her gaze slipped to his nose, its proportions more prominent than they had been when he was younger. His blond brows were sparse, his eyes wide, the blue of his irises appearing cerulean through the summer-tanned skin surrounding them. His face was narrow, though his jaw was pronounced. Puberty had been transformative to her son's features. She knew that Jace would change more, would look different a year from now. He would look different, too, a year after that. It couldn't be helped, this ever-changing growth and transfiguration. Her son was becoming a man, but it was happening too speedily for Brooke. As much as Jace craved autonomy, as much as he thought himself mature, she wasn't ready—for her son to date, though she could intuit that it would be happening soon—or for him to move farther from her side as he continued to seek out the lessons learned from friends and through societal expectations and social conformity. She wanted Jace to be strong of character. She wanted to believe that he'd be the outlier in a group of peers and wouldn't cave in to pressure, that he would act on his own desires rather than following the crowd. She wanted to believe that her son wouldn't experiment with any substances, wouldn't place himself in uncomfortable positions.

And yet she had been a teenager once. She remembered it well.

Even the best of kids made mistakes.

"I know you know," Brooke said quietly. "Just humor me."

Jace nodded. "If I start hanging out with a girl, then, yeah, you'll know who it is. But I don't think you need to know right now. Nothing's happening."

"I get that," Brooke said. "And I understand."

But her son's statement made her all the more curious. Was he actually interested in a particular person? And if so, who was it? Brooke knew that her son desired and deserved his space, his privacy. He was growing up, learning. And she needed to step back a bit in order to let him do so. But goodness, did she want to know! This was her son, after all. Her Jace. And he might be interested in a particular girl?

Brooke sighed.

It was beginning.

And again, she wasn't ready.

---

Brooke pulled into the garage and shut the engine off. She pushed a button on the bottom of her rearview mirror, and the garage door began its descent back into place. Jace opened the passenger-side door and squeezed himself out and into a standing position, the space tight. He walked around the back of the car and opened the door behind the driver's side as Brooke flung her purse over her shoulder and stepped out of the vehicle. Jace grabbed his backpack, and together, he and Brooke walked toward the thick garage door that led into the mudroom, but not before Brooke noticed Dan's stall was still vacant. Jace didn't comment on his father's absence. In fact, Jace had stopped commenting more than a year ago.

Once inside, Brooke hung her purse on a hook beside the door, and Jace let his backpack slip from his shoulder and to the floor. Brooke kicked off her shoes and walked farther into the silent house. She paused in the kitchen, looked around, and sighed. Jace passed her by and headed for the stairs. Brooke knew he'd be closeting himself in his room to do his homework and text with his friends. Their evenings had become ritualistic. Tonight's dinner out had been a deviation from their normal routine.

Dan didn't arrive home until Jace was brushing his teeth before heading to bed. Brooke had prepared herself for the following day at work and was in her bedroom and about to retire for the evening as well. The sound of the garage door opening was her indication that her husband had finally arrived from wherever he had been, for she instinctively knew he hadn't been at work the entire time.

Brooke contemplated remaining in her room; she wasn't sure she wanted to see her husband right now. But her conscience was telling her to welcome him home, and so respect prevailed over apathy.

Brooke descended the stairs and met her husband in the kitchen. She had left a light on for his arrival home, and it was this single light that gently illuminated the room. Her husband's back was to her as he grabbed a banana from the fruit basket on the counter. He turned, the contours of his face in shadow.

"You're home," she said. It wasn't a question.

He nodded ever so slightly.

"Well," Brooke said, her voice soft, resigned. "Welcome home. You were gone for a while."

Dan nodded again.

"No words tonight, Dan?" Brooke asked, annoyance creeping through her voice.

Dan merely stood there in the kitchen, a soft glow surrounding him, and stared at his wife.

Brooke gazed back at him, then her brows slowly began to meet. "What is it, Dan?" she asked. She knew her husband well, or at least, she had known him once upon a time. He never had been one for hiding emotion. His face portrayed it all, a canvas of expressive lines or merely a blank affect. Even when he was stoic, his physiognomy silently spoke. "What's on your mind?"

She watched her husband's chest rise with a large intake

of breath. She saw him physically exhale, and his face molded into a frown. Brooke narrowed her gaze.

"I'm leaving."

His words lingered in the still air. She wasn't sure she had heard them right or even, if she had, what they meant.

After a time, Brooke opened her mouth. Her voice sounded meek, even to her own ears. "What do you mean?"

"I'm leaving. You. Us." Dan paused and then said, "I'm moving out."

"What do you mean?" Brooke repeated, lacking the ability to utter any other words.

"I think you know what I mean, Brooke," Dan said, his voice filled with spite. "This isn't working, hasn't been working for a while. I don't love you. You don't love me. I make excuses just to be out of the house. I want out."

Brooke's mouth hung slightly ajar. She slowly blinked. "But... I..." She wasn't sure what to say, how to feel. What was she thinking? Although their marriage had been in shambles for a while now, her husband's declaration had surprised her greatly. No, they weren't happy in their marriage, that was clear. But they had coexisted. They had a son to care for, to think of, to love. Jace. What about Jace? "Where will you go?"

"Got a place on the other side of town for now."

"You... you already found a place to live? You've been thinking about this?"

Dan pressed his lips into a line.

"What... I... Dan, what the hell?" Brooke was feeling the anger arise within, eager to erupt, explode, escape the safe harbor of her mind, where it had been stewing, proliferating, for so many days, months, years.

"It's gotta happen, Brooke," Dan said, anger raising his

voice in turn. "You know it does. We—you and me—we don't work. Haven't for a long time. I'm not happy. I want out."

Brooke crossed her arms. "Yeah, Dan. You said that already. But what the hell about me? Sure, I've known that we weren't doing well. I've known for a while. But haven't I deserved a bit more?"

"A bit more what, Brooke? What the hell do you want from me?"

Brooke flung her arms out to the sides. "You just threw this at me, Dan. Gone all night, come home, tell me you're leaving for good? Couldn't you have worked up to this? Don't you think I deserved at least that? You've had so many opportunities to talk to me, to tell me how you've been feeling. But instead, here we go. This is how you break the news to me. Coming home and just laying it down."

"You coulda talked to me too!" Dan yelled.

"You have got to be kidding me, Dan!" Brooke's voice rose to meet her husband's. "I used to try to talk to you time and time again. I knew something was going on in that head of yours, I just knew it. Right after we moved here. Maybe before, but I didn't dare open my eyes. I tried talking to you. But you always shut me down! 'No, Brooke, nothing's wrong with me,' you'd say." Her voice was mocking. "'No, Brooke, I'm good, just a rough day at work.' 'No, Brooke, you didn't do anything wrong, I just want to sit my ass on the couch and watch TV with my dinner. Alone.' I *did* try to talk to you, Dan! All the time! Until I didn't. And that's on you! When I try and try and try and get nothing in return, I stop trying!"

"Just like you gave up on our marriage."

"Are you frickin' serious, Dan? Gave up on our

56

marriage. Are you even listening to what I'm saying to you right now?"

Dan lifted a hand, palm out. He shook his head, pursed his lips. "I'm done, Brooke. I'm out."

"Yeah, you go ahead and do that, Dan. Just check out. On your marriage, on your son. You go ahead and do that. It's all about you, after all."

Dan narrowed his eyes and glared at his wife. "And you wonder why I don't want to be home?"

"Then go!" Brooke flung a hand toward the garage door. "Get the hell out! We don't ever see you anyway!"

And then Brooke heard a sound behind her, watched her husband's eyes move from hers to look over her shoulder. She turned.

Jace.

Her son was staring at his father, daggers shooting from his narrowed eyes.

Brooke whipped her head back to her husband. His face softened the slightest bit, his shoulders rounded. To anyone else, the motion would have been imperceptible. But Brooke noticed.

She quickly looked back at Jace, her heart thumping, the sound accosting her ears, blood rushing to her head. She felt dizzy. She reached for the kitchen counter to steady herself.

Time elapsed in slow motion: Jace turning his back, retreating down the hallway; Dan reaching for their son, missing his target, and then pulling his arm back; her husband stomping into the mudroom, retrieving his keys, slamming the door.

The garage door opening, the truck's engine revving.

Her husband leaving, the sound of his muffler

decreasing in volume until the kitchen was silent again, and Brooke was left alone.

Lonely, confused, hurt, angry.

She wanted to slide to the cold tiled floor. She wanted to sob, to scream out her frustrations, her angst.

But she had to care for Jace now.

Her son.

On unsteady legs, Brooke walked down the hallway and climbed the stairs to the second floor. She knocked on her son's closed door. No answer.

She knocked again, a bit harder this time. "Jace?" After a pause, she asked, "Can I come in?"

Silence answered her.

She pushed softly on the door and peeked her head inside the room. Jace was sitting on his bed, his back to her. He was staring out the window. The moon's gentle glow spotted the off-white carpet.

She didn't turn the light on, merely stepped inside the room and slowly walked toward her son. She sat beside him on the bed. She heard it creak beneath her added weight.

Brooke placed her palm on her son's shoulder. He didn't flinch, didn't move. Didn't look her way.

"Are you okay?" She knew it was a loaded question, but she wasn't sure what else to say to Jace at the moment. What words could she use when Jace's father had just left his family without even a backward glance and no explanation to their son? She didn't know if he'd be back. She didn't know if Dan would attempt a conversation with Jace. She just didn't know.

She gently squeezed her son's shoulder. "Jace? Will you look at me for a minute?"

She watched his jaw clench, but he turned his head toward his mother. Even in the moonlight, she could see that his eyes had filled, the liquid threatening to jump the precipice of his lids, to mark his cheeks with angry stains.

"I don't know what to say," Brooke admitted. "But I'm sorry, Jace. I'm just so… I'm so sorry." Her lower lip quivered, but she attempted to keep her emotions in check. Jace didn't need to be affected by his mother right now. He needed Brooke to be strong, secure. He needed someone to lean on if he chose to act on his emotions. She needed to be her son's crutch. She was sure of it.

It was just so damn hard when she had been left utterly devastated and angered in the wake of what had, just moments before, transpired with her infuriating husband. "I'm here, you know. I'm here for you if you need to talk. I know you must be feeling a lot right now."

She knew that Jace was attempting to brush off his hurt. She could see it in the lines of his face. She let her palm slip off his shoulder and down his arm. She squeezed his hand and then placed her palm on her lap.

She sat on the bed beside her almost-fourteen-year-old son until her eyes began to droop with fatigue.

She didn't remember falling asleep, but she awoke in the morning, before the sun, to find herself on Jace's floor, curled into a fetal position. She sat up. Her body ached. She stretched and then slowly stood. Jace was under his blankets, his cheek against his soft pillow. He was breathing steadily, his eyes darting beneath his lids, his lashes clumped together.

Brooke extended her finger and gently brushed a tendril of loose hair off her son's forehead. He didn't stir. She sat beside him, careful not to disturb his slumber. By moonlight, she watched him sleep for a time, her heart aching terribly. Then she leaned over, brushed a soft kiss on his cheek, stood, and left the room, closing the door gently behind her.

Time didn't stop, not even when one's heart was breaking.

She had to trudge on.

---

Brooke watched Jace round the corner of the middle school the following afternoon. She had offered him the day off from school, what she deemed a much-needed respite, but he had refused, claiming instead that he'd prefer to be with his friends. Even from her vantage point in the parking lot, she could clearly see that he was winded. Coach was waiting for him in front of the main doors of the building as he typically did, but instead of her son running with Dustin, he had emerged alone.

Brooke watched Jace surge toward his coach and then stop so suddenly his knees buckled. She saw Coach's palm cup Jace's shoulder, saw the concerned expression upon his face. She watched as her son shook his head, turned, and picked his backpack up off the ground, slinging it aggressively over a shoulder.

And Brooke watched as her son—the son who, to her knowledge, had never disrespected an authority figure—retreated from the coach who was attempting to speak with him and stomped toward the car.

---

Jace didn't want to come out of his room for dinner, and Brooke wasn't going to insist he do so. She'd let him grieve any way he needed to, even if it was pulling her heartstrings so taut she was convinced the fragile threads would break at any moment.

She ate at the dining table, alone, heated leftovers she had found in the back of the refrigerator. She picked at her food, spread the morsels around her plate with the tines of her fork. The lights above the table hummed gently. Peepers sounded in the backyard, a sound she knew would fade along with the pleasant weather until a darkened stillness was left in its place.

She didn't finish her meal; instead, she scraped the food into the trash bin and placed her dirtied plate in the sink to wash later. She walked into the living room and sat in her favorite chair opposite the couch her husband had claimed as his own on so many past occasions. After pulling the string on a small lamp atop a stand to illuminate the immediate space, she picked up a book and removed her bookmark. Brooke began to read, but her eyes soon glazed over, and she realized she had been rereading the same sentence over and over again in order to focus her mind on the usually simplistic task, one she usually enjoyed when she found time to do it.

Brooke closed her book and returned it to its resting place on the stand. She pulled her legs up and folded her feet under her thighs. Crossing her arms, she stared at the wall closest to her.

Her eyes came to rest on a picture, large, square, and framed. It had been taken on her wedding day so many years ago, when she and Dan had been happy and in love and had believed they had the world at their fingertips, ready for the picking. A photo taken when neither of them could have ever believed that love faded, that life took unexpected twists and turns that set the course of one's future, even if those twists and turns seemed inconsequential at the time. The pair she was staring at, the woman in her wedding dress, the man in a black tuxedo and bowtie, wore their feelings proudly in their expressions, in the width of their smiles and the adoration in their eyes.

To the left of the picture hung another, this one smaller but also square and framed. It was Jace as a newborn. Brooke remembered well the day this photo had been taken. She had procured the services of an acquaintance who had a small photography business on the side and whose work Brooke had seen. She had been impressed and knew even before Jace was born that she'd very much like for the woman to capture her son in the manner she had captured other children. And to her unbridled pleasure, the photographer had done just that. She had instructed Brooke to remove Jace's clothes, leaving just his diaper on. She had then placed a small crocheted garment around the diaper, cream in color, and placed a matching cap on Jace's sparsely haired head. Jace had woken when the photographer had been handling him, but as soon as she placed him in a wide, shallow basket on top of a plush blanket, curled his thin, diminutive legs to his chest, and posed his palm on his thigh, Jace had fallen asleep. Not before startling, though, his posed arm shooting up to land over his ear, where it remained. And it was this pose the photographer had captured so beautifully. Her son. Her remarkable, new son who held such promise and purpose.

On the other side of her wedding photo hung a framed family portrait the exact size as Jace's newborn picture. Jace had been three years old when the image had been taken. It was a candid shot captured in the front yard of their old house, well before they had made the move to their current town. When Brooke closed her eyes, she could still remember the day: slightly overcast, summer, dandelions sprouting from the uncut grass. Jace had been pulling on his father's hand, attempting to get him to play a game of chase, and although Dan had been reluctant at first, he had soon acquiesced. The shot had been taken immediately before Jace had giggled profusely, screamed, and then darted away from his father's grasp, leaving Brooke, legs crossed, in the grass to look on with amusement. *Snap.*

The picture told a silent tale. Jace's lips were set in a determined line as he pulled on his father's hand. Dan was looking down at his son with a smirk, the corner of his mouth lifted. The softness of Brooke's gaze on her son conveyed her contentment.

A slight creak sounded on the floor beside her, and Brooke turned, pulling her gaze from the pictures on the wall. Jace was standing in the entryway. He looked at his mother, his face a blank canvas, revealing nothing of his thoughts or the motivation that had compelled him to leave his room. He hadn't spoken a word since she had picked him up from practice, and Brooke didn't expect he'd do so now. She watched as Jace slowly made his way to the back door and stepped onto the deck. He closed the door behind him, the click ringing loudly in Brooke's ears, though in reality, the sound was marginal.

The ensuing silence engulfed her.

Brooke left Jace alone for a time. She could see him from her angle on the chair. He had grabbed a blanket from the large storage container on the deck and set it out. He was lying on his back, gazing at the starlit sky, elbows bent, his head resting in his palms.

Eventually, Brooke stood from the chair and walked to the door. She slowly opened it and stepped outside. The air was crisp. She heard the rustling of leaves as the breeze tickled her nose and gently swept her hair off her shoulders.

She sat beside her son on the blanket and glanced over at him. Jace made no move to return her gaze. Instead, he continued to stare into the sky, pinpricks of light twinkling, a waning moon lending a sliver of light.

Brooke lowered herself, lying down on her back to mirror her son. She wasn't comfortable in the least, even with the blanket offering a fragment of softness to offset the unwavering rigidity of the deck. But she was with her son. In the same space and at the same time.

She'd take it.

After a few minutes of gazing at the stars, attempting to decipher the constellations—something she had failed to do time and time again—Brooke slid her hand over the blanket and touched the tips of her fingers to Jace's thigh. "Hey, babe?" she asked.

Jace made no reply, but she knew he was listening.

"I'm so sorry this happened," Brooke continued. "I wish there was something I could say or do. I guess I'm not good at this. I've never been in this position before." She offered Jace a wan smile, though he was still staring into the sky.

"I'm just here, okay? I'm here. Whenever you need to talk. Whatever you need. I'm here, Jace. I promise."

They lay in silence for several minutes. Brooke's back was aching, but she dared not move.

And then she heard her son speak. His voice was low and his words were drawn out. "He's an asshole."

Brooke had never heard her son swear before. She herself didn't swear often. Had things been different, perhaps she would have scolded him. If things were different, perhaps she would have spoken to him about finding a more appropriate word, especially to describe his father.

But times weren't different. Nothing would be the same

again. And yesterday had marked the day that, in Brooke's eyes, her son had been forced to grow up. Through all the confusion and anger he must be feeling, Jace would inevitably be forever altered by the choices his father had made.

So no, Brooke didn't correct him. She couldn't. She wouldn't.

"Yeah." Her voice was but a breath. "He's an asshole."

# Chapter 4

## *Now*

Brooke followed Officer Blunt and his partner—who she had since learned was named Detective Matthews —into a small, dimly lit room at the police station. She clutched Jace's upper arm and sat directly next to him at a small table centered in the square room. She looked from her son, who held himself rigidly in the chair, his jaw clenched, his countenance seething, to the round face of Officer Blunt, who had seated himself directly in front of her son. Even through her angst and trepidation, she found herself marveling at the youth of the man. Jace was sixteen, and Officer Blunt didn't look to be much older. What life experiences had brought him to this very moment? What had compelled him to become a police officer in the first place? And what could this man possibly be thinking about her son because of the information he had been given, which he hadn't fully imparted to Brooke?

What in the world was happening?

And Maddy Crawford? Had Maddy, this girl who had walked through Brooke's home time and time again through the years, the girl who had been Jace's first friend when they had moved to town, and the girl who had slowly morphed from friend to girlfriend—what had happened, truly happened, between Jace and Maddy that would compel Maddy to accuse him of assaulting her?

Rape.

She wanted to believe her son hadn't done this abhorrent deed, hadn't hurt Maddy in such a way.

But why would Maddy lie about something of such magnitude?

And if she hadn't, then that meant that Jace—

Brooke laced her fingers together, squeezing until the blood drained from her knuckles and they shone white on her lap. Her stomach roiled, and she found her legs were shaking. She tried to still them but couldn't. Her instincts had taken hold. And in that moment, even with all the thoughts flooding her mind, Brooke wondered why her body felt the need to shake in these circumstances. Wouldn't it intuit that she was in need of her senses, that she needed to be strong, bold? Instead, she felt as if she lacked the ability to control even the most habitual of movements.

Detective Matthews leaned back in his chair and cleared his throat. But it was Officer Blunt who spoke a moment later, looking directly at Jace.

"You know Madison Crawford?"

"Yeah." Jace didn't elaborate.

"And how is that?"

"Maddy lives down the street. We go to the same school. She's my…" Jace stole a glance at Brooke. "Ex."

Brooke's eyes widened. Ex? When had that happened? Just that afternoon, before the knock on the door that had changed the course of her day so drastically, she had been under the impression that Jace and Maddy were still going strong. Jace hadn't told her otherwise. If they had ended their relationship, that was absolutely a hefty piece of information that Brooke would have expected Jace to communicate. Why hadn't her son mentioned their breakup? And when had it occurred?

Officer Blunt steepled his fingers, propped his elbows on the table, leaned forward, and placed his chin on his fingertips. "So you know Madison intimately?"

Jace furrowed his brows at the officer, his eyes squinting. Brooke could still detect the clench in his jaw. Where Jace seemed to be livid, Brooke herself felt nauseated, the taste of the bile that had expunged itself from her stomach a half an hour ago still present. She feared more would follow at any moment.

"Not sure why you need to know that. It's personal."

"Not when you've been accused of rape," Officer Blunt replied matter-of-factly.

"Me and Maddy, yeah," Jace said. "We were intimate. We were together. But I never raped her."

"Why would she accuse you, then?"

Jace threw his hands into the air and expelled an exasperated sigh. "I don't know!" His raised voice showed that he was clearly incensed.

"Where were you a couple of nights ago?" Officer Blunt asked. "The night of—" he flipped a page in a file folder propped open on the table.

Brooke leaned forward in an effort to see what was typed out or written on the page, but to no avail. The table was too wide, and Officer Blunt was just far enough away that she was unable to detect the words.

"—November first," Officer Blunt finished.

Jace pursed his lips. It was a moment before he

answered. He crossed his arms and glared at the officer in front of him. "I was at Maddy's house."

"You were at Madison Crawford's house?"

"That's what I said," Jace scoffed.

Brooke leaned toward her son. "Jace, please," she pleaded in a whisper. Why was her son acting this way, so disrespectful and defensive? Didn't he know that right now, at this very moment, these officers held his life in their hands? Although she was sure that Jace heard her entreaty, he didn't shift his gaze from Officer Blunt.

"So you were with Madison on the night of November first." It wasn't a question.

"Yeah."

"Was anyone else with you?"

Jace paused before answering. "No."

"Nobody else was in the house with you that night?"

Jace uncrossed his arms and slapped his palms on his thighs. "That's what I just told you!"

Officer Blunt was nonplussed. "So you were at Madison's house Tuesday night, alone."

Jace's voice lowered. "Yes."

"What time did you arrive?"

Jace shrugged. "Probably sometime around six. I had practice then went home to take a shower."

Brooke managed a nod. "I was home that night." She knew she had been. These days, she didn't have much of a social life and was often home in the evenings.

"And after your shower, you went to Madison's?"

"Yeah."

"How did you get there?"

"I drove. Didn't want to walk, knowing it would be dark when I left. Why does that even matter?"

The officer didn't answer. Instead he asked, "What did you do once you were at Madison's house?"

"Why?"

Officer Blunt lifted his brow, and Brooke noticed a slight, uncomfortable shift in her son. He crossed his arms. Brooke looked into the face of Officer Blunt, who was staring directly at Jace. She pivoted her gaze to his partner, who was sitting across from her at the table. He met her stare, his posture languid, his expression unreadable. It was Brooke that looked away first.

"Okay," Jace capitulated. "Okay." He sighed. "We grabbed something to eat. Her parents weren't home, but her mom knew I was coming over, so she made us some quesadillas. Maddy texted to tell me her mom made them, so I didn't eat at home. After that we just… we talked."

Officer Blunt nodded, a minute gesture, for Jace to continue. The young man leaned back slightly, elbows still propped on the table, and lowered his fists onto the smooth surface.

"Yeah," Jace said. "So we talked. And then Maddy wanted to go to her room."

Brooke was no longer shaking. Instead, as her son relayed his tale, she felt her body stiffen.

"So we went to her room. She put some music on. She's always listening to music. And we just started… we started making out."

Officer Blunt nodded again.

"And—" Jace looked over at his mom then back to the officer. "Man, this is really awkward. My mom's right here. You don't really need details, do you?"

"We most certainly do."

Jace sighed again, and Brooke noticed his fingers clutching the material of his jeans. He shuffled a foot on the floor. "We were making out, and Maddy, she took off her shirt. Then took off mine. We had done a lot of fooling around before, but Maddy, she wanted, you know…"

"Know what?"

Jace stole a quick glance at his mother. "She wanted to have sex. She had for a little while. I just…"

"And had the two of you been intimate in that way prior to this night?"

Jace looked down at his hands, fingers still playing with the denim of his jeans. He shook his head.

"Out loud," Officer Blunt instructed. "With words."

Jace lifted his gaze. "No. I just… Look, I know it's weird, right? But I just… I… it didn't feel right. It always just felt weird to me."

"What felt weird to you?"

"Making that step, you know? With Maddy, anyway." Jace paused for a moment before furthering his explanation. "My mom's been talking to me for a while, respect and all that stuff. I know Maddy wanted to, but I just… I don't know. I've had a lot on my mind, lots of stuff going on. My dad visited not too long ago—that's a whole other story—and cross country. I'm on an elite team, and it just takes a lot, you know? Just a lot of stuff going on, like I said. I just… I just always stopped when she was pushing a bit. And she always got it, got me."

"And this night?" Office Blunt asked. "What happened?"

Jace pressed his lips into a line and then resumed speaking, his words slow. "We were making out, like I said. Before this night, we talked, me and Maddy, and when we talked, she said she wanted her first time to be with me, that she trusted me. She was ready. I told her I wasn't really ready just yet, not with everything going on and all, and I told her

71

that things were different with her, you know, because we had known each other for so long. We met when I was ten. She wasn't too happy. We talked a bit more, and I just saw her face, and I guess… I just changed my mind. So that night…."

"You changed your mind?"

"Yeah."

"So you had sex with Madison that night?"

Jace looked up and into Officer Blunt's eyes.

Brooke's stomach flopped, bile rising in her throat.

"Yeah," Jace said. "I said that already."

"And what you're telling me is that it was consensual?"

"Yeah."

"You didn't rape Madison Crawford?"

"Hell no!"

Officer Blunt leaned back in his chair, crossed one leg over the other. "Even when you say yourself that you had a lot on your mind, that you've been having trouble lately?"

"No."

"Then why would Madison say you raped her?"

"I have no frickin' clue!" Jace exclaimed in exasperation. "She asked me to. She wanted to have sex!"

Brooke's lower lip began to tremble. Her son was claiming that Maddy had wanted to have sex that night, that they had never done so before. He was claiming that he had wanted to hold off but that she had coaxed him into it. A flood of scenarios swam through her mind. The voices of so many women, past and present, shouted, pleaded, cried. Women who had been brave enough to come forward, to tell their stories. Women who had been taken advantage of, used, discarded. And those women who had been too frightened to speak of the crimes committed against them, the unthinkable crimes that had shattered their lives.

And then she thought of herself, thought about a day she had attempted time and time again to push back into the recesses of her mind, to forget about, to move past. A time in her life before she had met her ex-husband. A time in which she had met a man named Brian. A name she would never, never forget.

She felt the tears as they welled in her eyes and dripped to mark her cheek. Her nose began to run, but she didn't lift her fingers to swipe the secretions away. Her body had turned to stone. She was grounded, chained to her chair. Her son was using the age-old excuse of victim blaming.

*She wanted it.*

How had it come to this, she and Jace sitting at a table in a police precinct while Jace was interrogated about raping his girlfriend, a girl that Brooke had known for years now, the daughter of her best friend in town?

What had gone wrong?

The guilt she felt was immeasurable, not only because she still couldn't comprehend why she was sitting in this room right now but because, deep down, Brooke had to admit to herself that she didn't believe her son.

She didn't believe her own son.

What kind of mother was she?

"At any time, did she tell you to stop?" Officer Blunt asked Jace.

"No." Her son's answer was definitive.

"Did she make any indication that she wanted you to stop?"

"No."

"So again, let me get this straight: you're telling me that you did not rape Madison Crawford."

"Jesus!" Jace flung his hands into the air. "I already told you that. Why the hell do you keep asking me? No, okay? No. I did not rape Maddy. We had sex, yeah. But it wasn't rape. If anyone didn't want to do it, it was me!"

Brooke wrapped her arms around her chest as the tears continued to pour from her eyes. She squinted, shut her lids tight, attempted to look at her son, but all she saw was a blur, the contours of his figure, his face. Even as he sat only inches from her, she couldn't make out his features.

She let the tears fall. She let the liquid drip from her nose and onto her upper lip. She pressed her knees together and leaned forward, hunching over. She wanted to run. Run away from the situation before her. Run away from the men before her with their stoic expressions and their incriminating questions. And she wanted to run away from her son.

She needed to think, and she wasn't offered that opportunity sitting in a cold, hard chair in this police station. She wanted to clear her mind, though she knew that would be impossible. This wasn't something she could push aside. No, this was something of such magnitude that Brooke knew it would linger within her forever, ripping her, shredding her.

The questions continued, which only further angered Jace. She could tell her son was losing any modicum of composure, any thread, that he'd been able to hold onto. He'd snap soon. That was who Jace was, who he had become. Especially after his father had left two years ago. He was quick to anger.

"This is seriously bullshit!" Jace said.

Brooke shut her eyes forcefully, hastening the tears down her wet cheeks. She uncrossed her arms and raised a hand, swiping under her eyes, before blinking again.

"I didn't rape Maddy. I'd never do something like that to her. To anyone. What the hell? Seriously! Why'd she say that about me?"

"How have things been between the two of you since that night?" Officer Blunt asked.

Though her eyes still watered over, Brooke could detect the clenching of her son's jaw, the slight shift in his posture.

"Not so good."

"Meaning?"

"I broke up with her, okay?"

Brooke heard a gasp in the room. It wasn't until Jace turned to look her way that Brooke realized she was the one who had produced the sound. Yes, she had learned of their breakup just minutes before, but she hadn't realized Jace had broken up with Maddy and not the other way around.

"And when was that?"

"The next day."

Officer Blunt frowned. "The next day."

"Yeah."

"After you say, in your own words, that she wanted to have sex with you."

"Yeah," Jace repeated.

"Why?"

"Why what?"

Officer Blunt arched his brow. "Why'd you break things off? Didn't you tell me that you've known Madison for a while, since you were ten years old, was it? And you broke things off the day after you and she had sex?"

"Yeah," Jace said. "But…" He shook his head. "I don't know, okay? I was confused. I was… a lot is going on right now. I just… I couldn't."

"Couldn't what?"

"Be with her."

"Once you had sex, you mean," Officer Blunt said. "Once you got what you wanted."

Brooke gasped again at the exact same time that Jace yelled, "What the hell, man!"

Brooke's entire body was shaking now. She pressed her knees together more tightly and grasped Jace's arm with her fingers. "That's enough," she managed to croak. But the words weren't directed at Jace. She looked directly at Officer Blunt and repeated, "That's enough." Her voice was scratchy, coarse. "I'm taking my son home. That's it for tonight. I don't know what's going on. I don't know what went on, but that's enough. I think… I don't want you talking to my son again until I've found a lawyer." Brooke didn't want to admit that she had no idea how to go about such a thing, and there was certainly no way she was going to inquire about the process with either of the men across the table. She'd find a way. She'd do her research, and she'd find a way.

Brooke stood and looked at Jace. No more words were necessary. Jace stood, turned his back on the police, and made for the door. As Brooke followed her son and reached the threshold, she heard a voice behind her.

"We'll be in touch."

She looked back and into the rounded, youthful face of Officer Blunt. His lips were compressed, but his face was otherwise expressionless. Brooke blinked, breathed in deeply, and—on unsteady legs—walked out of the room.

---

Jenny fisted a hand, pulled her arm back, and punched the wall.

She wanted to scream, wanted to throw the first thing

she could get her hands on, but Maddy was upstairs in her room, and Jenny didn't want her daughter to hear her lose control. She had already witnessed that last night.

Her fingers were throbbing. She gritted her teeth. She regretted her rash decision, but what the hell could she do to exert her anger without further upsetting her daughter or possibly breaking a bone?

Jenny marched out the back door and onto the deck. She stepped off and into the grass of her backyard. Here, she stomped. One bare foot then the other, over and over again. The grass was dewy, and she felt the hard earth beneath her, the leaves, dirt, and pebbles. It hurt. And she welcomed it.

Eventually, she calmed enough to cease her stomping and, instead, dropped to the ground and sat. She bent her legs and pulled them closer to her chest, wrapped her arms around her shins, and rested her chin on her knees. No tears. Not for Jenny. She was too angry, livid, incensed. Her daughter had been raped. Raped! And by Jace Weatherbee. Never had she thought this could happen to her daughter. Not to Maddy. And not by Jace, the boy down the street, the boy who had strutted through her house time and time again, the boy who had pretended he was wholesome and kind. The boy she had always assumed treated her daughter well.

It had all been a lie.

It was amazing what one could project on the outside while harboring salacious secrets within.

Maddy had confided in Jenny last night, had told her everything: how she had thought that Jace loved her. How they had been alone in her room. How one thing had led to another and then—

*Mom, I was almost okay. But then I wasn't. I didn't want to do it. So I told him to stop.*

Told him to stop. And he hadn't. Maddy had been assaulted. And Jace had gone home.

And Jenny hadn't been there, hadn't been home to shelter her daughter. Hadn't been there to prevent this atrocity from happening.

*Why didn't you tell me what happened, Maddy? You know you could have talked to me. You know you could have talked to me when I got home. You could have called me right away to get me home sooner. Maddy...*

*I'm sorry, Mom. I'm sorry, I'm sorry. I was scared.*

But she had told her last night.

And it had changed everything.

Today had been a school day, but Jenny had kept Maddy home. There was no way she wanted her daughter in school. Not with that boy. Not after he had done this to Maddy. Not after he had stripped her of all innocence and left her hurt and scared and confused. And she knew now the truth behind Maddy's insistence on remaining home from school yesterday as well.

Her husband had been livid when he'd found out what Jace had done to Maddy. Jenny could have sworn she'd seen steam spurting from his ears, his mouth, as a red tinge spread to his cheeks and temples. Even his neck had turned red. Jenny feared that Gus was going to march over to the Weatherbees' house right then and there, break down the door, and accost Jace.

In her mind, she wanted him to do just that. Jace deserved it, no doubt. But they couldn't attack the boy, no matter how much they wanted to see him pay after harming their daughter in such a violent way. So after calming a hysterical Maddy, and once Gus had been able to ground himself well enough not to fly out the door, Jenny had picked up the telephone and dialed the police station.

Maddy had been hesitant to let Jenny do so. She claimed that she just wanted this all to be over with. She wanted to move on, to heal. She didn't want the news to reach the school, her friends, the teachers, the community. She didn't want to be known as the girl who was raped.

But Jenny had convinced her otherwise, stating that nothing would be done to Jace if they didn't come forward and that Jace could not get away with what he had done to Maddy. Didn't Maddy want to see him punished for his actions? Wouldn't that help her heal?

And yet, Jenny knew her daughter would never fully heal from something like this. Jenny herself had never been assaulted, but she had heard the stories: women who could never fully recover, girls who carried the trauma of their assault through the years, how it affected their relationships, their self-esteem, their coping mechanisms. Assault wasn't just something one could brush aside, no matter how much the survivor wished it so.

And now, it was her daughter who was a survivor.

Maddy's older brother, Michael, didn't yet know what had happened to his sister. And Jenny wasn't sure how her son would react to the news. He had remained introverted through the years, kept to himself. He didn't wear his emotions on his sleeve, and he wasn't one to talk about feelings, either. Even so, he had always been a protective older brother, and when he did find out about what had happened to his sister—no, Jenny didn't know how he'd react.

He was on campus right now, at a college in Boston. Should Jenny call him, tell him what had happened to his sister now? Or should she wait, holding onto the information for a while longer, perhaps until the semester was over so he could concentrate on his studies? She didn't know. What was right? What did Maddy want?

As Jenny pulled her knees closer to her chest on the hard earth, she fumed. Jace had taken something from Maddy that she could never get back, and it wasn't her virginity Jenny was mulling over. It was her daughter's innocence, her trust in other human beings, her trust in relationships and the opposite sex. It was walking into a room, meeting a boy, and not immediately wondering if he was capable of hurting her. What would her daughter do when, even years from now, she dated a man and he moved in to kiss her? What would she do when his hand slipped under her shirt? How would she feel, react, when a man wanted to explore further intimacy?

And Jace hadn't just defied Maddy's trust. He had affected Jenny's entire family. The police were involved. Jenny didn't know how it would proceed from here, but proceed it would, and she felt as if she was sinking. People would inevitably look at her daughter differently from here on. Maddy would walk into a room, and Jenny imagined a hush, a silence. The stirring of feet on the floor, the aversion of eyes. Surreptitious texting on phones. Or perhaps Maddy would walk into a room, and she'd be rushed by friends, sympathy prevailing, pity displayed on their faces. Would that be any better than ignoring her daughter altogether, though?

Jenny ripped the grass from the ground with a fist and tore it into smaller and smaller pieces. She threw the handful into the air before twisting and wrenching another bunch out of the dirt at her side. Once she discarded those pieces, Jenny rubbed her palms against her thighs, wiping off the moisture from the wet grass.

She wanted Jace Weatherbee to pay, and she vowed to herself and to her daughter that she would do all in her power to see her efforts prevail.

And Brooke—Jenny had truly thought that Brooke was an amazing person. Jenny had been thrilled to learn, six years ago, that there were new neighbors on their small, quiet street. Jenny was a people person, extroverted, and had many friends, but she always welcomed wholeheartedly the opportunity for more to enter her life. Her friendships fulfilled her, brought a sense of pleasure beyond that of motherhood.

And with Brooke, it had been so easy. No, Jenny hadn't been able to spend as much time with Brooke as she would have liked because of Brooke's work schedule, but the close proximity of their homes and their children's blossoming friendship when the Weatherbees had first moved to town —it had all lent an ease, really, a natural progression. Gus and Brooke's husband, Dan, had attended weekly poker evenings together in those earlier years, and once Dan had left his family, it had only intensified Jenny's relationship with Brooke, as Jenny had provided a crutch for her friend to lean on in her time of emotional need.

It was during this time, too, that Jenny had detected a change in Maddy's relationship with Jace. At first, the almost-fourteen-year-old boy had been reclusive, closing in on himself while he sorted out his feelings toward his father. Then, soon thereafter, he had moved closer to Maddy, spending more time with her, walking the rooms of Jenny's house more and more often after school, after practice, and on the weekends. Maddy had claimed that he was that way with all his close friends, but it still pleased Jenny. She liked Jace very much. He was polite, kind even. Although Jenny had still sensed him holding back, Jace had spoken to her openly about other matters: school, cross country, friends. She had felt close to him. As close as the mom of his good friend could be, anyway.

And now this.

What had she missed? Jenny prided herself on being an excellent judge of character, but she had clearly missed the mark with Jace, and now, she sat there in her backyard, pondering what she had missed, too, with his mother.

Brooke.

What had she been hiding? What kind of parent was she, truly, if her son was capable of causing so much pain, of harming another human being so fully, so wholly, and so permanently? Who was Brooke, really? And did Jenny know her as well as she thought she had?

No. No, clearly, she didn't. Brooke had to be manipulating their relationship. She just had to be. Jenny was just too trusting, always had been. She initially thought the best of people. She always gave a person a chance. No, that wasn't right. Not just one chance. She often found herself giving a person two, three chances before she made up her mind about their character. And until this point, her intuition had always been right.

But not with Brooke. It couldn't be.

What had happened with Jace for him to have done this to her daughter?

Was it his childhood? The move? His father leaving? Did he have as good a relationship with his mother as Brooke had convinced Jenny he had? Or could it be a combination of all these things commingling through the years, wreaking havoc on a young boy's life as his body changed, hormones , prevailed, and his adolescent mind struggled to develop?

What had happened in that very moment when he and

Maddy were in Maddy's bedroom—the very room she was in right now—that had propelled Jace to continue with an act that Maddy had clearly told him to cease?

Yes, Jenny was livid.

How dare he?

How *dare* he!

# Chapter 5

## *Two Years Earlier*

Apparently, their marriage wasn't the only thing that displeased Dan.

On a Saturday evening, several months after moving into his apartment, Dan announced during one of Jace's rare visits to his father's new residence—rare because Dan lacked the initiative to invite his son over, even when Brooke urged him to do so—that he wasn't content with his job—again—and had accepted a position out of state.

"Dad's moving."

Dan had dropped Jace off in the driveway after their time together, not bothering to step foot inside the home to have this much-needed conversation with Brooke. Jace had taken his shoes off in the mudroom and found his mother sitting in her favorite chair in the living room.

"He's moving?" Brooke asked, clicking off the television set. "Already? He just got this apartment a few months ago. Where in the world is he moving to?"

Jace frowned. "Back to Maryland."

"Wait," Brooke said, leaning forward in the chair.

"What? Maryland? When… I mean, what? When did he decide this?"

Jace shrugged. "He doesn't give a shit. Said he wasn't happy at work, so he found a new job. Moving back to Maryland in a few weeks."

Brooke didn't remark on Jace's choice of language, she had become accustomed to her now-fourteen-year-old son's profanity since his father had left.

"In a few weeks?" Brooke was incredulous. "How could he do this? You already don't see him often, and now he's moving so far away? How is this going to help your relationship with your father?"

Jace shrugged again. "Don't care," he replied.

But as much as Jace had tried to convince Brooke that his father's leaving didn't negatively affect him, Brooke knew otherwise. She could sense it in his speech, in the way he held himself more rigidly these days. She detected it in his lack of verbalizing his emotions, though she had to admit that his being a teenager could very well have something to do with that too.

And how could his father's absence *not* affect their son? True, he hadn't been around much when they were all inhabiting the same space, but he had still been here, had still been present. And now, Jace had only seen his father a total of four times in the few months that he had been gone. Four.

Brooke had called Dan later that evening when Jace was in his room. There was an audible sigh on the other end of the line even before her estranged husband grunted a hasty, "What's up, Brooke?"

"When were you going to tell me?"

"Tell you what?"

"Don't play dumb with me, Dan. I'm not in the mood.

When were you going to tell me that you were moving out of state? Farther away from our son. The son that needs his father."

"Figured Jace would tell you."

"He did," Brooke said. "But it's not our son's responsibility to be our liaison, Dan. It's your responsibility to tell me these things. And this isn't something light, either, is it? You're moving. Far away. Away from Jace. How are we supposed to coparent when you keep things from me? Big things."

She wished that instead of Dan being on the other end of the telephone line, she could look into his face, scrutinize his features to detect whether, as Jace had stated, he gave a shit. Because it certainly didn't seem that way right now.

Another sigh from her ex. "I need a change, Brooke. I need to get away. There's nothing here for me."

Brooke's eyes widened, and her jaw dropped. She paused for a moment before replying, not because she didn't want to throw a retort his way but because he had left her so shocked that she wasn't able to piece the words together. Eventually, she said, "Nothing here for you? What about your son?"

"That's not what I meant."

"No? Then explain it to me, Dan. What did you mean when you said you have nothing here for you?"

"You're blowing this way out of proportion."

"Oh, am I?" Brooke could hear the exasperation in her voice.

"Damn right." Dan's tone matched her own. "I only meant that I'm not happy here. Haven't been for a long time. I searched and searched and found a job that I think could be good for me. A new beginning."

Brooke didn't know if she could take much more

without exploding, spewing words she might regret in the near future. "A new beginning," she said, her voice low, seething.

"Yes."

"Away from your son."

"Jace knows that he can see me anytime he likes, and that won't change. I'll be in Maryland, but I'll fly him down."

"Oh," Brooke retorted. "Is that so? You'll just fly him on down, even when he's got friends, cross country, school? And when you've only seen him four times since you left us?"

"I didn't leave you both," Dan said. "I left you."

"Could have fooled me."

"I'm hanging up now, Brooke. I don't need this from you. I'm trying here."

Brooke laughed then, a low, dark, ominous sound that emanated from her throat. "You're a piece of work, Dan, you know that, right?"

"Bye, Brooke." And the line went dead.

Brooke threw her cell onto the sofa so hard that the device would unquestionably have shattered had it hit the wall instead. She brought her fingers to her temples, shut her eyes tightly, and let a deep grunt of frustration escape her lips.

At this point, she was indifferent to Dan's leaving her, but to essentially leave their son? She'd never understand that choice. And now a move back to Maryland? Dan had placed her in a precarious position. She was left to both pick up the pieces of their failure of a marriage and also do her best to support her son in his time of emotional confusion and turmoil. Again.

Damn Dan!

A couple of months later, in mid-March, Piper was sitting at the lunch table with Maddy, Princess, Jace, and Dustin. Jace and Dustin typically sat with their cross country friends, a table full of raucous boys, though Piper didn't think that either Jace or Dustin was nearly as annoying as their teammates.

Today, though, Maddy had asked Jace to sit with them, and Piper was delighted. Recently, her feelings toward Jace had morphed, and though she couldn't quite decipher them just yet, she knew she felt conflicted. When she looked at him, her stomach flopped, and at times, she even felt a slight tinge of a blush creep from her neck and spread to her cheeks.

She found herself staring at his features when he was otherwise occupied, and she thought perhaps she had memorized every line of his face, the way his nose curved ever so slightly to the left, his jawline, his cheeks, even his brows. And that hair. He had sported a similar style from the time she had first met him at Maddy's house the weekend he and his family had moved to town. His hair was still blond, though not as starkly so as it had been four and a half years ago, when Piper was nine and Jace had just turned ten. And that tendril—there was still that tendril that flopped down and, at times, covered a portion of his eye.

Piper didn't even realize she was staring at Jace until he turned, looked at her, and smiled—that genuine smile she had become accustomed to, the one he didn't offer all the time but that she fully appreciated. She hastily broke her gaze and looked down at the sandwich in her hands as she felt her chest constrict and warmth trickle up to mark the pale skin of her face.

She'd had this feeling before, she knew. She had had plenty of crushes. She was fourteen, after all. But this was Jace. Jace! They had only ever been friends. Didn't she want things to remain the way they were?

But no. When she was delving into her feelings, into the core of her heart, she knew she didn't want to remain friends with Jace Weatherbee. She wanted more. So much more. She wanted to touch his cheek without repercussions, without Jace thinking she was—as Piper's mom often expressed about other people—batshit crazy. She wanted to brush back that blond tendril of hair that she'd never dared touch, not even in a friendly manner, like Maddy had done. And she wanted—oh, how she wanted—to press her lips to his. What would they feel like?

Unlike her best friend, Piper hadn't yet been kissed. Sure, she had had crushes in the past, plenty of them, but nothing had come to fruition. She blamed it on her shy persona.

Yes, Maddy had been kissed. Almost fourteen now, Maddy had just broken up with her third boyfriend. None of the boys had lasted long, but Maddy was a go-getter. She was extroverted by nature, and what Maddy wanted, Maddy went for and often got. But she wasn't precocious. Piper knew that Maddy hadn't done much more than kiss those boys.

Piper often wished she was more like Maddy.

And Jace. Jace, too, had been kissed. Piper had seen this for herself. Though he wasn't currently in a relationship, Piper knew that he had had a girlfriend not that long ago, toward the beginning of the year. Back when his dad moved away. She knew about his dad. They all did. And

Piper knew, too, that it had really upset him, though he hadn't verbalized this. She could just see it, mostly back at the beginning of their eighth-grade year, but it was still there. It was in the way he carried himself and in the way he smiled sometimes, as if it was forced. And often in his eyes. Something was just… different.

But right now, as they sat at the lunch table, his real smile was back, and Piper couldn't help but look. His teeth were straight and white—his braces had done their work, that was for sure. And the way his lips parted when he smiled to reveal those teeth… Yep. Piper was a goner.

She hadn't confided her feelings to anyone, not even Maddy. And she told Maddy everything! She just didn't really know how Maddy would take the news or what she would say. Piper was sure she'd tell her best friend soon—that was what best friends were for, right? To confide in, to trust. Not just yet, though. She wanted to keep this secret to herself for a little while longer.

Piper was sitting next to Princess. Maddy was directly across from her. Jace was sandwiched between Maddy and Dustin. Maddy nudged Jace with her shoulder, a grin on her lips. "Hey, Jace," she said. "You goin' to the semiformal? It's the end of our last year of middle school, you know."

"Yeah, I know," Jace said. He took a bite of his turkey sub. "Don't know. Haven't thought about it."

"You should go," Maddy urged. "We're all gonna go." She motioned to Piper and Princess across the table. "How about you, Dustin?" Maddy leaned forward to better see her friend around Jace. "We've had fun at dances before."

Dustin shrugged.

"You guys suck," Maddy said teasingly. She flipped a lock of long brown hair behind her shoulder.

"Whatever," Dustin said, but he was smiling.

"We should just all go together," Maddy announced. "We, like, hang out all the time anyway."

"I can't wait," Princess chimed in. "It'll give me an excuse to dress shop!"

"See, guys?" Maddy was looking directly at Jace. "Be more like Princess."

Jace grinned. "Don't know," he said. "Maybe. I'll think about it."

"That's not good enough," Maddy declared. "But I'll let it go for now. I know I'll convince you."

"Oh yeah?" Jace chuckled.

"Yeah," Maddy said. "You know I will."

Jace lifted a brow and took another bite of his sub.

Piper found herself grinning. Jace might go to the semiformal! How amazing would that be? At this moment, Piper didn't even care that it was Maddy doing the pushing. If she could get Jace to go to the semiformal, then she, Piper, might have the opportunity to dance with him. She might feel his hands on her hips, feel the warmth of his body. She might feel his breath on her cheek. And it would give her a totally appropriate excuse to wrap her arms around his neck and hold him close.

Could this really happen? She'd have to talk to Maddy, convince her even further to get Jace to come. Maybe it was time for Piper to break her silence and get Maddy on her side. Maybe this could really work!

Lunch ended, and the friends parted ways, Piper heading for math class. Piper knew that Maddy and Jace were both going to the same social studies class, and she was so jealous that Maddy had this extra time with Jace, even when she knew they weren't able to socialize much when in class. They still occupied the same space at the same time.

The day ended, and Piper made her way to her locker to gather her belongings before heading to catch the bus. This weekend, she'd muster up the nerve to talk to Maddy. They already had plans to see each other anyway, so it was the perfect excuse.

---

"So…" Piper and Maddy were sitting on Maddy's bed. Piper looked down at her twiddling fingers. "I…"

"Spit it out, Pipes. You're acting super weird."

"I know," Piper agreed. "But it's kind of awkward."

"What is?"

"What I want to tell you," Piper replied.

Maddy leaned forward, her legs crossed under her thighs. "Ooh," she said with a smirk. "Then I want to know even more." She wriggled her brows.

Piper couldn't help but laugh. She didn't know why she was nervous. Maddy always had a tendency to make Piper feel good about herself, welcome and accepted. She could tell her this secret of hers, surely.

Piper looked into her best friend's wide, gray-blue eyes, the lashes surrounding them long and thick. They looked hungry for the news about to be relayed.

"Well," Piper began once more. "So, do you think you'll ask Jace to go to semiformal again? With us, I mean."

"Sure," Maddy said, narrowing her brows. "Why? That was super random."

"I know it was," Piper agreed. "But I think I just…" Piper let out a deep sigh. "I like him, Maddy."

"Well, duh," Maddy said. "What's not to like? Plus, I

know you like him. We all like him. He's, like, our best guy friend."

"No," Piper said. "That's not what I mean."

Maddy narrowed her brows even farther.

"I mean, I *like* him like him."

Maddy's eyes widened. "Seriously?"

Though she didn't do it often around her best friend, Piper found herself blushing. "Yeah."

"No freakin' way!"

"Yeah," Piper repeated.

"But he's, like, our best guy friend. He's… he's Jace. We tease him, make fun of him. We hang out. He's… he's Jace!"

"I know!" Piper said with a bit of exasperation, as if she, too, couldn't believe she had this particular crush.

Maddy tilted her head and squinted at Piper. "Jace?"

Piper nodded. "Jace."

"How did I not know? I'm usually good at figuring things out."

"Yeah, you are," Piper agreed. "But I didn't want you to know."

Maddy's lower lip fell, the expression on her face one of wounded pride. "Why not?"

"It's not like I didn't trust you," Piper hastily reassured her best friend. "I just know that…. You've known about all my crushes before, but this one is different because, like you said, it's Jace. Jace is different. He's in our group."

"Are you gonna do something about it?"

Piper bit her lower lip. "I was hoping you would."

"What do you mean?"

"You were talking about us all going to semiformal together at lunch the other day, and I thought, you know, I thought that you'd bring it up again. You seemed pretty determined to get him to go."

"I am," Maddy said. "Because he's one of our best friends, him and Dustin both. I know we'd all have a good time. I thought we'd have more fun if the guys were there."

"So... have you asked him again?"

Maddy shook her head while coiling a lock of hair around her pointer finger. "No. But I will."

"So I thought if you could convince him to go, then maybe, I don't know... maybe something would happen, right?"

Maddy shrugged a shoulder nonchalantly. "Don't know," she said. "Maybe? But why don't you just ask him? If you like him, don't you think you should ask him, like, on a date?"

Piper felt her stomach drop. "I can't do that."

"Why not?"

"You know I can't do that, Maddy," Piper said. "It makes me too nervous. What if he says no? What if he turns me down, and then everything between us is really awkward? And different?"

"What if he says yes? Then everything will be different anyway."

"Yeah," Piper said. "But different in a... well, in a different way. We'd be on a date. That's so much better than if I asked and he said no. Can you imagine? How weird would things be between us if I put myself out there and he turned me down?"

"Won't know unless you try."

"I guess. But, yeah... I guess I was just thinking that if you convinced him to go to semiformal, then I could try something there, right? I could ask him to dance. Even thinking about doing that makes me nervous, but it's so

94

much better than just coming straight out and asking him out!"

"Whatever," Maddy replied. "I don't know. I think you should just ask him out."

Piper shook her head. "Not yet. I'm not ready."

"Okay," Maddy said. Then, after a pause she asked, "Why Jace?"

Piper offered a close-lipped smile as her countenance softened. "Jace is so, so cool. He's such a nice guy, right? When you listen to him talk, the things he says. He's never mean to anyone. He's got a lot of friends but seems cool just hanging with us, with his closest friends. He's so good at cross country. And I think he just treats people really good. And he doesn't care what other people think about him, but not in a conceited way, you know what I mean? More in just a confident way, like he knows who he is. I still care what people think and say. But not Jace. I don't think so, anyway. And…"

"And?" Maddy prompted.

"He's so freaking hot!"

Maddy burst out in laughter, which set Piper off as well. The girls laughed and laughed, and eventually, Maddy grasped a pillow, hoisted it over her head, and whacked Piper in the face.

"Ow!" Piper protested, though she was still laughing. "Why'd you do that?"

Instead of answering, Maddy smacked Piper in the arm with the pillow.

"Hey!" Piper screeched. She grabbed another pillow from the bed, one of many, and slammed it into Maddy's chest.

Maddy squealed, and a full-out pillow fight ensued, the girls' laughter reverberating through the room, off the walls, and ringing in their ears. Eventually, panting, they ceased their fight, both girls plopping onto their backs on the bed, pillows discarded at their sides.

After catching her breath, Piper turned to Maddy. "You're my best friend," she said, her voice low, sure. Reverent.

"You're my best friend too. Promise not to keep secrets from me again, though?"

Piper smiled. "I promise. As long as you never keep secrets from me."

"Of course not," Maddy replied. "I've never kept secrets from you. And I never will. I love ya, Pipes."

---

Maddy did, in fact, convince both Jace and Dustin to attend the semiformal celebration at school.

It was now the night of the dance, a Saturday in mid-April, and Piper, Princess, and Maddy were getting ready in Maddy's bedroom. Maddy's mom, Jenny, was currently downstairs, making a fruity concoction that the girls would chug down, no doubt, before they hopped into Jenny's car and were whisked away to the school.

Piper had asked Maddy to keep her secret. Although she loved and trusted Princess, she kept her crush closely guarded. If anything came of it, then of course Princess would know. But for now, Piper didn't want the information to get out. Maddy had promised she wouldn't tell another soul, and Piper trusted her implicitly. Maddy was always truthful and had never given Piper a reason to lack confidence in her. Piper was certain that Maddy would always remain a true and loyal friend, and she was immensely grateful for her friendship each and every day.

"We're gonna have so much fun," Princess announced with a flourish as she spun in her skin-tight dress, strong legs exposed.

"Um, yeah, we are," Maddy said enthusiastically. "And Princess, you look hot!"

Princess grinned then bowed dramatically.

"You too, Pipes," Maddy said.

Piper glanced down at her dress. Nearly knee length, it was longer than both Maddy's and Princess's, and she knew that it would be longer than that of most every other girl at the semiformal dance, for that matter. Piper's legs were shorter and a bit thicker than her friends', and she often found herself a bit self-conscious.

"Yeah," Princess agreed. "That dress is perfect for you."

"Thanks, guys," Piper replied. "I do feel kinda good."

"Kind of?" Maddy said, widening her eyes. "You should feel super sexy. You look it! Hey…" She caught Piper's eye with a sideways glance. "Maybe there's a certain boy who will appreciate how you look tonight."

"Ooh," Princess said, looking at Piper. "A certain boy? You got someone in mind?"

Piper shook her head vigorously. "No," she said. "Nope."

"Ah," Maddy flicked her hand dismissively. "Just a boy. Or boys. Who knows. Whatever. I'm just saying that Pipes looks hot, and she's gonna make those eyes dart right to her."

Princess laughed. "We all are!"

"Hell yeah!" Maddy exclaimed.

The girls giggled, and then Maddy sat in front of her vanity. She fixed her hair and touched up her makeup. "Pipes, you sure you don't want me to do your makeup?

You know I'm good at it. I still can't believe you don't wear any."

"Even I can't believe it," Princess said. "I'd feel naked without mine."

Piper frowned. "I don't know…"

"Come here." Maddy stood and patted the cushion on the chair. "Sit. Let me do it just tonight. I promise you'll love it. And you're all dressed up. I won't do a lot, I swear."

Piper stared at her best friend for a moment then hesitantly sat. She looked in the mirror as Maddy clapped her hands and got to work, rummaging through her various eyeshadows and lipsticks. When she dabbed a bit of foundation on a sponge, Piper spoke up. "Maybe not that? It's too much. I'll feel weird."

"Aw, really, Pipes?"

Piper nodded.

"Fine. Whatever," Maddy said dejectedly. She picked up an eye pencil and held it aloft with a questioning expression.

"Yeah, that's okay," Piper said.

Maddy grinned and got to work. She lined Piper's eyes, swept mascara onto her lashes, brushed eyeshadow on her lids, applied a bit of blusher, and then spread a pale-pink lipstick on Piper's thin lips. Piper watched Maddy step back and inspect her work. "Take a look," Maddy said with a satisfied grin.

Piper looked into the mirror, and her lips parted immediately in surprise.

"I went easy," Maddy said. "But see? I told you I was good at this stuff."

Piper lifted her chin then moved her head slowly to the left then the right, inspecting her reflection. She had to admit that Maddy's work was transformative. And yet Piper didn't feel entirely made up, didn't feel the desire to swipe at her skin with a cloth to remove the cosmetics. She smiled. "I like it," she announced.

"Told ya," Maddy said. She moved to stand behind Piper and lifted her friend's straight brown hair off her back. "Want me to curl it like mine? I'm, like, super good at that too, you know."

"You don't think that would be too much?"

"Heck no," Maddy said. "It's the semiformal. If you want any excuse to dress up and pamper yourself, it's tonight."

"I suppose…" Piper said with uncertainty.

"You suppose right," Maddy said. "Let's do it."

"I'd do it if I was you," Princess remarked. "Can't with my hair." She ran her fingers down her incredibly straight, shiny black, chin-length hair. "But you can pull it off. Do it!"

Piper inhaled a deep breath and, upon exhalation, said, "All right. Curl away."

Maddy wriggled her brows in response, looking at Piper in the mirror. When the curling brush was ready, she got to work, coiling Piper's tresses. Piper watched her friend's movements, and eventually, Maddy pulled back, surveyed her work, and announced that Piper's hair looked incredible.

And Piper had to agree. She had never had it curled before, not even when fooling around with Maddy in her room. Between the makeup, the dress, and the hair, Piper felt like an entirely different person. Perhaps a person that was confident enough to make a move on Jace!

"Thanks, Maddy," Piper said wholeheartedly. She stood and pulled her best friend into an embrace.

"Welcome," Maddy said.

There was a knock on the door, and Jenny poked her head inside the room.

"You ready?" And then she pushed the door open more fully. "Holy cow, look at you three! I'm not sure I've ever seen three more beautiful girls. Oh, I miss dances. I went to semiformals. Did I tell you that, Maddy? I'm sure I did. And I went to prom my junior year and my senior year. Maybe you girls will be lucky enough to go your junior year too. Oh, you're just bringing back so many memories for me right now. You're going to have such a wonderful time." She clasped her hands in front of her. "Oh, how I miss dances. All the people and the music and the sights and the smells and the food and… that feeling I got inside. And—"

"Mom!" Maddy interjected.

"Sorry," Jenny said. "But look at the three of you. And Piper, look at your hair!"

Piper brought her fingertips to graze the tip of a curl. "Maddy did it," she announced.

"Leave it to Maddy," Jenny said. "I was just like her, you know. Always primping away. Lots of experimentation back in those days." She paused for a moment and then said, "You girls really do look incredible. What a fun night you're going to have! This is so wonderful!"

"Okay, Mom," Maddy said, rolling her eyes, which only elicited a laugh from Jenny.

"You girls all set?"

"Yep," Maddy said as Princess replied with a "yes" and Piper merely nodded.

The girls retrieved their clutch purses—acquired when they had gone shopping for their dresses together—and followed Jenny down the winding staircase and to the first-floor foyer. They passed the kitchen on their way to the garage, where Maddy's father was popping the top off a glass bottle of beer. He turned at the sound of their foot-steps. "Whoa," he said, eyes wide. "You kids are all dressed up."

Maddy frowned, lifting the corner of her mouth in a tell-tale annoyed expression. "Um," she said. "Yeah, kinda the point of a semiformal."

Her father returned Maddy's gaze with an expression of his own, a look that bespoke his acquired expectations of his daughter's teenage retorts.

"Well, you kids look great," Gus said.

"Yeah, Daddy… we're kinda not kids anymore."

"Okay," Gus replied. "Got the message. But you still look great."

Maddy smiled. "Thanks, Daddy."

For all her eye rolls and through all her complaints, Piper knew that Maddy held a special place in her heart for her father, a man who was both a stern and a comforting presence in her life.

"Pictures!" Jenny declared. "We need pictures before we go."

"Absolutely!" Maddy agreed. "Outside. It's still a little light. It'll make the best pictures."

"By the fireplace too," Jenny suggested, and the girls agreed. Piper reached into her purse and extracted her phone, handing it off to Jenny. Maddy and Princess did the same. Though these phones were not new for either Maddy or Princess, this was the first year in which Piper's mom had allowed her to join in with the majority of her peers. Piper knew that her mother feared social media and online bully-ing, but Piper had pleaded persistently and had finally worn her mother down.

The girls walked into the living room and stood in front of the wide fireplace, the pale stone extending toward the cathedral ceiling. "Smile!" Jenny instructed, then proceeded to snap photos with her camera as well as the cameras of all three girls. "Ooh," Jenny crooned. "I need to send these to your brother, Maddy. He'll love seeing you all dressed up!"

"Um..." Maddy said with a look of distaste. "I don't think Michael's gonna care about seeing me in these pictures, Mom, seriously. He's nineteen and in college. You think he's really gonna want to get pictures of me?"

"I absolutely do," Jenny declared. "Your brother might be older, and he might be busy, but he still loves you. And he wants to know what we're up to. I'm sure of it."

"Um... okay," Maddy said, her sneer clearly expressing her disbelief.

Once they finished taking photos indoors, the girls exited through the garage along with Maddy's parents. "Over there," Jenny said. "By the tree."

Maddy led the way, and the girls positioned themselves in front of a gargantuan tree by the side of Maddy's front yard. The thick, massive trunk, along with the blue sky and waning sun, offered the perfect backdrop. Maddy, standing between her friends, placed her arms around Piper and Princess and grinned into the camera lens. Piper liked the feel of Maddy's hand on her shoulder and wrapped her own arm around Maddy's waist. She felt the wind tickle her exposed skin, the evening air crisp and cool. Her curls bounced slightly in the breeze.

When Jenny had finished snapping photos, Maddy immediately took hold of her phone and scrolled through what her mother had captured. "Ooh," she said. "You got some good ones."

"I sure did," Jenny said.

Piper watched as Maddy tapped her phone's screen with the tips of her thumbs. "Done," Maddy announced, and Piper knew that Maddy had posted her favorites to Instagram, her social media platform of choice these days. Piper might post a photo, too, but she'd do so later.

Maddy kissed her father goodbye, and the girls piled into the back of Jenny's car. As she glided down the driveway, Jenny beeped at her husband, and Gus waved.

"This is gonna be awesome," Maddy said, and Piper and Princess agreed.

The girls giggled and chatted the entire way to the middle school, where Jenny pulled up to the curb behind other cars, and the girls exited onto the sidewalk. Jenny leaned over the center console of her car and shouted out the open passenger's-side window. "Have a great time!"

Piper and Princess smiled while Maddy raised her hand in acknowledgment.

Princess arrived at the main entrance of the school first and held a door open for her friends. Maddy entered, Piper following in her wake. Princess let go of the door, walked forward, and said, "Let's do this!" before flicking her black hair and strutting with playful exaggeration. Maddy laughed, her steps quickening.

The semiformal was in the gym. The girls made their way, joining a small gathering of seventh and eighth graders—this semiformal was not for the younger classes —as they, too, walked toward the festivities. The girls wore dresses, most of them short and strapless, and the boys wore khaki pants or dress slacks with collared shirts, some with ties and blazers. Most of the boys donned sneakers on their feet, while the girls wore sneakers, flats, or heels. Both Maddy and Princess were in heels, but Piper wore comfortable flats. She had attempted to walk in heels in the past, and it hadn't been pretty, to say the least. She felt awkward enough when walking; she didn't need to exacerbate her unsteady gait with a pair of shoes.

Piper heard the music wafting from the spacious room and into the hallway. The smell of pizza permeated the air, and Piper's stomach began to grumble. She had eaten a snack at Maddy's house, but the girls had been too eager for the dance to eat anything of substance.

When she stepped into the gym, Piper glanced at her surroundings. Though they had only arrived fifteen minutes after starting time, the floor was already packed with students. Some were dancing, but most were off to the side, chatting with friends, drinking, or snacking. A pair of boys had even found a soccer ball and were kicking it back and forth in the corner of the gym. Some adult chaperones were present, though not many.

Maddy nodded her approval. "Cool," she said. She spied some girls off in the distance, friends of hers, and she made her way over, Piper and Princess in tow. As the girls began to chat enthusiastically, Piper scanned the room again, attempting to ascertain whether Jace had arrived.

She didn't see him and immediately felt dejected.

She joined the conversation for a while, and then she, Maddy, and Princess broke off and made their way to the refreshment table. Piper ladled herself a cup of punch, took a sip, and then startled when she lifted her gaze and saw Jace across the room. Her heart thumped, and her stomach flopped. She held her cup a bit more tightly, the plastic crinkling between her fingers.

Jace. She could see the breadth of his smile even from this distance. He was wearing a slim-fitting pair of dark-gray slacks, so dark they almost appeared black. His jacket matched, and beneath it, he wore an off-white dress shirt, the top few buttons left open, and even from her vantage point, Piper could see that the shirt framed his chest and torso snuggly. To her, Jace always looked good. Even in a pair of jeans or sweatpants and a sweatshirt. But tonight—tonight, he looked incredible!

Jace laughed at something a friend had apparently just said, and then he looked to the side, and that was when his eyes found Piper's. He nodded and lifted his hand in a small wave of acknowledgment. She deposited her cup on the table, fearing that her shaking fingers might slip and spill the drink, before waving in turn.

"Jace and Dustin are here," Maddy announced.

Piper had been too involved in her own thoughts to realize that Maddy had also spotted their friends. Maddy popped a bite-sized treat into her mouth and then led the way to the boys. Piper followed, though her stomach protested more intensely with each passing step. She was thankful to be wearing a bit of blush on her cheeks. Maybe it would mask the warmth she felt creeping in.

She doubted it, though.

"Hey there," Maddy said happily as they approached the boys, her voice raised to be heard over the music.

"Madison Crawford, damn!" said Seth, one of Jace and Dustin's cross country teammates.

Maddy lifted her brows and smirked with pleasure.

"Looking good," Seth said.

"Thanks." Maddy beamed.

"You all are," Jace announced. He looked at Maddy with a smile then at Princess and, lastly, at Piper. Her chest pinched so tightly that she feared Jace could hear the beating of her heart.

"You're lookin' pretty good yourself," Maddy told Jace.

Piper wished in that moment that she had been the one to say something to Jace, to let him know that yes, he did indeed look amazing. But her voice was trapped, and she lacked the ability to utter anything intelligible, she was sure. She'd leave it to Maddy, her friendly, extroverted best friend. Her crush on Jace was no longer a secret between the two friends, and Piper knew that if anyone could help her out, it was Maddy.

The base suddenly ceased, and the fast-paced song that had just been playing was replaced by something much slower. Piper noticed some eighth-graders begin to dance, and then Seth took Maddy by the arm and said, "Dance? They don't play slow ones a lot. Let's do it."

"Sure," Maddy agreed. She took a step forward to follow Seth onto the dance floor but halted momentarily to look at Jace and say, "You should dance with Pipes." She turned her gaze to Dustin and said, "And you should dance with Princess. We can all be together!"

Although Piper was so nervous—she feared she'd be sick right then and there—she was also incredibly grateful for Maddy's attempt. Then, the notion hit her that perhaps Jace would refuse, and an entirely new set of emotions flooded within.

"Yeah," Jace said. "Okay." He offered a soft smile and extended his hand to Piper. Though relieved, she trembled slightly as she placed her palm in his and let him lead her to the dance floor. When he had found a suitable spot, he turned, let go of Piper's hand, moved in closer, and wrapped his arms around her waist.

She looked down. Her gaze settled on his shirt, and her breath caught.

Was this really happening?

Piper slowly lifted her arms, looking now at Jace's shoulder. She caught sight of the skin peeking out from under his pressed shirt, smooth and unblemished. She had to reach in order to place her arms around Jace's shoulders, and as she did so, she felt the material of his thin jacket, the hardness of his muscles beneath. He wasn't a large boy, Jace, but he was tall and lithe. His time and efforts in running were exhibited in the contours of his legs when he wore shorts to school, and Piper assumed he must make other efforts to keep his body fit and in shape, as she had noticed, too, the burgeoning muscles in his arms.

And now she was touching him. Actually touching him. Sure, her hands were splayed on his jacket and not on his skin, but it was still Jace. She was dancing with Jace. She had never been this close to him before, not in this way, at least.

"You having a good time so far?" Piper lifted her gaze at the sound of his voice and looked into Jace's eyes. So close. Right *there*! She had always known they were blue, but at that moment, only inches away, they were so much more —varying shades of blue mingling together, the pupils large at their centers.

Piper wasn't sure she could speak, but speak she must; Jace had just asked her a question. She nodded first, a slight movement, and then, barely above a whisper, said, "Yes."

"Good," Jace replied with a smile. She could still feel his hands on her hips, the warmth emanating from his body at such close proximity. "I'm not usually much for dancing. I didn't even know if I was gonna come tonight. But Maddy convinced us. It's a good time so far, though."

Piper nodded again. After a moment, her pink-hued lips parted, and she said, "I'm glad you're having fun."

Jace smiled.

*Come on, Piper! Say something else! This is Jace. You talk to him all the time!*

"How is cross country going? You're on a special team, right?"

"Yeah," Jace said, looking down at Piper. "It's not like school, where everyone on the team goes here. It's a team of kids from all of New Hampshire. And these kids are really freakin' good, too."

"But you're good. You have to be if you're on the team, right? And I've seen you run here. For the school, I mean." Her voice was still low, but her words were beginning to flow more freely now as her body relaxed in his arms.

Jace grinned. "I'm good," he said. "But not as good as some of these guys. You should see them, Piper. So fast!"

Piper paused for a moment, gathering her thoughts. She wanted Jace to know how she felt, but there was no way she was going to come right out and tell him. That would transcend her level of comfort. After a pause of several seconds, her gaze homed in on his shirt—she couldn't look him in the eye, not right now—and she said, "Maybe I could go watch you sometime?"

She could hear his smile in his reply—if that was such a thing—and it made her slowly tilt her head upward. "That would be great. But you don't need to do that. Matches aren't in town. They're usually at least a half an hour away and even out of state sometimes."

"I don't mind," Piper said. "I'm sure my mom would drive me. I'd… I'd like to watch you."

Jace shrugged, and Piper's hands elevated slightly with his shoulders. "You can if you want. I don't have any friends around here that are on the team, so my mom usually takes me to practices and matches alone. I'm sure she'd drive us if a bunch of us wanted to go and then grab pizza or something after a match."

*A bunch of us.* She obviously didn't know what she was

doing, how to convey her interest to Jace. Not for the first time, Piper wished she could channel Maddy's forthright personality.

Resigned, Piper nodded. "Yeah, okay," she said. "That sounds good."

"Yeah," Jace smiled.

Piper wanted to say something else, anything else, but the song ended, and Jace's hands dropped from her waist. He stepped back, and Piper suddenly felt cool air hit her stomach and chest and spread to the skin of her arms, leaving goose bumps in its wake. She crossed her arms and held her elbows with her palms. She pressed her lips together, feeling the waxy remnants of lipstick. She opened her mouth to ask Jace if he wanted to grab a drink, but a fast-paced movement caught in her peripheral vision and she turned her head to the side. Dustin leaped beside Jace, draped his arm over his friend's shoulder. Jace grinned widely in Dustin's presence, the beat of a new song blaring through the room and accosting Piper's ears.

"How's it goin', man?" Dustin asked. He turned to acknowledge Piper briefly with a nod before playfully punching Jace in the chest with his fist. Dustin had been wearing a blazer, but Piper noticed now that it had been discarded. The top button of his shirt was left open, the knot of his tie pulled down to drape lazily on his chest. Dustin began bobbing his head to the beat of the music.

"Food," he said. "I need food." Arm still hanging over Jace's shoulder, Dustin dragged him toward the refreshment table. Piper knew that Dustin wasn't attempting to be rude and hadn't meant to shun her. Dustin was just being Dustin: goofy, energetic. And in so being, he was just having fun. But he and Jace had left her standing in the middle of the dance floor nonetheless. Alone. Despondent.

Piper pressed her arms more tightly against her chest. She was about to turn and seek out a friend she could walk to when a set of hands grabbed her from behind, arms flung around her shoulders, and a warm cheek pressed against her ear.

Maddy turned Piper around, and Piper saw that her best friend was beaming. "How was it?" Maddy asked. "You danced with Jace!"

Piper managed a smile. "It was okay."

Maddy lifted a brow and pursed her lips. "Um… okay? Like, what does that even mean? I swear, Pipes, you need to talk!"

And then Piper smiled. She let her arms fall to her sides, the goose bumps having dissipated. "It was good."

"That's more like it. What did he say? What did he do? What did *you* do?"

Piper glanced around. Maddy was nearly shouting to be heard over the music, and there were too many people near them. They didn't appear to be eavesdropping, but Piper wasn't about to take any chances that her words would find their way to Jace's ear, so she shrugged and said, "We can talk about it later. Nothing much happened."

Maddy frowned. "Why not?"

Piper offered a close-lipped, wan smile. "We didn't have very long. We talked, but that's about it. I'll tell you all about it later, maybe when we're at your house tonight?"

Apparently, that was good enough for Maddy. She smiled brightly then took Piper's hands in her own and spun her on the dance floor.

Maddy started seeing Seth the following day. Princess had been picked up by her mother at the end of the semiformal and taken home since she had to awaken early the following morning for a family affair. It was just Maddy and Piper alone in Maddy's bedroom after the dance, and that was when Maddy, close to squealing, had told Piper that Seth had asked her out at the end of the semiformal.

"Really? Why didn't you tell me before?" Piper asked. "And where was I when this happened? We were together most of the night."

"You were in the bathroom, and like, I didn't have time when they were pushing us out the door, and we were walking with other people and stuff. And then my mom picked us up. I didn't want my mom to know. Not yet."

"Why not?"

"Because I wanted to tell you first! I didn't want to get in my mom's car and just blurt out that Seth asked me out. Then my mom would have been all gushy and asking me all sorts of questions. I just want to talk about it with you first."

"Your mom does talk a lot."

Maddy laughed. "Um… yeah!"

"But she's cool."

"I guess," Maddy said with a slight shrug.

"So, tell me everything!"

Maddy, who had been sitting on her bed with her legs crossed, leaped up onto her knees and crashed into Piper excitedly, hugging her tightly and knocking her over to land on her back on the bed. Piper laughed, and then both girls righted themselves before Maddy began to speak.

"Okay, so you know I danced with him."

"A lot," Piper said.

"A lot." Maddy grinned. "And I didn't really think

anything of it, I swear. It's Seth. He's just a super-friendly guy and all. I thought he was just being nice."

"Being nice to only you? He didn't dance with anyone else."

Maddy playfully swatted Piper's arm. "Shut up!" She laughed. "So, he asked me to dance at the end of the semi-formal again, and of course, I danced with him. I was having a really good time. And the song ended, and they didn't play another one because it was time to go. I was saying goodbye, but he interrupted me and said we should hang out sometime. So of course, I said yes. And he said that we should hang out, like, just the two of us. And that's when it hit me. He was asking me out. So I said that, yeah, that would be cool. And then he said 'cool' back. And then he said we should hang out tomorrow! Tomorrow, Pipes. He's taking me to the movies. So he's picking me up, and we're going to the movies!"

Piper's eyes widened. "Really?"

"Yeah, really." Maddy was beaming. She rocked side to side, lifting her shoulders in a pleased, celebratory manner, and then squealed again.

"You've got a boyfriend," Piper remarked. There had been a couple of previous boyfriends for Maddy, but those relationships had been fairly superficial. One boy in the seventh grade had lasted only a couple of weeks and hadn't progressed beyond hand holding and light kissing, and another at the beginning of this school year hadn't been serious, either.

"Maybe, maybe not. I'm not sure what we are right now. He's just taking me out, so I don't think he's my boyfriend yet, but…"

"So cool, Maddy!"

"I know!" Maddy spoke for a few more minutes about

Seth and then furrowed her brows and said, "So tell me about Jace. What happened?"

"Or didn't happen," Piper said forlornly.

"Aw, Pipes."

"I know," Piper said. "But it's my fault. I'm not like you, Maddy. I can't just say whatever's on my mind, especially not when it's something like this, like having such a big crush on someone."

"It's a big crush?" Maddy was smirking incorrigibly.

Piper sighed. "Yeah. Pretty big."

"I still can't get over it, though. I mean… it's Jace."

"I know," Piper said. "But he's just such a good guy, Maddy. And I know we've all been friends for a while now, but… I don't know."

"When did you start liking him? I mean, like, more than just a friend?"

"I'm not really sure," Piper admitted. "It just kind of happened. I started feeling differently when we were around each other and when we'd talk to each other. It just kind of happened."

"Okay," Maddy said, satisfied. "So tell me about the dance."

"The dance?" Piper's confusion was evident. Was Maddy asking about the semiformal as a whole?

"Um… yeah. The dance. When you danced with him. You said you'd tell me more about it when we got here. Now we're here. Spill."

"Oh," Piper said. "Yeah." And then she found her cheeks warming and her lips curving upward. "It was really nice."

"Ooh…"

"But I just… I couldn't really talk to him. We talked a little, but I wanted to… I asked him about cross country and the team he's on right now, and then I got up enough nerve to tell him that I'd go and watch him. I thought maybe he'd get the clue, right? But I don't think he did. He said that it would be good if I came to watch him compete but that we should all go as friends. You, me, other people. He said his mom could drive us all and then we could get pizza after. So I don't think he got it."

Maddy shook her head. "Definitely not. You should have just told him that you wanted to go out, like, asked him on a date. Like Seth did to me."

"No way," Piper said.

"Aw, come on, Pipes. You can do it!"

"I really don't know," Piper said.

"I think boys are stupid," Maddy remarked. "They just don't get it sometimes. Jace is awesome, but he's clueless, you know? I think you need to tell him how you feel. Obviously, he doesn't get it if you tried to ask him out and he said we should all go out together."

"Or he did get it but just didn't want to go out with me alone."

"Aw, Pipes," Maddy said soothingly. "I don't think that's it."

Piper frowned. "I don't know. Maybe I'll just tell him again that I want to see him run at a meet. At lunch or something? We can make plans and see what happens."

"I guess," Maddy said. "But if we do, then, for sure you need to make a move."

Piper sighed. "I'll try."

The following week at school, Piper was sitting with Maddy, Princess, and a few other friends when she saw Jace walk into the lunchroom. He was with a girl that Piper only vaguely knew, a girl named Sam. She was smiling coyly at him, and he was grinning back. And then he reached over, took her hand in his, and didn't let go. He led her to the table where Dustin and some of his other cross country friends were gathered, and he and Sam sat together, side by side.

And then Piper watched as Jace leaned over and kissed Sam on the cheek.

Piper's lower lip fell, her chest went heavy, and tears began to well in her eyes.

Jace Weatherbee had a girlfriend.

# Chapter 6

## *Now*

The officers had interrogated Jace for what felt like hours to Brooke. She knew she had to get a lawyer; she had never been placed in such a position before and felt confused, frustrated, lost... But most of all, she had been left feeling nauseated.

When they arrived back at home later that night, Jace had instantly climbed the stairs and slammed the door to his bedroom. Brooke let him go. She didn't know what to say to her son right then. She lacked the ability even to sort through the myriad thoughts and feelings that accosted her mind, leaving her feeling spent, barely able to trudge farther into her house. She turned on the light over the counter in the kitchen and, with shuffling feet, walked into the darkened living room, where she sat in her favorite chair. She stared out the window into the November night sky, where the stars were plentiful and the moon full. On any normal night, she'd have marveled at the beauty. But not tonight. No, not tonight.

Tomorrow was Friday, and Jace was due at school.

She'd be keeping him home, though. This she knew with certainty. How could her son attend school and pretend that everything was okay when it clearly was not? How could he walk through those halls when Maddy might be there, when his friends would be there, when the news would spread like wildfire that her son, her Jace—and at the thought of the ensuing word, her chest constricted and her body began to quake—was a rapist?

Brooke shut her eyes tightly. She lifted her legs and placed her heels close to her bottom, wrapped her arms around her shins, and placed her forehead on her knees. She clenched her thighs and ground her teeth.

Images stirred in her mind, unwanted, unbidden.

*A dark dorm room, the smell of dirty socks pervading her nostrils.*

*A bed, small and unkempt.*

*A beer handed over, though she had already had too many.*

Brooke clenched her jaw tighter, begged the images to flee from her mind.

*A face, close now. Lips on hers, dry and chapped.*

*The bitter taste of beer.*

*A push, though soft, guiding her down.*

*Her mind reeling, swimming. Dizzy.*

*Sitting up.*

*Another push. Harder. Forceful.*

*Protestations.*

*Protestations.*

*Begging.*

*Kicking.*

*Flailing.*

*Then nothing.*

*She was gone.*

Tears welled behind her closed lids. Brooke raised her forehead off her knees and opened her eyes, the moon's rays the only discernible gleam of light. She looked out the window and into the sky once more, her gaze focusing on the beauty of the moon, full and glorious. Unwavering.

A mother was supposed to believe her son. A mother was supposed to be her son's most avid supporter. A mom was supposed to lift her son up, tell him that everything would be okay, even when she wasn't entirely sure of the validity of her own words.

A mother was not supposed to feel like she did right now: confused, dejected. Angry as all hell. But her feelings weren't directed toward Maddy. They were directed at Jace.

How could he? How could he have done this? Especially after everything he knew that had happened with his own mother. How did it come to this?

Because, after all was said and done tonight, Brooke had to admit to herself that she believed Maddy. Despite not having spoken to Maddy herself, she believed her. Because she had lived this truth. She had been there, in Maddy's shoes.

And nobody had believed Brooke.

But now? Now, this involved her son. The son she had borne. The son she had looked down upon in the hospital room and promised the world to. The son who had looked to her as an infant and a toddler for unconditional support and love and to whom she had given both fully and wholeheartedly. Her life had changed the very moment her son was birthed because then she was living for someone else. Another human being, a part of her, fragile and trusting.

She had watched him grow, watched him learn, watched his curiosity about the world around him. She had loved with him, cried with him, grieved the loss of his father with him. She had thought that she and Jace had as a strong relationship as a mother and son could have, especially a teenage son with all his emotions and constant attempts at figuring out his place in the world.

How had she been so blind?

And now this son, this boy who was such an integral part of her life, her identity, had hurt another human being in one of the most abhorrent ways imaginable.

And in so doing, he had crushed Brooke as well.

And again, Brooke's mind began to reel.

What had gone on that night?

The blame was entirely too much. The guilt felt all-encompassing.

Where had she gone wrong?

---

Brooke awoke the following morning, Friday, with a sore neck and back. She had fallen asleep sometime in the night in the chair in the living room. She ran her tongue along her teeth, felt the grime, and winced. The early-morning sun was seeping through the windows.

Brooke extracted herself from the chair, placed her palms on her lower back, and stretched. She then rubbed her fingers along her eyelids, picked at the crust that had developed overnight in their corners. Perhaps she had wept in her sleep. That wouldn't have surprised her.

Brooke made her way slowly to the kitchen. She looked at the clock on the stove. Just past seven o'clock. She had slept in. Jace knew he wasn't attending school today, so Brooke was sure he was still up in his room. Brooke startled as she realized then that she hadn't called in to work, and they'd be expecting her soon.

Where had she left her cell phone? She typically had it on her at all times, but last night, she had obviously misplaced it in her emotional state. She scoured the kitchen. Not there. She walked back into the living room. Not there. Brooke was wearing her Apple Watch, so she tapped the screen, and soon, a dinging rang out close by. She followed the sound and found herself digging between the cushion and the armrest of the chair in which she had fallen asleep. Her fingers wrapped around its case.

Brooke dialed work. No receptionist was on duty at this time, she knew, but she left a message. Typically, she'd have felt terrible for the short notice, but this particular morning, she was beyond caring. She had entirely too much on her mind and even more to do as far as calling her ex-husband, procuring a lawyer, and dealing with her own emotions, let alone those of Jace. Plus—and this was going to prove the most difficult task at hand—she needed to speak with Maddy and Jenny at some point.

After leaving a message for work, Brooke grabbed her laptop, sat in the living room chair, and opened the computer, bringing the screen to life. She'd have to research how to procure a lawyer since she hadn't the slightest idea how to do so. She didn't believe any of her friends or acquaintances had ever had to do this, either.

And who was she kidding? Friends *and* acquaintances? She had several acquaintances, yes. She had spoken on several occasions to other parents when helping out with the PTA or attending school functions, but with her work schedule and tendency toward introversion, Jenny was really her only good friend in town. And there was absolutely no way she could ask Jenny if she knew how to acquire the aid of a lawyer to help Brooke's son fight the allegations that Jenny's daughter had made against him. Absolutely no way on God's green earth.

So she was left to her own devices. Maybe Dan had the

knowledge and ability to help. He was more of a go-getter. But at this moment, Brooke couldn't bring herself to call Jace's father. Despite the fact that he had every right to know what had occurred last night and the complicated agonizing logistics it would bring to the near future, she didn't want to make that call just yet. She didn't want to be berated over the telephone. That was the last thing she needed right now, especially since she was already placing the brunt of the guilt on herself. She didn't need Dan to grind that in even further.

Brooke spent about half an hour online before she felt the inclination to check on her son. She closed her laptop, stood, and set it down on the chair's cushion. She'd get back to it in just a moment. She climbed the stairs to the second floor and knocked softly on Jace's bedroom door. She didn't want to wake him, but neither did she want to walk in on him if he was dressing for the day. When there was no answer, she knocked a bit louder before turning the knob and pushing the door open a crack. She peeked her head inside, then opened the door more fully.

Jace wasn't there.

Brooke flung open the door and hastened to his bed. She knew he was gone because she could clearly see the rumpled comforter. But reason eluded her. She yanked the blankets off his bed so her eyes caught sight of only his bedsheet. She ran to his closet door. Why in the world her son would be holed up in his small closet, she didn't know, but she was compelled to check anyway. She was panicking. She hurriedly opened the door. No Jace.

There was nowhere else he could be in his room, nowhere to hide, alone, so he could lament the state of his life at the moment.

Brooke ran out of Jace's room and to the second-floor

bathroom. He wasn't there. She looked into the spare bedroom. Not there. And then she headed to her own bedroom, the bedroom she had once shared with Jace's father but that now felt large and empty. Jace wasn't there, either.

In a panic, Brooke flew down the stairs and called Jace's name. The house was uncannily quiet, and she didn't find him anywhere. And then it hit her: the garage. She pulled the hefty garage door open, and that was when she saw that Jace's car wasn't in its stall. He had taken it at some point without her even hearing the engine rev or the garage door lift. Had she been sleeping in the chair when he'd left the house? Had he left this morning, or had it been last night? And where in the world had he gone?

Brooke was breathing heavily now. How was she going to find Jace? What was he capable of doing to himself or to another person in his current state?

Brooke grabbed her phone and, with shaking fingers, brought up the Find My app, something she rarely used and had nearly forgotten she could access. It took her a few attempts to click her thumb on Jace's name, but she eventually succeeded. With bated breath, she waited. It only took a moment, but to Brooke, that moment felt eternal.

And then her stomach plummeted when the phone told her that it couldn't find her son and that, in fact, his phone was no longer connected to hers. When had he done that? Brooke tried to think back to the last time she had utilized this application and realized that it had been at least a couple of months ago if not more. Jace had always been a trustworthy boy, and Brooke had never felt the need to check up on him. She had placed her faith in him and had always thought it prudent to offer him his freedom and autonomy. Now she immediately regretted so many of the decisions she had made.

"Damn it!" Brooke flung her phone with such force that it swept through the room and, with a loud thunk, hit a mudroom cubby. Brooke fell to her knees and wept. What was she supposed to do? What was expected of her? How were they going to get through this?

And where in the world was her son?

---

Maddy was still sleeping when the doorbell rang. Jenny was expecting a friend from out of town this morning. Eager for a supportive listening ear, she hastened to the front door.

Jenny pulled the door open in a hurry, but instead of her friend on the front stoop, it was Jace Weatherbee. Jenny's expression immediately transformed. "What the hell are *you* doing here?"

The young man before her, this sixteen-year-old whom she had known since the very weekend he had moved in down the street and who had been in her home countless times, the young man who had always exuded confidence, stood before her, wringing his hands and wearing a weary expression.

"Can I talk to Maddy?"

"You most certainly cannot talk to Maddy. Why the hell would you think I'd ever let you talk to my daughter again after what you did to her? Who do you think you are? And the nerve of you… coming to my home, knocking on my door. Never did I think…" Jenny shook her head vigorously. "No. Get out, Jace. Go home. And don't come here again. I don't ever want to see you again or talk to you again unless it's with the police. I swear to you, Jace, I swear... you'll pay for what you did to my daughter."

"But I didn't do anything!"

Jenny was seething now. "How dare——"

"Mom?"

Jenny whipped around and saw that Maddy was standing on the bottom stair behind her, her daughter's bare foot hovering over the foyer floor as if it wanted to complete that last step but couldn't recall the movement necessary to do so. Her hair was a matted mess, and her cheeks were pink and splotchy. She had slept in her clothes, and they were now disheveled. Jenny noticed that Maddy was shaking slightly.

"Maddy, go back to your room."

"But I think——"

"I said," Jenny repeated through clenched teeth, "go back to your room."

Maddy hesitated but turned and began to ascend the stairs.

"Maddy!" Jace called, and Maddy slowly turned to look at the boy peeking over the threshold of the front door. "Why'd you do it, huh? This is bullshit, and you know it. This is gonna ruin everything, Maddy. I——"

And that was when Jenny lost any semblance of composure. "Get the fuck off my property, Jace!" She was screaming. Her arms flailed, and she stomped her foot. She then grasped the edge of the door with her fingers and slammed it closed.

"Mom, I..."

Jenny held up a hand. "No. Not right now," she said. "Go back to bed, baby. Get some sleep. You need it. We both need it. I wish your dad stayed home today. He would have handled that boy much better than I did. What the hell was he thinking coming over here today? Is he that deluded? I mean, seriously? What the hell, you know?" She paused for a moment as Maddy stared down at her from the middle of the stairwell.

"Yeah, go back to sleep, baby. We'll figure this out. I promise you, we'll figure this out."

Jenny walked up the stairs with outstretched arms and met her daughter. She wrapped her arms around Maddy's neck and pulled her in for a tight embrace, emotions poured into the gesture. Maddy's shoulders began to quake, and she sobbed into Jenny's chest. Eventually, she settled down enough to take a deep breath and part from her mother's arms.

Maddy looked up and into Jenny's eyes, gray blue like her own. "Maybe we should... I don't know, Mommy. I... maybe I should take it back, call the police..."

*Mommy?* Jenny couldn't remember the last time her daughter had called her Mommy. She had moved beyond that term of endearment long ago, back when she had graduated from the mentality of a toddler and into that of a little girl. And that was all it took for Jenny, that one little word that held an abundance of meaning.

"No way," she said. "Maddy, we are not going back to the police. Not unless it's to fight this. That boy deserves what he gets. He needs to be punished for what he did to you. Way too many boys get away with hurting girls and women, way too many. I've read the statistics, you know. Most girls are too afraid to come forward. But not you, Maddy. Not you. And oh, baby, I'm so proud of you. Have I told you that yet?" She saw the few straggling tears that trickled down her daughter's cheeks. Jenny lifted a finger and wiped them away.

"I'm so proud of you, baby girl. You are so strong to

125

come forward. You're so strong to make this boy pay for what he's done to you. This way, he won't be hurting anybody else, I promise you. The police are on our side. How could they not be? I wish you would have come forward sooner, right after it happened, but we won't go there. No. No blame. But—no, Maddy, don't cry again. Oh, okay, baby. I know…" Jenny wrapped her arms around her daughter again, bringing Maddy's cheek to her chest. She kissed the top of her daughter's head.

When Maddy broke away, she walked forlornly up the stairs. If she closed her bedroom door, Jenny wasn't aware of it. There was no sound.

Jenny made her way back to the first floor of her expansive house and to the kitchen. Fortunately, her friend would be here soon, and Jenny could pour out all her feelings then.

Yes, she'd make Jace Weatherbee pay.

Nobody did that to her little girl!

But first, a call to Michael. It was time. He had a right to know what had happened to his little sister.

———

Piper spent a good deal of the weekend with Maddy. Princess was there for a few hours on Saturday but then had to head home. Her mom had made plans for the family. Jenny knocked on the closed door of Maddy's room time and time again, always offering sweets or drinks. Piper loved her own mother, really, but when she was at Maddy's house, she was constantly impressed with how attentive Jenny was to her daughter. Maybe it was the whole not-a-working-mom thing. Piper knew that her own mother was super busy, so she guessed she got it. But Jenny—yeah, to have a mother like Jenny would really help Maddy right now with what she was going through.

Maddy didn't want to talk about the rape. Not like the other day when she had confided in Piper, the day that had set this whole thing in motion. She wished Maddy would talk to her now. Didn't she need to get it off her chest? She was a talker, Maddy. Piper knew this. She always had been a talker, just like her mother. But maybe this was different, right? Maybe Maddy just *couldn't* talk about what had happened to her. Maybe she was traumatized. She *had* to be traumatized. Piper didn't know how she'd react herself if she went through something as massive as Maddy had. Especially when it was Jace who was the cause of all this pain.

Jace. Piper still couldn't believe that Jace had raped Maddy. Well, of course she believed it, because she'd always believe her best friend was telling the truth. It was just that she never would have thought that Jace was capable of something so violent. Sure, he had changed a bit when his dad left, but she had never seen him hurt someone else so viciously. Never. His words were strong sometimes but not his actions. He angered quickly sometimes, too, but Piper had always seen him eventually curl into himself and walk away when he got like that.

She just didn't know what to think, how to feel. She ached for Maddy. With her whole being, she ached for her best friend. But she was also utterly befuddled. She had liked Jace for as long as she had known him—first as a friend and then as something else: a crush. She had seen something in him that she hadn't seen in any other boy, something special. And now she was confused and hurt and, yes, relieved even. Relieved that it wasn't her that had been attacked. And that sent her into an absolute flurry of guilt. What kind of best friend was she that she was relieved this hadn't happened to her? Did that mean she was happy that it had happened to Maddy? No! Of course not! She wouldn't wish something this brutal on her worst enemy, even!

But when she thought about the scenario, when she thought about the few details that Maddy had divulged to her... Piper went over and over it in her mind, this nightmare scenario. And always, it was her that she saw instead of Maddy. Piper in Maddy's place. Just last night, she had woken in the middle of the night, her cami drenched in sweat.

And if this was how Piper was reacting, how had Maddy endured this? How would Maddy *continue* to endure this?

It was Monday now, and Piper was in school. Maddy was still out, but Piper was planning to take the bus to Maddy's house when school was over. She wished she was sixteen and had her license. Then she could drive herself. Well, if she had a car, that was. And she probably wouldn't have access to one during the weekdays even when she did have her license.

The bell rang out at the end of the day, and Piper walked to her locker. She removed her math textbook—most of her work was done online, but her math class used an actual textbook—stuffed it into her backpack, then made for the main entryway to the school where the buses lined up, ready and waiting for the students they'd transport home. Piper had needed a bus pass in order to ride a different bus home, but her mother had willingly written out a note for the office.

The bus that Piper would take to Maddy's house was toward the end of the line. Piper walked and walked some more. In the near distance was the student parking lot, and it was there that Piper saw a scuffle begin in her peripheral vision. Something was going on. Something out of the ordinary, it appeared. Piper squinted in an attempt to make out the scene playing out in front of her. And it was then that she saw not only Jace but Michael too. Maddy's older brother.

What was he doing here? Wasn't he supposed to be at college?

Instead of boarding the bus, Piper ran toward the commotion without making a conscious decision to do so. Her legs just carried her of their own volition. She approached the small crowd that had gathered. She didn't comprehend the words that spewed from Michael's mouth, but she wasn't fully listening to them. They just burst into the air, their explosive sounds left to hover above him. She didn't know what Jace shot back. Her mind wouldn't allow that information to settle. She just heard shouting.

And then she saw it: a fist flew through the air as if in slow motion. Piper's stomach plummeted as if a heavy stone had settled within it and weighed her down. Nausea erupted. Piper's lower lip fell, and she began to cry, though she didn't realize in the moment that she was doing so, not even when she watched the scene unfold before her through a blur of tears.

Michael's fist found Jace's jaw. Jace's head whipped to the side, and he staggered backward. Another fist, this time in Jace's eye. Jace stumbled, lost his balance, and fell to the ground.

But Michael wasn't done.

A boot to Jace's thigh. Again. Again. Another to his back.

Piper watched as one boy in the crowd smirked and

held his phone aloft, capturing the fight with his camera. She closed her eyes. There was shouting, but from whom? One person? Two? More? What were they saying? She couldn't decipher the words. Her mind had closed, attempting to protect her.

Eventually, she opened her eyes. Michael was walking away from the scene, fists clenched at his thighs. Jace was cradling his jaw in the palm of his hand, blood dripping from his nose. His eye had already begun to swell. The small crowd that had formed began to disperse. Nobody offered to help Jace up from the ground, not even Dustin, who stood with his arms crossed, looking down at his best friend with an unreadable expression.

Jace turned and caught Piper's eye. Blood stained the collar of his shirt.

Piper blinked once then twice. Then, on trembling legs, she made her way back to the bus that would take her to her best friend.

———

"He did what?" Maddy almost screeched when Piper told her what Michael had done to Jace back at the school.

"Yeah," Piper said. "I'm not kidding. Jace looks terrible. I was afraid maybe someone would have texted you already. I thought Michael was at school."

"He was. He came home this morning. He's only got one class on Mondays and told his professor that he needed to be out. Didn't seem to be an issue. He wanted to be at home with us right now, you know? But I thought he left to go back to Boston."

"You've got a great big brother," Piper remarked.

"I guess," Maddy said with a shrug, and then she

added, "Yeah, he is. He's always been quiet, and even now, I think he keeps to himself. I don't know, whatever. But he's been really supportive. I've never seen him this angry."

"He has a reason to be angry."

Maddy pressed her lips into a line. "Yeah."

"What's going to happen from here?" Piper asked. "I mean with Jace and you and the police and all."

Maddy sighed. "I need to talk to the cops again tonight. We're doing it when Dad gets home from work so he can be there."

"Well, that's good."

"Yeah." Maddy's expression was stoic. She bounded off her bed. "I need to go to the bathroom. Then I'll get us something to eat. You hungry?"

"Sure," Piper said.

"Be right back."

"Okay."

Piper sat on Maddy's bed for a few moments, looking around the room. It was eerily quiet, not even enlivened by the sound of music that she and Maddy so often played. Piper looked from a poster on Maddy's wall to the string of Christmas lights that she kept up year round for ambiance to her white wooden dresser, one of the drawers partially open. And then her gaze settled on Maddy's windowsill and, on it, her journal.

She didn't know what compelled her to stand and grab it. Her feet walked, her hands moved, and before she knew it, she was holding the journal open before her. She skimmed its many pages. Judging by the first date written, Maddy had begun it when she was nine years old, her handwriting large and sloppy, copious spelling mistakes apparent throughout. She had gone many months without an entry at one point when she was eleven.

Piper flipped toward the end of the journal. She caught sight of her own name in Maddy's sixteen-year-old curly script, penmanship that had evolved since she was nine. There—her name again. And then Jace's. It was Piper's crush. And then, farther along, it was Maddy's sudden, yet —once they had begun dating—progressive interest. She skimmed from sentence to sentence, never reading an entire entry. She came to the last few pages, and Jace's name caught her attention again. She homed in.

And then, eyes moving rapidly from left to right, Piper felt her heart drop.

"What are you doing?"

Piper turned abruptly and saw an incredulous Maddy standing just within her room, a tray of crackers and cheese in her hands.

"I… I…" Piper had no excuse, but she also couldn't unsee what she had just read. Her lips trembled. She tried desperately to keep her emotions in check, but there was no helping it. She closed the journal and threw it onto Maddy's bed. "I thought I was your best friend."

Maddy walked forward. "You are my best friend."

"I don't believe that," Piper said. "Not anymore."

"What do you mean?" Maddy was still holding the tray.

"You're not telling me the whole truth, are you?" Piper asked. "Not all of it. If I was your best friend, you would tell me everything. I tell you everything, Maddy! I always have."

Maddy's face contorted into an expression of anguish. She deposited the tray on her bed, never taking her eyes off Piper. "I couldn't tell you all of it," she said. "How could I?"

"But this," Piper spat, pointing at the discarded journal. "This… this is just… I don't get it! How could you keep this from me? How could you not tell me everything that happened?"

Tears began to pour from Maddy's eyes, and in a pleading voice, she said, "It was too much. I couldn't tell anybody!" With outstretched arms, she walked toward Piper. "I was so hurt, Pipes. You know that. So hurt. He hurt me. I didn't know what to do."

"The police need to know this, Maddy. All of it. What he did to you, yeah, but all of it. All of it!"

Maddy attempted to fling her arms around Piper, but Piper backed away from her touch.

"I think I need to go home," Piper said. "I love you tons, Maddy. I'll always love you. No matter what. You're my best friend. And I'm here for you. Give me a day to let this settle in, okay? I just can't believe you didn't tell me the whole truth."

Maddy looked to the ground. "I know," she mumbled. "But I couldn't. How could I? Nobody would understand my feelings after he did what he did."

Piper sighed. "I get it. But…"

Maddy looked up.

"I'll talk to you tomorrow, okay?"

"How will you get home?"

"I'll start walking, and then I'll call my mom."

"I need you right now, Pipes."

Piper shook her head. "I know," she said. "We'll talk tomorrow."

Then she walked out the door.

# Chapter 7

## *One Year Earlier*

I t was the summer before Jace's freshman year, almost four months after the middle school semiformal, when Brooke found herself comfortably seated at the bar of a restaurant about half an hour away from her home. The city in which she was currently enjoying herself wasn't overly large by any means. If residents of her state craved history, nightlife, and a bustling atmosphere, they drove into Boston. This city, however, boasted some of the best restaurants in New Hampshire, and seeing as it was a Saturday evening and Jace was out with a group of friends, Brooke was thrilled to be out of the house. In fact, Jace was staying over at Dustin's that night, so Brooke felt relaxed and unrushed. The following month—September—would mark the one-year anniversary of her husband's departure, and even though their marriage had been in shambles for years prior to his leaving, Brooke had found herself feeling exceptionally lonely these past months. She had rummaged through her closet when Jenny invited her out, looking at one dress and then another, hoping to prepare for the evening to come, before she had retired to her bed in a fit of depression at the meagre choices. She hadn't realized until that very moment how long it had been since she had purchased a new outfit for herself. And that, in turn, saddened her even further. So after a few minutes of self-pity, she had reached for her cell and texted Jenny.

Brooke: No clothes. Ridiculous. Want to feel good when we go out. Let's shop?

Jenny: Hell yeah! Eek Gonna feel like a teenager again

Brooke: I'm free this weekend. I think Jace is busy with his new girlfriend. Friday after work?

Jenny: It's a girl date

They had spent an afternoon shopping while Jace met Dustin at the high school's track to practice once school let out. He had told his mom that his girlfriend and her friend would be joining him and Dustin afterward so they could head to the mall. Jace had told Brooke that he'd catch a ride back to the house with Dustin and his mom if Brooke was still out. This put her at ease, and she spent a leisurely, pleasurable late afternoon with Jenny. Brooke had tried on dress after dress then several pairs of slim-fitting pants and blouses. Eventually, she settled on a pair of black slacks with a black-and-white checkered, loose-fitting, sleeveless blouse. She opened the door to the dressing room to garner Jenny's opinion.

"What, are we trying to break into jail? Oh my God, Brooke, you wear that and you'll scare everyone away. I mean, I thought you wanted to have a good time, you know? You wear that and people will think you should have a tight bun in your hair with a pair of huge glasses and you work somewhere, I don't know, like in a stingy office or something. We're going out, girl! We need to dress the part. And by we, I mean you. How long has it been since you've gotten any? I mean—"

Brooke raised her hand, palm out. "Hold up," she said. "Who said anything about sex?" She could feel the blush radiating from her cheeks. She shook her head. "That's not why we're going out. I just want a nice night out with a good friend. That's all. And I want to feel good."

"Yeah… you want to feel good to attract attention." Jenny winked. "I like feeling good around other people too. Nothing like a confidence booster to feel like you're out there, can hold your own, own it, you know?"

Brooke's eyes widened. "No," she said. "I do not know."

"Pfft." Jenny rolled her eyes. "Dan left you, the asshole that he is. You've been moping around your house—"

"I have not been moping—"

"And we need to get you out. Even if you're not gonna do anything about it, if you feel good, if you look hot, you'll go home happy. I guarantee it. Been there, done that. Now, get those clothes off of you. I don't know why I let you bring them into the dressing room in the first place. Seriously… here. Take this dress." She pushed a dress forcefully into Brooke's arms.

"No," Brooke said with a shake of her head. "I told you before that I can't pull off this dress. It's too… not me."

"Confidence, Brooke. It's all about confidence. Trust me…" She raised a brow. "Try it on."

Brooke sighed, but she slipped back into the dressing room, where she proceeded to take off the slacks and blouse, place them back on their prospective hangers, then thread her arms through the spaghetti straps of the skimpy black dress that her friend had chosen for her. Never in her life had Brooke owned a dress made of such little material, but she'd humor Jenny and try it on, even if she knew it would go right back onto the rack, where someone with more self-assurance would pick it up. And it was not as if Brooke lacked confidence in herself. No, that wasn't it at all. She was very comfortable in her own skin, knew who she was, and was proud of it. She just didn't think one needed to own a slim black dress to exert their personality, especially when one's disposition was rather modest.

The material of the dress was smooth, and it slipped nicely down her torso to stop at midthigh. Brooke smoothed her palms down her stomach and then looked up and glanced in the mirror.

And she was shocked.

Sure, it was a skimpy black dress she was wearing, but—damn! Was it really her own reflection looking back? While she'd thought she'd feel entirely uncomfortable wearing such an item, the effect it elicited upon first glance was quite the opposite. She felt good, giddy even. What was it that Jenny had texted her? *Gonna feel like a teenager again.*

Brooke smoothed her palms down her stomach once more and then moved them to her thighs. She turned and looked over her shoulder. Yes, the dress was much shorter than she was used to, but it still covered a good amount of skin. The material was thin, but it didn't appear to be transparent. The back of the dress drooped, and she could see her bra clasp. That, she didn't like. In fact, she could see a good deal of her bra since the straps were so narrow, but when she leaned over, thankfully, an abundance of cleavage didn't peek out.

There was a knock on the dressing room door. "Let me in," Jenny said. "I want to see."

"I like it, Jenny, but I still don't think it's for me. I can see my bra all over the place. That's just... not right."

"Ugh," Jenny said, her voice playfully annoyed. "Just let me in."

Brooke unlatched the door, and Jenny slipped in with an expectant smile. And then her eyes widened. "I haven't lost my touch," she said. "You look hot."

"This dress is for someone in their twenties," Brooke said. "Not a mom of a teenage boy in her forties. Like I said, it's a nice dress, and yes, it makes me feel good, but it's not me."

"That's a load of crap, you know," Jenny said. Brooke raised her brows, and an amused smirk played on her lips. "This is so you! I'm telling you, Brooke, you'll turn heads in this dress. You look so, so wonderful. Just wonderful! And you said you wanted to feel good. Don't you feel good? How could you not feel good in something like this?"

Brooke grasped the strap of her bra and pulled. "Because of this," she said.

"That's easy," Jenny said. "Take your bra off."

"Excuse me?"

"You heard me," Jenny said. "Take your bra off."

"There is no way I'm taking my bra off."

"Oh, don't be such a prude," Jenny said. She grasped Brooke by the shoulder and turned her so she was facing the mirror. "Take it off. Trust me."

Warily, Brooke slipped the straps off her shoulders with careful fingers so that her dress still covered her breasts. She liked Jenny and felt comfortable with her but not *that* comfortable. In fact, she had never exposed her breasts to another woman before, with the exception of her primary-care physician and the mammogram technician at the local hospital during her yearly preventative appointments.

Holding the material of the dress at the chest with one hand, she used the other to unclasp her bra and then shimmy it off her shoulders and down her arms. She hung it on a hook in the dressing room then looked at Jenny expectantly and with a slight frown.

"Okay," Jenny said. "Turn around."

Brooke did as instructed, and Jenny helped her slip the thin dress straps back up. Jenny lightly grasped Brooke's wrists and lifted her arms to the sides. When she released her hold, Brooke let her arms drop.

"See?" Jenny said with a grin. "Hot."

With wide eyes, Brooke exclaimed, "You can see my nipples."

Jenny flicked her wrist dismissively. "Easy fix," she said. "You don't want to go strapless because, well, you'll still see the bra in the back. Plus, this dress is so fine that you'd see the outline even if the back wasn't so low. Don't want to go there. I've got some adhesive bras at home. Just use one of those. You're little like me. It'll do the trick."

Brooke raised her brows. "Adhesive bras?"

"Yeah," Jenny replied. "You know. Adhesive. Sticky. They stick on. Just on your breast so you're not showing your nipples to the world."

"Oh my God, Jenny."

"Hey, it's no big deal. You're worried about your bra showing. I've got a solution. I promise you, it'll work. And you'll get this dress. And you'll wear it. And you'll look hot." She squeezed Brooke's shoulders. "Just look at yourself."

Brooke gazed at her reflection. She had to admit that although this dress wasn't one she would have typically picked out for herself, Jenny obviously knew what she was doing. Brooke felt good. No, more than good. She felt confident, sexy."

Brooke sighed. "Okay," she relented. "I'll get the dress."

"Yeah!" Jenny replied with zeal. "We're gonna have the best night!"

So here they were, the following Saturday night, sitting at the bar of a well-known and highly frequented restaurant in the city. Music played from the speakers, the sound of glasses clinking filled the air, and voices carried to Brooke's ears. She was on her second martini when two men approached. One of them sidled up next to Brooke, nearly grazing her arm, and sat in the thick, wooden bar chair beside her. Brooke thought nothing of it and continued to converse with Jenny at her opposite side but then saw her friend's smile transform and a devious smirk play on her lips.

Jenny leaned in toward Brooke and whispered, "The guy next to you is gorgeous. No ring—I checked already. And I can tell you, he's been stealing glances. Yep, at you. You know, this is awesome, just what needed to happen. We're having fun, but now you can have fun in another way. Know what I mean?"

Brooke felt her face flush. "That's not going to happen."

"Hey, you were the one who told me you wanted to have a good time." She leaned back, crossing one leg over the other in her burgundy dress. She ran her fingers through her long brunette hair.

"Not that kind of a good time. And I already *am* having a good time. With you!" Brooke's whispers were strained, almost pleading.

Jenny laughed. Her gaze darted over Brooke's head,

and Brooke saw her friend's smirk alter again—knowing, expectant. Amused.

And then Jenny leaned forward over the bar and spoke loudly to the man seated beside Brooke. "Hey there. I'm Jenny." She held out her hand, her elbow grazing Brooke's chest. Brooke reclined, her back pressed up against the hard chair, the smooth, cool material sending a shiver through her body.

The man smiled and, for the first time, Brooke dared look his way. He was so close! She hadn't realized just how close he'd sat, but then again, of course he would be this close to her. The seats at the bar were practically touching one another. His proximity meant nothing, surely.

He was taller than Brooke. She could easily ascertain this even from a seated position. She had to lift her gaze in order to look him in the eyes—dark, like umber. Wide-set, with thick, short lashes. He had a prominent nose, and his lips were neither thin nor full, but they seemed to fit his features perfectly. His chin was stubbled, and his brown hair was shorn close to his scalp. Jenny had been right; this man was very attractive.

Brooke watched as Jenny shook hands with the man. When she retreated to her seat, she said, "This is my good friend Brooke."

When the man looked directly at Brooke, her blush deepened, and she immediately chastised herself for acting like a schoolgirl. She was in her forties, for goodness' sake! This wasn't her first go-around at meeting a man. He offered his palm, and Brooke shook it.

"I'm sorry, what did you say your name was?" Brooke asked. She knew he had verbalized it when Jenny introduced herself just a moment before, but somehow, it had eluded her.

"Steve."

"Yes, okay," Brooke said rather awkwardly. "Hi, Steve."

"Hi." Steve smiled, displaying a set of slightly crooked white teeth, which Brooke found endearing. "This is——" Steve pivoted, but when he found his friend speaking with a person who had seated themselves beside him, Steve turned back to Brooke. "Doesn't matter. Looks like he's busy."

"That's okay," Brooke said.

Steve motioned to Brooke's nearly empty martini glass. "Can I buy you another?"

"Oh, no, that's okay——"

"That is so wonderful of you," Jenny chimed in amiably. She nudged Brooke's shoulder inconspicuously then whispered, "Brooke, you should go for it. Fun night, right?" And there was that smirk again.

"Oh, I don't know…"

"Not a problem," Steve said. "Thought I'd offer."

Brooke looked into his eyes and scrutinized his expression. She could feel Jenny's eager presence beside her. "Okay, then," she said. "Maybe just one more." She could feel the effects of the first two martinis she'd consumed. It wasn't often she allowed herself to enjoy an alcoholic drink; only when she was out with friends, and that was rare enough. In fact, she didn't even stock any alcohol at home. But one more martini wouldn't hurt, surely.

Steve waved down the bartender. He asked Jenny if she'd also like another drink—she declined—before kindly ordering another martini for Brooke and a beer for himself.

"We're celebrating," Jenny supplied when the bartender turned her back.

"Oh yeah? What?"

"Divorce," Jenny said matter-of-factly.

Mortified, Brooke watched Steve's brows pinch.

"This girl right here, Brooke? Her ex, well, let's just say he's not the best guy. But now he's gone and she's... single." Jenny smiled slyly, and Brooke knew then that Jenny had brought up her divorce for the mere purpose of inserting her single status into the conversation. "So we just had to go out, you know? Celebrate life. But it's all good. He's been gone for a while now. Almost a year, right, Brooke? Not that we girls really needed an excuse to get out, though. I mean, sometimes you just don't want to be home, you know? Sometimes you just want to be out having a good time, with good company..."

"All right," Steve said. "I can get on board with that."

Jenny leaned into Brooke again, so close that Brooke could feel the warmth of her body and the tickle of Jenny's lips on her ear. "I'm gonna head out. What do you think? You okay with that? You want me to go?"

Brooke whipped her head to the side and stared at her friend. Jenny smiled before leaning back in.

"I can see where this is headed, and you need a good night out. I drove, so I'll drive myself home. Maybe you can Lyft? Whatever you do, do not go home with him. I listen to way too many true-crime podcasts, and you seriously don't need to be murdered. Okay, I know I'm being ridiculous, but you know... So I'll head out, but you stay here with Steve. His friend is busy, Steve is clearly interested, and how long has it been for you?"

Brooke turned to look at Jenny again, this time with a frown.

Jenny laughed, whispered again in Brooke's ear. "Be safe. There are tons of hotels around here." And then after a slight pause, "Do you want me to stay?"

Brooke pondered the question for a moment. She stole a glance at Steve, who was taking a sip of his newly acquired beer. She noticed the way his arm was lifted, how he had rolled up the sleeves of his button-down shirt. How the first few buttons were left undone at the neck, the skin exposed, revealing a sparsely haired chest. She watched his Adam's apple bob as he swallowed. She turned back to Jenny and shook her head.

"No, I think I'm okay." Her stomach was in knots, but she felt compelled to continue her evening with Steve, to speak with him and see if things progressed further. "You can go. But... is that rude? Shouldn't we end the night together?"

"Hell no," Jenny said. She eyed Steve again then slipped off her chair, waved, and walked away.

It took Brooke a moment to turn her gaze back to Steve. It had been years since she had been in this position, and she wasn't sure what she was supposed to say or do. She felt entirely out of her element. With a slightly trembling hand, she smoothed down the sheer black material covering her thighs, surreptitiously glanced at her breasts to ensure the adhesive cups were still in place—what had she been thinking when she'd agreed to wear these things?—and, satisfied, she looked back at Steve.

"She had to go." And then Brooke felt herself wince. *She had to go?* Any man in their right mind would see right through that excuse.

But Steve didn't move. Instead, he turned his body so it was directly facing Brooke, smiled, and asked her what she did for work. A safe start to their solo conversation.

"I'm a nurse."

"Ah," Steve said. "Noble profession. Where?"

"At a doctor's office. Not too far from here, actually." Jenny's warnings of safety had unsettled her, and she found herself impelled to hold back particular personal information.

"And you like it?"

"I do, actually, yes. I like it well enough. It's not my favorite position of all the jobs I've had, but it works, and it pays the bills, and the schedule couldn't be better. The people are nice for the most part. What about you? What do you do?"

"I'm an engineer. Work and live here in the city."

Brooke nodded. "And how about you? Do you like your job?"

"Yep," Steve said, lifting the glass of frothy beer to his lips. " I do." He took a large gulp.

"How long have you been where you are?"

"Since I graduated from college. Got the job, never looked back. So that would put me at... oh... more than twenty years now."

"Wow. That's quite impressive. I've had several jobs over the years. I don't know many people who have been in the same job for over twenty years."

"But now you do," Steve said with a grin.

Brooke nodded. "Now I do." She lifted her martini glass by its stem and took a small sip. The room was swaying slightly, so she thought perhaps the first two drinks had, indeed, been enough. She'd have to be cautious. She had forgotten how strong martinis were and didn't want to become inebriated. Not when she was sitting next to a stranger and would have to request a Lyft driver to pick her up from the restaurant. If that was the course she decided to take. She needed her wits about her.

Steve's friend nudged him with his elbow, and Steve turned around. Brooke saw him nod, and then he swiveled to face her once again as his friend walked off with a woman.

"So," Steve said, taking another swig from his glass. "Divorced, huh?"

"Yeah," Brooke replied. "I'm divorced. Dan—my ex— lives in Maryland. We don't see him often anymore."

Steve pursed his lips. "We?"

Had she said too much and too soon? She really wasn't good at this, was she? But it couldn't be helped. She did have a son, after all, and he was the most important presence in her life.

"I have a son. Jace. He'll be a freshman when school starts up at the end of the month. He's almost fifteen."

"Tough age? I don't have kids."

"Not really, no. Not with Jace. He's a good kid. I suppose there are typical things. I'm sure he doesn't tell me everything on his mind—he's a teenager, after all." Brooke smiled. "I can't imagine he wants to be best friends with his mother. He'll lean on his friends for those conversations. He does well in school, runs cross country. I think he's just an all-around good kid, so no. Not really a tough age right now." And then she laughed. "I hope that's not coming!"

Steve shrugged. "Don't know. Like I said, no kids here."

"What are you doing out tonight?"

"Meeting you," Steve said with a grin.

Brooke chuckled. "I suppose you are."

"Pets? Do you have the obligatory dog or cat? Or maybe it's a rabbit?"

With a grin, Brooke said, "No, no pets. It was an area of contention when my son was young—he really, really wanted a dog, but it hasn't come up in years. And it wouldn't be fair, either. I'm gone at work all day, Jace is at school. And then he has practice, or he wants to go here or there. If we had a pet, they'd be alone a lot."

"Makes sense," Steve said. "No pets for me either. I live alone. Like it that way."

"I see," Brooke said.

Steve brought the glass to his lips, but before taking a sip, he looked down at Brooke's lap. "I like your dress," he said. He sipped, swallowed, and brought his glass back down to the bar.

Brooke felt herself blush and was thankful for the dim lighting. "Thank you. It's new." *It's new?* Why had she said that?

"Looks good on you."

"Thank you," Brooke repeated.

They chatted for a while longer, conversation superficial but flowing. Brooke felt comfortable in Steve's presence and had no desire to end her evening.

Eventually, Steve leaned in toward Brooke. She could feel his warmth on her bare arms, detect the smell of soap on his skin. Her stomach lurched with anticipation.

"I hope this isn't presumptuous of me," Steve said, "but would you like to come back to my place?"

Brooke swallowed. Her chest tightened, and she suddenly felt exposed. She wrapped her arms around her stomach and looked down nervously at the bar top. "I..." she began. She could do this, she *could!* "I think... not back to your place, but maybe... maybe we could get a hotel room?"

Steve leaned back in his chair, and the smile on his face intensified. "Sounds good to me. Shall we?" He slid from the chair and held a hand out—palm up—for Brooke.

With trepidation and a racing heart, Brooke stood, pressing her small black clutch to her chest. She smoothed down her dress, took Steve's hand, and let him lead her into the cool August evening. The city lights shone down on them as they walked. Brooke glanced up at Steve, caught her heel in a crack on the sidewalk, and stumbled forward.

"Whoa there," Steve said as he tightened his grip on her hand and helped pull her upright.

Mortified, Brooke placed one foot in front of the other and continued to walk, paying more mind to where she stepped. "Where are we going?" Her voice was barely above a whisper.

"I thought maybe just right there?" Steve motioned with his chin. There was a five-story hotel just a block away.

Brooke swallowed. "Okay." She feared her voice was shaking.

She followed Steve through the revolving door of the hotel and into the spacious, well-lit lobby. Steve squeezed her hand and smiled down at her. Brooke returned a slight smile of her own.

At the front desk, Steve dropped Brooke's hand, and she was surprised at how cold and empty it felt. She laced her fingers together in front of her and let her arms hang limply. "We'd like a room for the night if you've got one," Steve told the attendant, a young woman in her twenties with her dark hair swept back in a low ponytail.

"Let me see." She punched a few keys on the keyboard of her laptop then looked back up at Steve. "I've got a room. Second floor. One queen bed. Two-fifteen for the night."

Steve looked at Brooke, and she nodded her assent. "We'll take it," Steve told the attendant.

"Very good." She typed in Steve's identifying information as he relayed it and then said, "Credit card, please." Steve slipped his fingers into his pants pocket and pulled out a slim leather wallet. He rummaged inside and offered the attendant a card.

"I can help," Brooke said. She lifted her purse.

Steve shook his head. "I got it."

Brooke nodded, swallowing the lump in her throat. It felt as if it was expanding with each moment that passed, a swelling mass that threatened to restrict her airflow.

After completing the check-in, Steve was handed a key card. He led Brooke to the elevator. He pushed the up button, and they waited, side by side. Brooke could hear the whooshing of the elevator as it made its descent, a low rumbling sound. It was otherwise still and quiet around her save for the rapid beating of her own heart.

The elevator opened its doors, welcoming them inside. Steve stepped in first, and Brooke followed, her heels clicking on the solid floor. The doors closed, and Brooke suddenly felt confined in the heady air. She flushed, though it wasn't from embarrassment this time. Beads of sweat broke out on her forehead.

The elevator halted suddenly, and the doors opened onto the carpeted landing. "I think…" Steve said. "Yeah. This way." He grasped Brooke's waist with his hand, bringing her closer to his side, and they exited the elevator together, turned left, and made their way down the hall. In just a moment, Brooke found herself staring at the door of their hotel room.

Steve unlocked the room with the key card and pushed the door open. He stepped inside and motioned for Brooke to join him. She walked over the threshold and into the room. There was nothing special about the room, just a small space with a bathroom, a desk, a dresser. And there, in the center of the room, was a queen-sized bed.

The door shut behind Brooke, and she startled slightly.

Steve wasted no time, wrapping his arms around her waist and pulling her toward his chest. She felt the heat of him and smelled his aftershave.

He lowered his head to hers, and their lips met. His were soft, smooth. But he tasted of the beer he had drunk. She had thought she would like to be close to a man again, feel wanted. But something about this, about *him*, felt wrong.

Brooke broke from the kiss. Her feet wouldn't budge. Her hands trembled even as she felt Steve's arm around her back and viewed his quizzical expression. A flood of memories pervaded her mind: a room, a bed, a boy.

Brooke leaped back, breaking Steve's hold. "I can't do this!" She felt panicked, her mind concurrently alert and drunk, though how that could be was a conundrum. "I'm so sorry, Steve," she said, near tears. "I can't do this. I thought I could, and you seem very nice, and you're very handsome, and it's been…" She shook her head. "I can't do this. I'm so sorry!"

She paused for a moment and then sped off as fast as her feet would take her, out the door, down the hallway, and toward the exit sign. She whipped open the door to the stairwell and descended in a high-heeled flurry to the first floor. She sped through the hallway and out into the late-night air. Brooke hunched over, palms on her knees, and gulped in a large breath of fresh air, close to hyperventilating. Two plump tears dribbled down her cheeks.

She felt terrible for leaving Steve so hurriedly and without further explanation, especially after he had already paid for the hotel room. She had thought she could do this, she really had. She had thought she *wanted* to do this. Goodness knew she had lacked any sort of intimate companionship for what felt like ages. Her body ached to be touched, to be appreciated. But not like this. Not right now. Not here. And not with a man she knew next to nothing about. It just wasn't in her nature. This had been a mistake.

When she had calmed enough to use her phone without trembling fingers, Brooke hailed a Lyft. She walked two blocks over and waited in front of a different restaurant than the one she had been in that evening, just in case Steve decided to head back. She didn't want to chance an encounter with him outside. She was already feeling terribly ashamed and awkward. She didn't need the added humiliation.

When her driver arrived, Brooke slid into the backseat of his car, and they set off. Although he attempted conversation, Brooke made it clear that she had a lot on her mind and preferred silence. It took twenty-five minutes for her driver to pull up in her driveway, and during the entire drive, Brooke's mind had reeled. She couldn't stop thinking about that one night back in college. The hotel room, Steve —they had both been triggers for her, somehow, and now she felt tormented, nausea roiling in the pit of her stomach.

Brooke exited the car, clutching her purse to her chest. She thanked the driver with a croak of a voice. He nodded and set off before Brooke had a chance to enter the security code to open the door. She entered her home, closed the door behind her, and deadbolted it. The house was silent and dark. Jace was at Dustin's, and though she knew he would be, it only intensified her anxiety and made her feel even more lonely.

What the hell had just happened?

Brooke swiped at a tear, steeled herself, and walked farther into the house. She flicked on the mudroom light and then the kitchen light as well. She deposited her purse on the counter and heard a clang as the metal clasp hit the granite countertop.

Her phone chimed. Brooke extracted it from her purse and looked at the screen. It was Jenny:

Hope you're having fun. Whoo whoo.

Fun? Her current emotional state would argue otherwise.

Brooke disregarded the message; she'd talk to Jenny at a later date. Tomorrow, in fact, as she knew all too well that Jenny would text her again in the morning to check in. And she was a gossip, her friend. She'd want all the details played out like a steamy romance novel. Brooke shut her eyes tightly. Her friend was going to be sorely disappointed at the turn of events.

Brooke shut the lights off and ascended the stairs, the house so silent that she could hear the creaking of the floorboards. She stopped off at Jace's room and opened his door. Dirty clothes littered the floor, and his bed was unmade, the blankets left askew and the pillow hanging precariously on the edge. She sighed and shut the door.

In her room, Brooke plonked onto her bed. She kicked her heels off and curled up into a fetal position, cradling her knees with her arms. Her pillow was soft and welcoming, but the images in her mind, as well as the feelings those images elicited, wouldn't leave her, no matter how hard she pleaded.

Eventually, Brooke shut her eyes, still in her new dress and uncomfortable adhesive bra. Eventually, she fell into a fitful sleep, full of dark corners and disturbing dreams.

Sunday dawned, and Brooke awoke with a sour taste in her mouth and her eyelids crusted shut. She rubbed her eyes and sat on her bed, her dress wrinkled and disheveled, one adhesive bra cup resting uncomfortably on her stomach. Feebly, she stood from the bed and made her way to the bathroom, where she turned on the shower, removed her clothes, and looked at her haggard appearance in the mirror above the sink. The previous night came flooding back, with all its hard edges. What had she been thinking? Really, what in the *world* had she been thinking?

But that was just it, wasn't it? She knew what she had been thinking. She was lonely. She was an adult. She had the power to consent, to decide what could or could not be done with her own body. Initially, it had filled her with desire to be wanted the way Steve had wanted her last night, to be looked at a certain way, to be treated like a woman, when she had lacked any sort of intimacy from a partner for such a long time. She had known what she was doing, what she had craved.

But then, the room. The kiss.

Brooke blinked and leaned over the counter to gaze in the mirror. Her eyes were bloodshot, red streaks on a white background. Gobs of crust still clung at their corners. There was puffiness in the tender skin under her eyes and a red tint to her cheeks. Her hair was a bedraggled mess. Brooke took a deep breath. She was happy Jace had spent the night at Dustin's house; she didn't want her son seeing her like this.

Yet what she knew she had to do once he arrived home —she'd look a mess then, too. She was sure her emotions would play out plainly in the lines of her face no matter how hard she attempted to keep them at bay.

But it couldn't be helped.

He needed to know.

And it was her tale to tell.

Brooke climbed into the shower and let the water cascade down her shoulders and back. She tilted her head and wet her hair, closing her eyes and allowing the warmth to seep through her skin.

She remained in the shower until the water ran cold. She turned the faucet off, grabbed her towel from the rack, and stepped onto the hard tiles of the bathroom floor. She dried her body then wrapped the towel around her head before moving into her bedroom and grabbing a pair of jean shorts, a plain yellow T-shirt, and undergarments. Back in the bathroom, she dressed, unwound her hair, and brushed it out. One more glance in the mirror, and Brooke made her way down to the first floor of her home, the silence berating her, taunting her. She started the coffee machine, and soon, the smell of hazelnut filled the air, a welcome distraction. Brooke rummaged through the refrigerator, but she wasn't hungry. Not now.

Soon, Brooke sat in her favorite chair in the living room and sipped from her mug. It was there that Jace found her when he arrived home later that morning from Dustin's house. Brooke was thankful that Dustin's mother had dropped Jace off. If she had been obliged to pick him up, she wasn't sure she would have had the ability to muster up the motivation for superficial small talk with Dustin's parents on this particular morning.

"Hey, Mom," Jace said, his lips extended into a wide smile, though the droopiness to his eyes made it look as if her son wanted nothing more than to climb under the blankets of his bed and fall asleep.

"Hi, Jace."

"Whatcha up to?"

"Nothing much," Brooke said softly. "Just… thinking."

"Thinking?"

"Yeah," Brooke said. She looked at her son, at the smile that was still present, though not as wide.

"'Bout?"

"I'll let you know in a minute, but first, tell me about your night."

Jace walked farther into the room. "Nothing much to tell," he said. "Didn't do anything different. But I was glad to be with Dustin."

"I'm sure you were," Brooke said.

She paused momentarily, allowing herself time to figure out how she'd start this much-needed conversation with her son. She had pondered the entire morning and still wasn't entirely sure how she'd get the words out. How did a mother confide in her teenage son that she had been raped at an age not much older than he was now? How would he take this news? Would it affect their relationship with one another? Surely, it would, yes? Brooke didn't know. But she was certain that she couldn't harbor this immense secret any longer. If she had any promise of raising her son to be a kindhearted, caring young man, a man much the opposite of the one she was about to tell him about, then she knew she had to let him in on her past. He had to know the gravity of her situation, especially now that he had been dating for a little while.

For years, Brooke had been conflicted about what she'd say to Jace about her assault and when. Ever since he was a little boy still in diapers, really. They lived in an era of women finally being heard, given a voice, and actually believed. They lived in a country where there was still victim blaming, yes, but it had become a bit less prevalent. Or so she thought. Women sometimes felt more confidence

155

when compelled to come forward and confront their attackers.

And this filled Brooke with hope. Hope that there would be consequences, retribution for the men—and women, yes—that assaulted others. She hadn't felt this back in college. She had been filled with such shame, such divergent perspectives. Brooke had made the choice to go out that night. She had made the choice to follow her attacker back to his dorm room. She had walked inside. She had kissed him willingly. She had gone out that evening wanting to meet someone. She hadn't been sure at the time where she wanted that desire to lead her, but she knew she had gone out with an open mind, ready and willing to attach herself to another. And she had been drinking. Heavily.

Add all of those factors together, and who would have believed her? Who would have sided with Brooke when she told them she had willingly entered his room, had willingly kissed him? Who would believe Brooke when it was her word against his? Her parents had certainly been skeptical when she had finally mustered up the courage to tell them.

And oh, the shame. She had stumbled back to her dorm that night, traversing pathways on campus at one o'clock in the morning so that other late-night revelers wouldn't see the despair she was in. Had she welcomed this? Had she actually asked for it through her actions, her body language, her words? She knew now that she had not, but then—those were the thoughts that had swum in her mind in the days following her assault.

"Have a seat, Jace." Brooke motioned to the couch.

"What's goin' on?" Jace was wary as he sat on the couch and faced his mother.

Brooke heavily lifted herself from the chair and sat next to her son so they were in close proximity, so she could look him intently in the eye, so she could ensure he was listening to the words she was about to speak. Words that she felt would alter their relationship forever. Words Jace would remember, would think about when he looked at his mother. But what thoughts would cross Jace's mind when he did so? What opinions would he construct about her? That was what frightened Brooke the most: what her son would think.

"I need to tell you something." She heard the croak in her voice though she tried desperately to hide it, to enter the conversation with self-assured forthrightness.

"Okay…" Jace's voice lingered in the air between them.

Brooke felt her chest rise with her next breath, detected the nausea that had settled in her gut. "How are things going with Isabelle?" Isabelle was Jace's new girlfriend, a girl Brooke had met only twice.

"Fine."

Brooke nodded. "I'm glad to hear it."

Jace looked sideways at his mother. "Don't know where this is going, though…"

"I know," Brooke replied, her voice soft and unsure.

Jace eyed Brooke questioningly.

"I don't know how to say this to you or even where to start. I've been thinking about it all morning. No, that's not right. I've been thinking about it for years, maybe even before you were born since I had always known I wanted a child. But… this is really hard for me, Jace, so you need to bear with me. Just listen, all right?"

"Okay," Jace said, the word expressed with unease.

"I've never known when to tell you what happened to me. But I think it's time. I think you're old enough, and I know you'll understand. To a degree, anyway. And now that you're dating…"

Jace frowned but made no verbal reply.

"It was in college," Brooke continued. "I was young. We've talked about alcohol and drugs but probably not as much as we should have. I guess I still think of you as being a little boy, but I know you're far from it. A boy still, but not little. Motherhood, Jace—motherhood is just… it's complicated. When I birthed you, when I held you in my arms— it's hard to describe what a mother feels at a time like that. Your father and I, I know we're not doing well now, but we were then. We were very much in love. And you, Jace. You were—" Brooke shook her head. "I can't even describe it." She smiled wistfully, holding back tears. "I held you in my arms. There you were, this tiny little boy that had grown inside of me. You couldn't do anything unless it was instinctual, reflexive. You relied on me for everything, and that feeling as a mother, that feeling that burrows itself inside of you when another human being relies on you like that. I can't even describe the amount of love I had for you from the very first moment I held you in my arms. And I know you're almost fifteen years old, and you're growing up. But that's not something that you'll understand until you go through it if you choose to do so.

"But there we were, you and me. And your father, yes. But there's a special sort of bond between a mother and her son. I really believe that with all my heart. And then you started to grow and to thrive. You've become such an amazing boy, Jace. But…" Brooke paused again, pondering her words. "There are things that I never thought I'd have to worry about, and having a boy, I worry."

Jace's brows creased. "What do you mean?"

"Jace, I need to tell you what happened to me. I think then maybe you'll understand my worries." Brooke shrugged. "I don't know. But you deserve to know. You have a right to know. And if I can help you to become a man that is kind and gentle, a man that respects women…

"It happened in college. I went to a party with some girlfriends. We did it a lot, especially when I was a freshman. Everything was so new. I was out of my parents' house, I had a sort of freedom I had never felt before. I was on my own, making my own decisions. There's something about the experience of living on campus when you're in school, something else that's tough to describe unless you live it.

"But I was at this party, and I was drinking. A lot. More than I should have. It's just… it's tough, Jace. When you have one beer, and you're having a good time with your friends. That one beer turns into two, and by the time you've downed the second, you're not thinking straight. It's so easy to drink that third. It's easy to lose count, to go overboard, and then you've put yourself into unsafe territory. When you've been drinking, things become blurred. Decisions you would never make sober, you make when you're drunk. And consent…

"I met a boy at that party. We were having a good time. It was really, really late. My friends were done, but I wasn't. I told them I was fine, told them to go back to their dorms. We were young. And there's a sense of invincibility that comes when you're young. I know I'm talking to you right now, and that you, too, are young. I could go into an entire conversation about how your brain isn't fully developed and all that, but that's not where I want this conversation to go. I just…" Brooke's lower lip trembled, and she bit down on it with an upper tooth.

"What's goin' on, Mom?"

"I was at that party," Brooke continued, her words soft and spoken slowly. "My girlfriends left. I was having fun with this boy I met. And he invited me back to his dorm room. He said his roommate was gone for the night."

Jace's eyes widened in understanding.

"I went, Jace. I went back to his room. We were alone. We had both been drinking. And I... we were kissing. A little more happened."

Jace looked clearly uncomfortable as he stared at his mother, just inches away on the couch.

"He... he wanted to have sex. He... I let things go a bit further, but then I... I just felt like things were wrong. I didn't want to be there with him, in his room, alone. I wanted to leave. I told him I wanted to leave, that I wasn't comfortable, that I didn't want to be there any longer. I told him. But he...

"I don't know what he was thinking, but he didn't want to stop, and he didn't listen to me. I'm not going to go into details because I don't think you need to know those, but what I do think you need to know is that I was raped that night." Although she had desperately attempted to hold back her tears, her emotions won over. She swiped under her eyes, but the tears still came.

"I've struggled with this for a long time. Even now, I struggle with it. Even after all these years. It's not something that leaves you. Ever, I think. And I guess I just... I think about you. I know I've been telling you since you were a little boy that you need to treat people well. And I know we've talked about bullies, kids being disrespectful, and how it's tough to treat someone well when you're not treated well by them. I know we've touched on so many topics, especially now that you're at an age where you can better understand.

"But this is just... it's different, Jace. So different. And I really hope that by telling you this—I hope that you can

160

really understand more of where I'm coming from when I tell you to treat others with respect. Especially women. Especially girls that you are dating. I just... I worry. Every day, I worry. I worry about you. I worry about others."

Jace looked aghast. "You seriously think I'm gonna be like that asswipe that hurt you? Holy shit, Mom!"

Brooke had become accustomed to her son's swearing. It had only intensified once his father had left them both. She typically didn't mind. Not so much. And his profanity was exerted almost strategically—when he was incensed, when he needed an extra push to verbally exert his feelings. No, she didn't mind.

And right now, at this moment, she almost welcomed the choice of words. She knew that her son had heard what she had to say, and she knew that he was angry. But she felt terrible that Jace had immediately come to the conclusion that she thought he'd walk in the footsteps of the person who had committed that atrocity against her.

"No, that's not what I mean at all, Jace! I know you'd never hurt anyone. But I also know that things are different these days. Things are different than they were when I was your age or when I was in college. Back then, a boy could touch me in an inappropriate place, and it was perceived as a joke. Nothing was wrong with it. Even if it made me feel really uncomfortable, had I told anyone about that back then, they would have thought I was crazy to have the feelings I had. Today, though. If you were to touch someone on the bum, for example, purposefully, you'd get in trouble. That's really very inappropriate behavior.

"Even if you're in a relationship, Jace, you need to be careful. I guess what I'm trying to say is that even if it's your girlfriend, you need to ask. Maybe you haven't kissed yet? Then you should ask her before you do it. And you absolutely should ask if you can touch her. I don't mean holding hands, of course, but if you want to touch her on the bottom, or—" Brooke watched as Jace averted his eyes and a pink tinge lined his cheeks.

Brooke rested her palm on her son's thigh. "I know these things are uncomfortable to talk about, but I need to say this, and you need to listen. Consent. It's a real thing, Jace. If you ask your girlfriend, then you are showing her that you respect her—her body and her feelings."

Jace turned to look back at his mother. "I know this."

"Even so," Brooke said. "I need to say it all again. Especially because of where I'm coming from, because of what I've been through. Can you understand that?"

Jace nodded. His eyes remained on his mother's.

"This is so important, Jace. It really is. Consent, respect. Things are different now. But for a reason. Boys were able to get away with so much when I was growing up, and now… there's still work to do, but it's different. I don't know any other way of describing it."

Jace nodded. "Okay," he said. And then after a pause, he asked, "Did anything ever happen to that guy?"

Brooke shook her head slowly. "No."

Jace frowned, looking disgusted. "Why not?"

"I never said anything."

"Why?" Jace's voice rose.

"I was confused, Jace. I had been drinking. I followed him back to his room. Like I said, things were different. I felt… ashamed."

"Why?"

"It's hard to explain."

"But he did that to you!"

"It's not that simple," Brooke explained.

"But why not?"

162

Brooke sighed. How could she explain? "It just wasn't. And I suppose it still isn't. Even now."

Jace shook his head with revulsion. "So that asshole did that to you and got away with it?"

Brooke swiped another tear away and nodded.

"What the hell? That's bullshit!"

"I agree, but I just… I didn't know how to come forward. Not then. It's hard to explain how I was feeling, Jace. Some things aren't so black and white."

"Well," he said, "I wish they were."

"When it comes to this, I wish they were too."

They sat in silence for a while. Eventually, Jace said, "I'm sorry that happened to you."

"Thanks, Jace."

"Did Dad know?"

"Yes. Not right away, but yes, I did tell him eventually."

"Does anyone else know?"

Brooke slowly shook her head. "No. I haven't told anyone else. Except my mother and father."

Jace's eyes widened. "Really?"

"Really."

"Why?"

"I never felt comfortable. It took me a very, very long time to realize that this wasn't my fault, Jace. And I wasn't close to my parents growing up. I almost didn't tell them, and once I did, it was hard for them to believe me, and that just…" Brooke shook her head. "I don't need to go into those details right now. I'm not close to my parents. You know that. They live so far away, and we have our life here together. We talk to them, sure, but we're not close. I never could bring myself to open up to them more fully about what happened to me. And then I graduated from college and moved out of their home. We grew apart."

"Do you… do you think maybe things would have been different if you'd explained it more to them?" Jace asked.

Brooke shrugged. "I don't know," she admitted. "I suppose it's something I tried to tuck away and deal with myself, especially when it first happened."

"That's not good," Jace said.

"No," Brooke agreed. "It's not. But that's what I did."

"Do you think you'll ever tell anyone else?"

"I don't know," Brooke said, and she felt the honesty behind the statement.

After a time, Jace said. "Sorry again."

"Thank you."

"And I get it."

"Get what?" Brooke asked.

"What you're trying to tell me," Jace replied.

Brooke offered a wan smile. "I'm glad."

"Was it… is it hard for you to tell me?"

"Yes," Brooke readily admitted. "Very hard."

Jace nodded. He averted his gaze, seemingly lost in thought. When he looked back at his mother, he said, "I'm still mad."

Brooke chuckled wryly. "So am I, Jace. Believe me, so am I."

# Chapter 8

## *Now*

How the hell could this happen?

Jenny was beyond furious, but not at her daughter for dropping the charges. She was angry beyond belief at Jace Weatherbee for assaulting her daughter in the first place and angry that Maddy had been so conflicted, hurt, and scared that she'd felt it necessary to retract the charges against him.

Maddy had come to her just last night, Monday, after Piper had spent time with her daughter and left the house so suddenly—and why had Piper left the house in such a hurry, anyway? She always said goodbye to Jenny—and told her mother that she no longer wanted to pursue charges against Jace and that she just wanted to try and forget anything had ever happened.

Forget anything had ever happened? How in the world could Maddy ever do that? Although Jenny had never been assaulted herself, she knew full well that it wasn't something one could ever just forget had happened! What was her daughter thinking? But then again, that was it, wasn't it?

Jenny didn't entirely know what her daughter was thinking, the feelings she was struggling with, or the turmoil that boiled within. Jenny had only ever read about cases such as her daughter's, and that wasn't nearly enough to fully understand, was it?

Last night, Maddy had opened up to Jenny. Although Jenny had kept Maddy home from school again yesterday, Piper had told her daughter that Michael, Maddy's brother, had confronted Jace in the student parking lot at the high school. Piper had witnessed with her own eyes when Michael had beaten Jace so badly that Jace had fallen to the ground. Piper told Maddy about the blood, about the face that was already beginning to swell. And Jenny had been pleased when she'd heard this news. Good. Served him right!

But what the hell had Michael been doing at the high school in the first place? Jenny hadn't known he'd be there. And as the thought had crossed her mind, Jenny had once again felt pleased. Pleased that she had raised a boy to stick up for his younger sister in any way possible, even if it came to a physical altercation. Typically, Jenny didn't condone physical violence, but in this case, it was more than warranted.

She had called Michael the previous night once Maddy had gone to bed, and he was back at school. She had spoken to him and confirmed Piper's tale. Why he hadn't visited her after the altercation, Jenny didn't know. He had been at the house that morning and into the early after-noon for emotional support, but as far as Jenny knew, he had been on his way back to college when he'd stopped off at the high school and confronted Jace Weatherbee. Perhaps he didn't want his mother to see his outrage. Perhaps he didn't want her to notice his scuffed fists or the splatters of blood that marked his shirt. Jenny, though, would have welcomed it.

They had spoken about the situation with Maddy and their path forward. And she hadn't berated her son for his attack on Jace. On the contrary, she had thanked him. Especially because Maddy had told her mother that she wanted to drop her charges, and she had been vehement about it too.

"What?" Jenny had shouted. She immediately felt guilty about her tone of voice, but it couldn't be helped. She was utterly shocked at the turn of events transpiring right before her. "Why in God's name would you want to drop the charges? After all that boy did to you?"

Maddy had been crying, and based on her puffy eyes and the prominent red streaks in her sclera, the tears had begun before Maddy had approached her mother with her request. Maybe they had even begun before Piper had left the house so abruptly.

"I can't do this, Mom. It's just too much. Like, it hasn't even been a week, and I can't even… I don't want to do this anymore. Too much is going on, and I haven't even been back to school. What will people think? This is too much for me, Mom."

"Why would you worry about what other people think about you? You're the victim here, Maddy. If people are going to think anything, they're going to be on your side. Who wouldn't after what happened to you? Maddy, you can't drop these charges. If you do, then nothing will happen to Jace."

"That's not true," Maddy had insisted. "Michael already beat him up."

"And rightly so!" Jenny had exclaimed.

"Maybe that's enough," Maddy suggested. "People already hate him. Maybe that's enough?"

"No way!" Jenny said. She took her daughter's hands in her own, forcing Maddy to look up and into her mother's eyes. "What your brother did to that boy, Maddy, it's not enough. Not nearly enough. The police, they can really make a difference, you know? Without them, without these charges, he gets away with what he did to you. Do you really want that?"

Maddy's tears were plentiful as she meekly shook her head.

"I didn't think so," Jenny said, her voice forceful. "If you let this go, then that boy gets away with everything he did to you. And he could do it again, you know. He could hurt someone else. Do you want that to happen?"

"No," Maddy said with a sniffle. "But it's so hard, Mom. Everything that's happening. I don't think… I guess I didn't think about all of what would happen." She turned her red, tear-streaked face up to her mother, and in a whisper, she said, "I'm scared."

"Oh, baby." Jenny leaned into her daughter and wrapped her arms around Maddy's shoulders, pulling Maddy into her chest. She smoothed her daughter's hair at her forehead with her long fingers as Maddy's tears wet her mother's sweater. "I'm so sorry this is happening to you. I'm so sorry you're going through this. Never in my wildest dreams did I… but never mind. Whatever happens to that boy, he deserves, Maddy. Whatever happens. To hurt you like that…" She kissed the top of her daughter's head as Maddy continued to weep.

They'd had their scheduled meeting that evening with the police. Maddy's father, Gus, had been there too. And it was then that Jenny had learned that if Maddy was unwilling to speak out against Jace Weatherbee, there was next to nothing that Jenny could do. It was Maddy's word against his, and now that Maddy wasn't willing to speak out against her attacker, the case was at a standstill.

But Jenny wasn't done. She wasn't willing to concede this loss. Instead, she was determined to do whatever was in her power to stand up for her daughter and other girls and women out there in the same position, struggling not only with what had physically been done to them but also with the emotional turmoil such an attack induced.

These past few days had been torturous not only for Maddy but for Jenny as well. Jace's actions had affected their entire family, and Jenny would not rest until Jace Weatherbee was held accountable for them.

---

Jace wasn't in school on Tuesday, but Piper spied him on Wednesday in the lunchroom. He was sitting at an otherwise vacant table in the corner of the cafeteria with Dustin across from him. Other students were keeping their distance from Jace Weatherbee as if he had an extremely contagious viral plague. His posture was slouched and his eyes downcast. He nibbled on his food rather than eating it. And his face was a canvas reminiscent of Picasso's best work, his nose slightly crooked, one eye puffy and partially obscuring his vision, his cheek red and swollen.

Piper didn't notice Jace's phone anywhere near him. That didn't surprise her. She had seen the video that had been taken of Michael's pounding circulating through social media. Piper imagined that Jace had been receiving many jabs because of it. If the video had been of her, Piper would have thrown her phone away!

Piper's feelings toward Jace had vacillated this past week from anger to pity to loathing to confusion to obstinacy. She hadn't realized until she had found out about the Maddy-and-Jace catastrophe that she had been capable of so many varying emotions. It had clearly taken something of such magnitude for her mind to conjure them and then spit them out, leaving Piper feeling thoroughly exhausted.

The truth of the matter was that she loved Madison Crawford; she had loved Maddy since the day they had met, her best friend, her confidante. But she loved Jace too. It had begun in a friendly manner because of his easy, light-hearted demeanor and his way of always making Piper feel comfortable and welcome in his presence. Then that love had morphed fully and, she had always assumed, uncondi-tionally.

And then this.

She didn't know how she felt about Jace any longer. Did she still love him? Confusion wasn't even a strong enough word to describe how Piper felt when she was alone with her thoughts, attempting to sort them out into some semblance of meaning. These days, she felt as if she was inhabiting a dream, a nightmare, really. Piper, Maddy, Jace, and their friends were all intertwined with one another yet separate.

And then Maddy and Jace. Then Maddy. Then Jace. And Piper was left by the wayside.

And yet she was the one that Maddy had confided in prior to going to the police department with her allegations. And it was Piper who had convinced Maddy to speak with her mother. She had been desperate for her best friend to do so despite her conflicted feelings for Jace Weatherbee. What Maddy had confided that day, coupled with this assault, changed everything for Piper.

Everything.

And now here they were: Maddy still at home with her mother, Jace back at school with an unrecognizable, painful-looking face, and Piper with the knowledge that Maddy had dropped the charges against the accused.

And it was because of her, Piper. She was sure of it.

Again.

She felt a pull toward Jace as she sat at the lunch table with her friends. Princess chatted away, but Piper was so preoccupied that her friend's words were lifted into the air and carried away before she had a moment to comprehend them. But what would she say to Jace even if she did eventually muster up the courage to approach him?

No, Piper knew she couldn't speak with Jace. Not right now. Not yet. Not after everything that had happened. She was just struggling with too much right now. She needed to be alone to sort this all out.

Piper threw her unwanted food into her lunch sack, zipped it closed, and made for the door, not bothering to say goodbye to her friends or let them know where she was headed. Princess would probably ask her later that day why she had rushed off, Piper knew. Piper would probably just tell her that everything was getting to her and she was thinking too much. Princess was such a good friend, but Piper couldn't confide in her. Not about this. Not about all the feelings wreaking havoc within her.

Piper wasn't sure she could speak with anyone, really. Not even her mother. Not about this. She knew what her mother would say if she knew every intimate detail; she could hear her mother's probable words in her head right now. But Piper didn't want to hear them.

She passed Jace and Dustin as she hastily made her way out of the cafeteria, and no matter how stringently she instructed herself not to look at him, she did so anyway. And it was a mistake. In the moment in which their eyes made contact, Piper saw in Jace—in those eyes and in his countenance—a desperate plea. His expression spoke volumes. Even though Jace said nothing, she could plainly see the torment he was feeling.

And the entire situation hit her anew.

Never, never had Piper ever thought something like this would happen.

But here they were.

Maybe one day soon, Piper would approach Jace, the boy she had spent countless hours with and toward whom she had always felt an affinity. Yes, Piper knew that she would. She needed to hear what he had to say and how he could explain away his actions.

As she passed him and exited the cafeteria, all Piper could think was that she had to make it to the bathroom, and fast. She felt the bile in her throat, its acidic taste lining the back of her tongue. Her mouth began to salivate, her stomach roiled.

Piper pushed the bathroom door open with such force that it banged against the wall. She rushed into a stall, and without even closing the door, she bent over the open toilet, palms cupping the bowl, lunch sack hastily discarded to the cold, stained floor. Her eyes welled, and she could still detect the bile in her throat, but blessedly, it was slowly dissipating. Eventually, with a quivering lip, Piper leaned back onto her heels and inhaled deeply, the nausea subsiding.

When this year had begun, she had wanted it to be a good one. A year filled with friends and get-togethers and laughter. She had assumed her only worries would be about homework and getting to class on time, earning good grades, and what she'd do in slightly uncomfortable situations. Her typical worries, really.

But then had come Maddy's revelation.

After a time, Piper extricated herself from the floor, closed and locked the stall door, and sat on the open toilet seat. She heard another girl enter the room, the sound of her boots echoing on the floor. The faucet began to run, followed by the sound of teeth being brushed. Piper paid no mind; underclassmen with braces often brushed their teeth in the girls' bathroom after lunch or a snack.

Piper had never had braces. Her dentist had told her she didn't need them. She had a slightly crooked lower tooth, and a couple of her molars were marginally misaligned, but Piper didn't care about those minute imperfections, and neither had her parents, so she had counted herself lucky.

Most of her friends had had braces at one time or another, and Piper had seen how difficult they were to maintain. Even Jace had had braces. She remembered it well. It wasn't that long ago, really. They had come off just a couple of years ago when she and Jace were in the eighth grade. She had found his braces endearing in a way. Jace always seemed to know how to wear something, even if that something was metal stuck to his teeth.

Jace.

The thought of him sent her spiraling again, and the image of his tormented expression just minutes ago played in her mind, eliciting both pity and anger.

Piper wrapped her arms around her chest tightly, closed her eyes, and spent the remainder of the lunch period sitting on the toilet seat. Alone.

Jenny had just finished dinner with her family that evening when her cell phone rang, startling her from her reverie at the kitchen sink as she scrubbed stuck-on cheese from the lasagna pan. She wiped her hands on her jeans, removed her phone from her back pocket, and looked at the screen. Brooke. Screw that. There was no way she was going to talk to Brooke Weatherbee right now. No way in hell!

Jenny repocketed her phone and resubmerged her damp hands in the sudsy, hot water. Her fingers found the sponge. She squeezed it and then slowly let it go. She leaned forward, palms on the bottom of the sink, and sighed through gritted teeth.

No. That was not how this was going to go down. She had entirely too much to say to simply ignore that phone call.

Jenny lifted her hands from the sink, wiped them on a kitchen towel, and called Brooke. Her former friend answered on the third ring.

"I'm glad you called back," Brooke said.

Jenny detected a wariness to her voice, a tremble almost.

"I wasn't going to," Jenny said, her voice on edge and her words forceful. "But I want to talk to you, you know? I mean, what the hell, Brooke? I thought I knew you. I thought I knew Jace. I thought you were a great family. I thought we were great friends."

"We are great friends," Brooke said, her voice almost pleading, hopeful.

"To hell with that," Jenny said aggressively. She almost wished she was looking Brooke in the eye. She wanted to see the look on her face when she spat out what she had to say to the woman.

"I know our kids aren't us, Brooke, but what our kids do

reflects on us. All the time. I don't get how a kid can do what your son did to my daughter and not have it come from somewhere. Didn't you ever teach your son the difference between right and wrong? Didn't you ever teach him about respecting boundaries? I mean, what the hell, Brooke? How could Jace have done such a thing? Seriously, how?

"Not only has he hurt my daughter, but he's hurt my entire family. I can't even... I can't even wrap my head around this. Do you know what it's like to have a daughter come to you and tell you she was attacked by her boyfriend? No. You don't. And you never will because you don't have a daughter. But what if it was Jace that was hurt in this way somehow, huh? Can you imagine it? What would you do? What would you say?

"I can't even talk to my daughter without thinking about what happened to her. That's so wrong, Brooke. On so many levels. I can't even talk to you right now without wanting to punch a wall. How could your son have done something like this?"

"I don't...I don't know what to say," Brooke whispered.

"Then why the hell did you call me?"

"I needed... to hear your voice. I needed to tell you..."

"Tell me what, Brooke?"

"I don't know," Brooke admitted. "I don't understand this at all. I'm hurt just like you—"

"Oh hell no!" Jenny exclaimed. "You do *not* get to go there! You don't know how I'm feeling. You have no idea! My daughter was raped, Brooke. Raped! And by your son! How can you even live with something like this, huh? How?"

Brooke didn't respond, but Jenny could hear soft weeping emanating from the phone.

"I can't do this," Jenny said with exasperation. "I mean, I don't even know why I called you back. You know what? That's a lie. I do know. I called you back because you need to hear these words. You will never have any idea what your son has put us through, Brooke. Never. I am so mad. And that's not even a good word. I'm furious! Absolutely furious!

"And now Maddy's dropped the charges, which is ridiculous. She should go after your son for what he did to her. He needs to pay. He needs to know that what he did was wrong on so many levels.

"I can't even believe I'm having this conversation with you right now. I thought I knew you. I really did. But there's no way I knew you, Brooke. Not if this has happened. There's just no way. Not the whole you. I always hear people saying things like 'you never know who lives next door,' and it's so true. But I guess I just didn't realize how true those words are until this happened.

"Was Jace just always good at hiding who he really was? Has he always been capable of hurting a girl like this? And then I get to thinking, you know? Has he done this to another girl? Maybe he has, right? Maybe we just don't know because that girl was too scared to say anything, just like Maddy is too scared to follow through with the charges against your son like she should be doing! I'm so mad, Brooke. So mad!"

Jenny pressed her finger against the end call button and slammed her phone on the kitchen counter. Normally, she'd have felt terrible for using such force when speaking to a friend, but they weren't really friends, were they? Not now. Not anymore.

Plus she had needed to say what she had just said. It was what she was feeling, and the words rang true. Brooke had needed to hear them. What had happened to Maddy should never have happened. Never. Jenny couldn't even imagine Michael doing something like that to a girl he was dating. She had raised him to respect other people. Had Michael punched anyone other than Jace Weatherbee, Jenny would have been appalled, but when she'd found out what Michael had done to Jace, Jenny had admittedly felt a sense of pride almost. A sort of relief. Vindication.

But it wasn't nearly enough.

Maybe Brooke had needed to hear Jenny's words so she could really home in on the gravity of the situation. Maybe she needed to hear those words so she could talk to her son, so she could compel him never, ever to accost another girl. Never!

And still, it wasn't enough.

Her heart broke for her daughter. The images her mind conjured of that night were enough to send her teetering over the precipice.

Yes, she was convinced that Brooke Weatherbee had needed to hear her words.

---

The line went dead and, with trembling hands, Brooke placed her cell on the table beside her chair in the living room. She was thankful Jace was in his room because Brooke didn't think she was capable of maintaining the last remnants of her composure after her conversation with Jenny.

She had known she needed to speak to her friend. She had wanted to do so soon after the police had come knocking on her door the previous Thursday. But even as her finger hovered over Jenny's number on her phone's screen time and time again, Brooke had hesitated. She hadn't been sure what she would say. What words did one use in a situation such as theirs? "Hey, Jenny. Look, I know your daughter just accused my son of raping her, and I'm sorry?" Sorry? Yes, she *was* sorry, but the word was futile, meaningless.

No, she hadn't known what she would say to her friend, but she couldn't simply ignore Jenny entirely and pretend nothing had happened. And the guilt Brooke felt was immense and all-encompassing. She hadn't been able to eat more than a few bites of food each day for nearly a week now and hadn't been able to push her lurid and disturbing thoughts to the back of her mind. She hadn't been sleeping well and had been distracted at work to the point that her supervisor had spoken to her in an attempt to ascertain Brooke's alteration.

She was sure the woman had heard the news. How could she not have? Theirs wasn't a large community, and although Brooke worked in a small city about half an hour's drive from her home, word got around quickly. And something of this magnitude? Yes, Brooke was sure her coworkers had been apprised of her situation, though nobody had approached her about it.

It frightened Brooke that she had been spoken to about her performance on the job. She had never been criticized about her work, not in all her years of employment in several positions in two different states. And it had shaken her up. She couldn't afford to lose this job. Not now. Not when she needed the funds to maintain her household and to pay Jace's legal fees.

Dan, her ex-husband, had helped her procure the services of a local attorney. Dan had always been more aggressive than Brooke, and at this moment, Brooke wished that he was still living at home. She needed him now. And Jace needed his father.

But Dan had told her that he'd remain in Maryland; had claimed he couldn't leave work at the moment. Not even when his son had been accused of raping his girlfriend.

But he had picked up the telephone and, with his forceful and persuasive nature, had acquired a lawyer. Yes, Brooke had been informed that Maddy had dropped the charges against Jace, but she still wanted to protect her son. And a lawyer could help with that. Who knew if Maddy would change her mind once again? And if that happened, she wanted to be prepared. Well, as prepared as she could be, anyway.

Brooke put one foot in front of the other and realized that with her legs trembling so severely, there was no way she was going to make it past the living room. She sat in her chair and allowed her emotions to prevail—Her body shook, her lips quivered, and her eyes welled with unshed tears. Although she had known that her conversation with Jenny would not go well, now that Jenny had hung up on her and Brooke was reflecting on the exchange, she realized that she had held a fragment of hope that perhaps Jenny would listen to what she had to say. Hope that they would be able to speak to each other with even a minute amount of civility.

But no, that was not how the conversation had gone, if she could even call what had just transpired a conversation. Jenny was furious. And Brooke understood. She really did. She'd be angry too. She had been in Maddy's position, not that Jenny knew that, of course. And if Brooke had had a daughter—hell, if something of the sort had happened to her son, Brooke would be enraged too.

She just didn't know what to do or where to go from here. Although the charges had been dropped, there had been no closure. She didn't know what had occurred that fateful evening between Jace and Maddy. Not really. She only knew what the police had told her and what her son had said at the precinct, and Jace hadn't really been very forthcoming. Not so much, anyway. And when Brooke was being honest with herself, she feared that conversation if it ever occurred. She didn't want to know exactly what had transpired because she was scared—scared to know and scared to learn that her son truly was the monster that Maddy had accused him of being.

Jace had arrived home first on Monday, just two days prior. When Brooke had arrived shortly thereafter, she had taken one look at her son's face, and her expression had contorted into one of pure shock and distress. He had clearly been punched or slapped or kicked. The fact of the matter was that her son had clearly been physically assaulted, and much to her chagrin, he refused to tell her what had happened or who had done it to him.

Brooke had called the school only to get the answering machine. Apparently, office hours were over. She didn't leave a message; instead, she called the school the very moment the office opened the following morning and, after jumping through hoops, had finally been connected to the principal. It had been extremely difficult to quench her anger, but she had succeeded in speaking with the man civilly, explaining her son's physical state and telling the principal that she was sure the attack had happened on school grounds, though as the words left her mouth, she realized she wasn't entirely certain if they were true. Jace hadn't told her what had happened or where. She had only assumed.

The principal had told Brooke that there had been no complaint. He wasn't aware of something of the sort happening on school grounds, and therefore, there was nothing he could do. Brooke had tried to protest, but the principal had been adamant, and Brooke had eventually hung up the phone in defeat.

"Why won't you tell me what happened to you?" She looked at her son across the kitchen counter just minutes after she'd first spotted the signs of assault. She wanted to rush to him, hold him in her arms. But she knew, just by the look on his face, that he'd push her away.

"Because it doesn't matter."

Brooke was incredulous. "What do you mean 'it doesn't matter'?"

Jace shut his eyes and ground his teeth. "It doesn't," he scoffed.

"Jace, that makes no sense. Have you looked at yourself in the mirror? Of course it matters. I wish you'd tell me who did this to you. And I think we should go to urgent care."

"I don't need urgent care."

"I think you do."

Jace shook his head.

Brooke walked around the counter and planted herself in front of her son. She lifted her arm slowly. She brushed her finger along the puffy skin under Jace's eye, and he winced, jerking his head back.

"I'm sorry," Brooke said. "Is it just your face or... do you hurt somewhere else too? Jace, a doctor can check to see if you have internal damage, if... maybe... have you been kicked or hit with something else, some sort of object?"

Jace shook his head again. "I'm okay, Mom."

"You look far from okay."

"Stop it, all right?" Jace attempted to bypass Brooke and head for the stairs.

She grabbed his shirt and spun him back toward her. "Why are you doing this, Jace? Why are you acting like this?"

"Like what?"

"Like…" Brooke looked from his forehead to his chest then back to his face. With her palm out, she waved it in a circular manner, indicating his entire self. "This. You. What you're doing right now. You're hurt. That's obvious. I wish you'd let me help you. Why won't you let me help you?"

Jace pressed his lips together and averted his gaze, and it was in that movement that Brooke noticed the liquid pooling in his eyes.

"Jace, what's going on?" She took a step toward her son. "Please, tell me."

He refused to look her way.

"I can't send you to school if this is what's going to happen. It's not safe. I don't want anyone else to hurt you."

It took a few moments for Jace to reply but, head still tilted away, Jace said, his voice a whisper, "Maybe I deserve it."

Brooke's stomach plummeted. She reached out and lightly grasped her son's hand. "Why do you say that?"

It was then that Jace looked his mother in the eye. There was no verbal exchange, just watery blue eyes looking into brown. Brooke gently swept a tendril of blond hair off her son's forehead.

"Please help me understand what you're going through," she said. "Why you…" She didn't know how to continue.

Jace gently broke free of his mother's grasp, and a single

tear dribbled down his cheek. He turned his back on Brooke and walked out of the room.

———————

Brooke was on lunch break the following day at work—Thursday, one week after the police had knocked on her door—when her cell rang. Brooke's cell didn't often ring, so she was curious and a bit nervous to see who was calling. Was it the school? Had something else happened to Jace? Could it be Jenny?

She put her fork down and looked at the screen of her phone. She was surprised to see that it was the number of the elite cross country team that was composed of athletes throughout their small state, which Jace was part of. Jace had been thrilled when he'd made the team. Not only did he love to run, but he knew this team would better his chances of getting into a great cross country program in college. The team would be starting up soon now that the school's varsity season had ended.

Brooke answered on the third ring, confused.

"Mrs. Weatherbee, Phil here from Stars."

"Yes," Brooke said, the word elongated with uncertainty.

"We need to speak with you about your son's participation with Stars this season."

"Okay." She felt even more confusion now.

Phil cleared his throat on the other end of the line.

"We are backtracking our invitation."

"I'm sorry, what?" Brooke asked, her mouth hanging open.

"I regret to inform you that we will be backtracking on

our invitation for your son to join us this season," Phil repeated monotonously.

"You regret to inform me," Brooke said. "You have to be kidding!"

"We are not," Phil said. His voice was firm.

"But," Brooke spluttered, "how can you do that? Jace ran for you last year. He was one of your best. You were hanging all over him, telling him you hoped he'd be a part of the team this year. How could you do this? And—" Brooke closed her mouth. She sat at the table in the small, stuffy breakroom of the doctor's office. "This isn't fair."

There was a pause on the other end of the line, and then Phil spoke again. "I'm sorry you feel that way."

"Of course I feel that way. Why are you doing this?" But she knew.

"There have been... there are... we were informed about what Jace did to that girl."

"What Jace did to that girl," Brooke retorted. "You mean, what Madison Crawford said about my son? The charges were dropped."

"That doesn't matter," Phil replied. "We can't have... Jace is not welcome on the team. We can't have this level of... we can't have it."

"And how is it you're able to do this?" Brooke asked, her voice thick with distaste. "You already invited him. We've already paid."

"You will receive a refund of your payment by this evening."

"That's not the point! Jace, he relies on your club. All the scouts that are at meets, all the... you can't do this!"

"I'm sorry," Phil said. "But it's done. We reserve the right to—"

"Reserve the right?" Brooke was nearly shouting now.

"I.. I can't even believe this is happening. I… let me talk to your supervisor."

"I am the supervisor," Phil informed her.

"Then let me speak to someone else, anyone else, that can set this right!"

"There is no one else. That person is me. The decision is made. You can look for your refund later today." And with that, the line went dead.

Brooke removed her cell from her ear and looked down at the screen in disbelief. How was she going to tell Jace that his dream of being scouted this year through this high-profile elite team had just been shattered? He was going to be devastated. And there weren't any other programs in their state that were nearly as competitive as this one. She didn't know what to do.

She didn't believe there was any way to fight this. The club had the right to accept or deny anybody. Plus, even if she did fight Jace's removal from the team, where would that lead them? Jace had already dealt with enough, but if Brooke made a fuss in an attempt to get him reinstated, then his purported actions against Maddy would be spread even further, and that was the last thing that Jace needed right now.

She'd talk to their lawyer. That was what she'd do. He'd know whether or not this was legal and if there were any steps Brooke could take.

And yet, she knew, deep down, there were not.

# Chapter 9

## *Five Months Earlier*

"Jace broke up with his girlfriend," Maddy said to Piper at school in early June. This had been Jace's third relationship as a freshman, the girls knew.

"Oh yeah?" Piper asked nonchalantly.

Maddy side-eyed her. "Yeah," she said. "Hey, Pipes? You, like…" She coiled a strand of brunette hair around a finger then released it, standing up straight. The girls were in front of Maddy's locker, about to head to their first period classes. "You haven't really talked about Jace, you know? Like… about how you had a crush on him last year. Remember? I mean, we talked about it a bit after that, and then you just kinda let it go."

"All right," Piper said, not knowing in which direction this conversation was headed.

"I mean… you don't like him anymore, do you?"

Piper shrugged. Maddy was right. Piper hadn't pursued Jace after the semiformal. He had come to school the following week with a girlfriend, after all. There was nothing Piper could have done then. Maddy had been insis-

186

tent that Piper make advances toward Jace at the dance and shortly afterward as well, but instead of her friend's actions bolstering Piper's confidence, Maddy's urgings had left her feeling dejected and uncomfortable. So Piper had dropped it. She had feigned indifference, and that apparent apathy had persisted from one of Jace's girlfriends to the other and until this very moment.

But she hadn't stopped liking him. Not at all. Quite the opposite, actually. She liked him more and more as time went on and the more she got to know him. They still hung out pretty often. They met as a group of friends, of course, but she was still in his presence, still talking to him. And she didn't think he had any idea that she liked him. Not unless Maddy had said something, but Piper had always trusted Maddy to keep her secret. Plus, if Jace did know, wouldn't his attitude toward Piper have changed? At least a little bit?

No, she didn't think he knew.

And she was pretty sure that Maddy wasn't aware she still had feelings for Jace.

Piper looked at Maddy now, tilted her head to the side. "Nah," she said, flicking a hand in the air. "I don't like him anymore." She felt the lie spread within. And she felt an immense amount of guilt. She had never really lied to Maddy before. Not outright. Not telling Maddy about her persistent feelings for Jace was a lie of omission, and that felt very different for some reason.

"Oh," Maddy said with a grin. "Okay. Good. Because..." She wriggled her brows.

Piper's stomach flopped. "Because why?"

"Because I think I'm gonna ask him out."

And there it was.

Piper felt a weight bearing down on her chest. She inhaled sharply, and the motion proved difficult to do.

"What?" Her voice was low, no more than a mumbled whisper.

"I'm gonna ask him out. I swear I didn't know it."

"Know what?" Piper asked. She could detect the angst in her voice, though thankfully, Maddy didn't seem to notice.

"That I liked him. I think I didn't know until just now. Now that he's not with that girl."

"She has a name."

"Yeah," Maddy said, shrugging one shoulder. "I guess. But she doesn't even go here. We didn't even really know her."

"But she was still Jace's girlfriend."

"I guess," Maddy repeated impassively. "But now she's not, and I think…" She pursed her lips and squinted. "Yep. I'm gonna ask him out. He's changed, don't you think?"

"What do you mean?"

"This past year, he's changed. Especially the past few months, right? He's just… I don't know. He looks taller and older, and he's so hot. Like, I would have said all that stuff to his face because we're good friends and all, but now that he's not with that girl…" Maddy lifted a shoulder again. "It's just different. I looked at him yesterday, and it just hit me. Jace has always been such a cool guy, but now? I swear it just happened!

"But yeah, I'm gonna ask him out. They always say the best relationships start when the two people are friends, right? So that would mean that Jace and I will be great together. And I deserve a good guy, don't I? My last boyfriend—and, ugh, I'm not even gonna say the asshole's name—didn't last long, and he didn't treat me good, and we definitely weren't friends before. So maybe this will be good for me, right?"

"Don't you think," Piper said carefully, "that maybe it will ruin your friendship. If you don't work as a couple, I mean."

"Umm… no! Pipes, you know me. And you know Jace. Even if things don't work out, we'll be good. We have to be. We've been friends for way too long. We know each other really good."

"But this would bring things to a whole new level."

"I know. But that's what I want right now. With Jace. When my mom picked him up to give him a ride to school, I seriously don't know what happened, but when I saw him... I have no clue why it changed then, but it did. But Pipes, I swear it changed. For me, anyway. So I'll talk to him. And no, I don't think it will change things between us at all." And then Maddy looked questioningly at Piper. "Why? You do? That's why you asked? "

"I don't know, Maddy. Maybe? How could it not? If you two end up together, then it won't just be Maddy and Jace the friends anymore, it will be Maddy and Jace the couple. You'll be… closer. We talked about things like this back when I liked him, too, remember? Don't you think things will change once you," Piper's breath caught in her throat, "kiss him?"

Maddy smirked. "I hope so."

Piper felt nauseated, her stomach roiling to the point that she wanted to flee this conversation, run down the hallway and out the door to fresh air and freedom. But what would that prove? If anything, it would let Maddy know that Piper was vehemently against her best friend pursuing a relationship with Jace, the boy that Piper herself had pined over for more than a year. Piper, always in the shadows, and Maddy, always at the forefront. Perhaps this was the way it was supposed to be.

Maddy frowned. "What is it?" she asked. "I see your face. You don't, like, think I should do this? Oh my God, Pipes. You seriously don't still like him, do you? You just said—"

Piper shook her head. "No, it's not that."

"Then what?"

"Nothing," Piper said. "I guess maybe… maybe I just worry about you?"

Maddy grinned. "Awe. I love you too, Pipes!"

The bell rang. "Gotta go," Maddy said. "See you at lunch?"

"Yeah," Piper said. "I'll be there."

Maddy lifted a brow, smiled, and walked away.

Piper stood at Maddy's locker, watching the retreating figure of her best friend, feeling as if the world was crashing down around her.

Maddy and Jace.

Perhaps things wouldn't work out after all. Maybe Jace didn't want his friendship with Maddy to change. Maybe Jace didn't feel for Maddy what she had suddenly come to feel for him.

There was always hope.

Lunch arrived and, with it, both Maddy and Jace.

Piper made herself comfortable beside Maddy. Princess was there, too, as she often was. Jace sat across the table from Maddy with Dustin beside him. The pair were nearly inseparable these days. They were surrounded by various boisterous friends.

The lunch period began as it often did, with the friends starting to chat before bottoms hit the seats. Smiles abounded, laughter was heard and even bellowed by Dustin.

At one point, Jace smiled at something Dustin said, and

Piper looked at him across the table, at the teeth revealed by Jace's parted lips, at his downward-cast eyes, and at the blond hair that dipped to cover the corner of a brow. And she felt it, that feeling that overcame her from time to time. She wanted to lean over the table and brush the tendril of hair from his eye. She wanted to caress it between her fingers. She wanted to sense his body next to hers, much like she had done at the semiformal dance last year.

Oh, how that one dance she had shared with Jace had filled her! She had felt the heat from his body, smelled the soap on his skin. She wanted that now. And now that she knew what Maddy was going to do, Piper wanted it more than ever. But deep down, Piper knew it was futile. Piper and Jace as a couple: that was just a dream. But for Maddy, it might be reality.

And Piper didn't know how she'd tolerate it, much less hide her feelings toward Jace and her jealousy toward her best friend.

Piper picked up her sub and took a small bite, not from hunger by any means but to occupy herself so she wasn't caught staring at Jace with tears running down her cheeks.

That was all she needed!

"So, are we all set for the weekend, guys?" Maddy asked the immediate group surrounding her. "Last weekend before school is out!"

A chorus of cheers erupted from the table.

"This is gonna be the best summer ever," Dustin said enthusiastically. "My man Jace here, me and him, we're gonna head to the track every day, play video games, all the good stuff. And no school."

"I've got to work," Jace reminded him.

"Whatever, man," Dustin said. "But you're not working a lot. We'll still have the best summer."

"No, not working a lot," Jace agreed. "But I have practice."

"I know," Dustin said. "But even that's just, what? Two days a week?"

Jace nodded, shoving a cracker into his mouth.

"And nights, remember," Dustin said. "We've got our nights. And when school starts up again, you'll have your license soon after, and even that car your mom got you, junker that it is—"

"Don't go there," Jace said with a grin. "I'll have a car. And you?"

"Yeah, point taken," Dustin said. "But I'll get my license soon too. You'll see. No car, but that's where you come in."

"Now it's coming together," Jace said. "That's why we're friends, is it?"

Dustin draped his arm over Jace's shoulder. "You know it," he said. "That's what I was thinkin' back when we were kids. I was thinkin' 'Dustin, this kid's gonna have a car, he's gonna take you places, just you wait and see. Better be friends with him now so you can take advantage of him then.'"

"I'm sure that's what you were telling yourself," Jace replied playfully. "And here I thought you wanted to be friends with me so you'd have more cross country opportunities."

"Oh," Dustin said, removing his arm. "I see how it is. Jace Weatherbee thinks he's some sort of star or something, yeah? Man, you've got an ego!" He laughed.

"If he's got an ego, he has a reason," Maddy chimed in.

"I'll say," Princess agreed.

Jace offered a shy smile and looked down at the cracker in his hand.

Dustin whacked him on the back with a palm. "Jokin'," he said. "You know you're the best. That's why you're on that superstar, gonna-get-you-into-college team."

"He doesn't even need that," Maddy said. "He'd get in because of his grades anyway."

"Yeah. Suppose," Dustin agreed. "What? Athletic *and* academic scholarships? I'm tellin' ya. There was a reason I chose you for a friend." He laughed, and Jace lifted his gaze, returning a grateful smile.

"So," Maddy said. "We're good? For the weekend?"

"Yeah," Dustin said. "I'm good. I'll bring my football, and we've got that game, what's it called? The one with the net and the ball?"

"Spikeball," Piper said softly.

"Yeah, that's the one," Dustin agreed. "Spikeball. I've got that one. I'll bring it along. Supposed to be a nice weekend, so we'll get some sun and all. It is the beach, right? And that's what you do at the beach!"

Maddy smiled. "I have a huge blanket that we always used when I went to the beach with my family when I was younger. We went all the time. My mom loves it. I know she still goes when I'm in school. We go sometimes together in the summer but not as much. My brother's a loser and doesn't like the beach."

"He's not a loser," Piper said.

"No. That's not what I meant. Just saying it's crazy that he doesn't like the beach, you know?"

Piper nodded. "I'll bring snacks. We have a really big cooler."

"Anything you want me to bring?" Princess asked. "Other than Sean?" Sean was a boy that Princess had just begun to see. He went to a neighboring high school and was two years above them. Princess had met him through a mutual friend.

"Maybe we all just bring what we want for ourselves, and Dustin will bring the games and Pipes will bring the cooler, and we can stuff things in there? I'll bring the blanket, but we don't need anything else. Is Sean still driving?"

"Yep," Princess said.

"A friend might come," Dustin said. "Told him about it the other day. Okay with you all if he does?"

"Okay with me," Maddy said.

"Me too," Princess agreed.

Piper nodded.

"Good thing Sean's got three rows of seats," Maddy said. "And…" Maddy's voice dropped an octave. "Jace, I was thinking after the beach, you and me, we can go out somewhere."

Jace looked up from inspecting a smooshed strawberry. His face was expressionless. "What?"

Maddy smiled confidently. At least, she looked confident to Piper. Maybe inside, she was screaming. But this was it, Piper knew. Maddy was going to ask, and Jace would answer, and any of Piper's last hopes would come crashing down, buried forever.

"You and me," Maddy said. "I was thinking. We should go out. Do something. Together."

"Together?"

"Yes, together," Maddy said with melodic laughter.

"You and me?"

"That's what I said," Maddy replied. "You and me. Alone." And then after a slight pause, she added, "A date."

"A date?"

"Hello?" Dustin said. "Earth to Jace. Man, are you dense? The girl's asking you out."

Jace blinked. Once, twice. "Where'd this come from?"

Maddy shrugged. "Don't know. But it's a good idea, right? You're not seeing anyone. I'm not seeing anyone. So we go out together."

"Holy crap," Princess said, her voice near to screeching. "Why didn't you tell me?" She wore a smile that only intensified with each passing moment of realization.

"Don't know," Maddy said. "Guess it just came to me. But seriously, Jace. I think it's a great idea. Just one date. We'll see if we want to be more than friends after that."

Piper dropped her hands to her lap and looked down at the table. Her vision was swimming, and her ears felt clogged, like she was being held underwater.

Jace took a while to reply, but when he did, Piper's heart felt near to breaking. "Okay," he said.

Maddy beamed. "Great! Maybe a movie since it'll be late. Or... you can even come back to my place."

Piper leaped from her seated position, all heads turning to look at her. "Sorry. I... need to go to the bathroom." She didn't wait for a reply, didn't look at Maddy, and didn't dare look into Jace's blue eyes. She knew she couldn't handle it. Not right then.

He had said yes.

Jace and Maddy. Maddy and Jace. Whichever way she thought about them, they were a pair now. A pair that didn't include Piper.

---

Saturday morning arrived, and Brooke said goodbye to her son in the driveway as he threw a large bag into the trunk of a car owned by a kid she had never before met. Princess was in the passenger seat, her window rolled down. Maddy and Piper were in the middle of the car. Brooke knew that Dustin and one of his friends would be joining them as well, but she didn't spot them now.

"Make sure your friend drives safely, especially with all those kids in the car." She didn't want to embarrass Jace in front of his friends, so she made her voice low, but she was nervous for this boy to be driving her son and his friends.

"I know."

"When you have a lot of people in the car, you can get distracted, take your eyes off the road. And if you take your eyes off the road for even a second, your hand can follow, and you'll turn the wheel, and there's oncoming traffic, and—"

"I know." Jace smiled at Brooke, though she could tell he was only humoring her.

"Sorry," Brooke replied. "It's just, what was it your driver's ed teacher said? Something like it takes eight years to become even an okay driver? Something like that. And I remember how I was when I was your age. I was a good kid but still did some very stupid things and made poor choices. "

Jace arched his brow.

"I just think—"

"Okay," Jace lifted a palm in the air. "I'm sure Sean will be careful." He leaned over and gave Brooke a brief hug. "And oh, I forgot to tell you." He looked at Brooke and ran his fingers through his hair.

Brooke eyed her son. She knew him well, knew his mannerisms, and the Jace before her was clearly trying to hide his discomfiture. Brooke tilted her head. "Tell me what?"

"It's nothing. I'm just... Sean's dropping everyone off after the beach but me and Maddy. We're..."

"Yeah?"

"We're gonna go out after."

Normally, this news wouldn't have alerted Brooke at all. Maddy and her son had been good friends for years now. But the way Jace was leaning, the way his fingers were fiddling just the slightest bit, Brooke knew this news meant so much more.

"Out where?"

"Don't know yet. Maybe even just her house. But I'll be out."

"Just the two of you?"

Jace nodded.

"And," Brooke said, "I'm thinking maybe this is a date?"

Jace nodded again.

"Wow," Brooke said. "That's some big news."

"Okay."

"You don't think so?"

Jace shrugged.

"All right, then," Brooke said. "You be careful, please. Have a great time with your friends. And with Maddy. Will Jenny be driving you tonight if you go out, or do you need a ride?"

"Jenny's got us, I think. Maddy said, anyway."

"All right. Home by midnight."

"Midnight?" Jace grimaced.

"Midnight," Brooke repeated decisively. "You might be a bit older than your friends, but you're not sixteen for another four months, Jace. Midnight is late enough."

"Okay," Jace said.

"And you know I'll stay up to make sure you get home. You know how much I worry."

"I know, Mom," Jace said.

Brooke stood on tiptoes, leaned in, and planted a small kiss on Jace's temple. "Be safe," she reminded him.

"I will."

"See you by midnight."

"See you." He opened the back door of the SUV and climbed in between Maddy and Piper. Brooke waved as she watched Sean back out of the driveway, and the friends set off.

Brooke hadn't been back inside her house for more than a few minutes when her cell chimed on the kitchen counter. She was cradling a morning mug of coffee in one hand, and with the other, she lifted the phone and saw that it was Jenny. Brooke smiled. Of course!

"Hellooo?" Brooke said, her voice a purposeful song. She knew what this phone call was going to be about.

"Holy crap, Brooke!" Jenny exclaimed. "Do you know yet?"

"Know what? Oh, you mean do I know about my son and your daughter?"

"Yes!" Jenny screeched. "No, you know what? I'm headed to yours. You around for a bit?"

Brooke laughed. "I am."

The phone went dead without even a goodbye from Jenny, and not two minutes later, Brooke heard tires in her driveway. Jenny knocked loudly on the garage door and then let herself into the house, charging straight through the mudroom and into the kitchen, where Brooke still stood with her coffee in hand.

"Holy crap! I can't believe this!" Jenny said, hands in the air. She smacked them down upon her thighs and settled joyfully beside Brooke. "Maddy and Jace! How wonderful is this? Just wonderful. I mean, Maddy's had boyfriends, and I know Jace has dated a lot, but Maddy and

Jace together. Holy crap! I'm just so excited. Maddy didn't tell me until this morning, can you believe it? Not until right before she left the house. What the heck is up with that? Maddy and I are super close, so why didn't she tell me before this morning? But oh well… it is what it is, and I know now. Wait, did you know before this morning?"

Brooke smirked behind her mug before shaking her head and taking a small sip.

"No? Good! I mean, not good, that's not what I mean. But yes, good, because I would have been so upset if you knew and didn't tell me! They've been friends for so long, and I don't even know how this happened or who made the first move, or… damn, I don't know much of anything, but you better believe that I'll be talking to Maddy tonight and then again tomorrow because I just have to! Jace is such a good boy, Brooke, and you are so wonderful, and Maddy's my daughter, and we all want the best for our kids. I couldn't ask for a better boyfriend than Jace."

Brooke lifted her brows. "You think they're that serious?"

"Suppose I don't know," Jenny admitted. "Maddy just said they were going on a date after the beach today, asked me to drive, which, of course, I will, right? And made it a point to tell me that she and Jace would be alone. So maybe they're not serious? Or maybe just not serious yet, you know? Things take time. But then again, they've had so much time, as friends, anyway. Looks like they're taking another step right now.

"Oh, I hope it works out, don't you? I know lots of young relationships don't work out, but I met Gus when we were both in high school, and look at us. So things do work out when you're that young sometimes, and then I just think about Maddy and I think about Jace, and… why didn't she tell me before? Why did she wait until Sean was picking her up to tell me this? Holy crap! Maddy and Jace."

Brooke couldn't help but laugh at her friend's fervor. "I think you're a little excited," she said. "They're going to be with their friends for the entire day, and then tonight they'll be alone, sure, but they've been alone a lot before. This isn't new. And like you said, they're young. We don't know what's going to happen, and we definitely don't want to push anything. They have their entire lives ahead of them."

"Oh, I know that," Jenny said airily. "But a girl can dream, right? I know that anything can happen. I'm not naive. But like I said, this is so wonderful, you know? They're already such good friends, and they're both great kids, and I think they could be really happy together. They could have a healthy, strong relationship. And I know they're young, but again, Gus and I were young, and look where we are today. Things can happen, you know. Can you just imagine…" Jenny wriggled her brows, and Brooke laughed in return.

"I can see you're very happy about this," Brooke remarked.

"Darn right I am," Jenny replied. "Even Michael likes your son, and Michael's still so surly. He hasn't changed much since you first met him, has he?" Jenny smiled. "But my son has always been a good judge of character, and even though he's not at home anymore, I know he likes Jace. That's saying something for sure." Jenny stood up straight and began to walk slowly through the kitchen. "Dum dum dum dum," she chimed, humming the wedding march.

"Oh my goodness," Brooke admonished playfully. "You are ridiculous!"

Jenny giggled. "I know. But I'm only teasing. I'm happy

but definitely playing this up. I can have some fun with this, you know."

"I guess so," Brooke said with a grin.

"All right," Jenny said, clasping her hands in front of her. "Whatcha got going on today?"

"Not much, actually," Brooke replied. "I've got to get some groceries. We're out of milk and eggs and even bread, I think. It's just me and Jace, but Jace eats like a—well, like a teenage boy." Both women chuckled at the remark.

"That's no fun," Jenny said. "I'm glad I can get to the store during the week. Less people then. Weekends suck at the supermarket."

Brooke scowled then took another sip of her coffee. "Yeah, they really do," she agreed. "But there's no way around it. I suppose I could get some shopping done after work, but there are other things that need to be done. I need to get Jace from practice when cross country's in session, and he always seems to be on a team. He's got one he does a couple of times a week in the summer. Until he starts up again in the fall, that is. When we get home, I start dinner. It's always what I've done, so I do my shopping on the weekends, mostly."

"I can see that," Jenny said. "Doesn't mean I envy you, though." She smiled.

Brooke motioned to the coffee maker on the kitchen counter. "Would you like a cup? I've made plenty. Always do."

"I've got to get back," Jenny said. "When Maddy told me she was headed to the beach, she got me thinking. I want to go to the beach too! And when I checked the weather and saw the day we're supposed to have today, that's all it took. Called some girlfriends, and we're headed over soon."

Jenny eyed Brooke. "Hey, why don't you come with us? It'll be fun! It's gorgeous outside but still early in the season, so it won't be packed. I don't think you know the ladies I'm headed over with, but they're wonderful. You'll love them. Won't be able to spy on Jace, though. I promised Maddy I'd head to a different beach. Now I'm rethinking my promise! What I wouldn't give to see those two together today!"

Brooke smiled. She leaned over, lowering her elbows to the cool kitchen counter, hands still cradling her mug. "I don't think so, Jenny, thank you. The beach sounds fun, but not today. I think I'm going to have a leisurely morning here at home with my coffee and a book or television show, and then I'll head to the grocery store. Work has been kind of crazy lately, and I could use the respite. A relaxing day sounds right up my alley."

"You could relax at the beach." Jenny wriggled her brows. "Lie in a chair or on a blanket, close your eyes, soak up the sun."

Brooke smiled. "Hear the screaming kids, get sand kicked into my eyes, get sunburned, just to come home with sand in places sand should never be—yeah, sounds great."

Jenny pouted. "Well, you're no fun."

"I like the beach," Brooke said. "But a day at home sounds better to me today."

"Okay, then," Jenny conceded. "But you're comin' to the beach with me some other time this summer. Deal?"

"Yeah," Brooke said. "I can do that."

"Then we'll make plans. But for now," Jenny turned on a heel, "it's back home for me."

"Have a great time at the beach," Brooke said.

"Thanks, girl. You know I will! And hey—tomorrow, we've *got* to chat. I'm gonna get info out of Maddy if it's the last thing I do!"

Brooke laughed. "And I believe you too."

Jenny smirked, opened the garage door, and walked out of the house.

---

Piper had spent Friday night at Maddy's house along with Princess. Logistically, it was easier to plan out the carpool when Sean wasn't required to drive to each end of town in order to pick everyone up. Princess's boyfriend would meet them at Maddy's house and then pick up Jace just down the street. Then he would drive to Dustin's house, where he'd grab Dustin and Dustin's friend, Greg. Sean's vehicle would no doubt be at full capacity with the seven passengers, as well as all the beach belongings crammed into the trunk.

It was Saturday morning now. Typically, Piper would have been looking forward to the trip they were about to take, but right now, no. Not so much. Not when she knew that Jace and Maddy were set to go out later that night. What would today reveal? Piper had imagined herself so many times with her arms around Jace's waist, with her head against his chest. She had imagined reciprocal feelings. But now, she'd have to sit there at the beach, feigning a good time, when her best friend was living out Piper's dream.

She knew she should be happy for Maddy, and why shouldn't she be? Maddy was amazing. She was Piper's best friend and had been since they were both little girls. And Piper had made the conscious choice not to confide in Maddy further about Jace after the eighth grade semiformal dance, right? Had she been more forthcoming, maybe this day would play out in an entirely different manner. But she had held back. For whatever reason, she had held back.

And because of it, Maddy had every right to ask Jace out. And, of course, Jace had every right to say yes. Neither of them knew the internal struggles Piper was dealing with right now. And that was her own fault. If only she had been more confident. If only she had broken out of her comfort zone and done something about her feelings for Jace. She had had plenty of time and plenty of opportunities, that was for sure!

But instead, here they were.

"Maddy," Jenny called from the foyer. Maddy and her friends were currently in the kitchen, downing some orange juice and snacking on homemade banana bread. "Sean just pulled up. I see him in the driveway."

"Eee," Maddy said, her voice a squeal of delight. "We're gonna have so much fun today!"

"Sure are," Princess said. She wrapped her arm around Maddy and pulled her in close, pressing their cheeks together.

Maddy grinned widely.

Jenny walked into the room. "All set? I just waved to Sean and told him to hang out in the driveway so he didn't have to get out of the car."

"Yeah," Maddy said. "We're all set." She turned to her friends. "Right?"

Piper nodded, and Princess said "Yeah" before she tilted her head back and swigged the last bit of orange juice. She deposited the glass in the empty kitchen sink and popped the last large chunk of banana bread into her mouth with a grin.

Maddy led her friends to the front door, lugging a beach bag over her shoulder. Piper trailed behind, pulling a large wheeled cooler that the kids had filled up with drinks and snacks. Maddy turned the knob on the door but paused, then pivoted so she was facing her mother again. "Forgot to tell you that Jace and I are going out after the beach," she said.

"Okay," Jenny replied. "Where are you headed?"

Maddy shrugged. "Don't know yet. We'll figure it out. But can you drive?"

"Sure," Jenny said. She turned to Piper and Princess. "Will you girls be joining them?"

"No, Mom," Maddy said. "Jace and me, we're going out alone." She lifted a brow.

"Alone?" Jenny asked.

Maddy gave her mother an annoyed look. "Alone."

Jenny's face was expressionless for a moment, and then her eyes widened, and she stood more erect. "Oh!" she said. "Alone!"

Maddy rolled her eyes and turned back to the door.

"Details," Jenny said, stepping closer to her daughter. "You and Jace alone? On a date?" she asked, her voice hopeful.

"Yes, Mom," Maddy said with exasperation.

"Oh, how wonderful!" Jenny exclaimed. "When did this happen?"

"I don't know," Maddy said, her back turned to her mother. "It just did."

Maddy walked outside, hefting her large bag farther onto her shoulder. When Piper passed Jenny at the threshold of the door, she noticed the older woman was beaming. She supposed her mother would be beaming, too, if it was Piper that was going out with Jace that night. Piper's mom had met Jace on a few occasions and had spoken of his demeanor. She had described him as "the boy next door, only cuter. And not batshit crazy." Piper had been embarrassed at the time, but she understood her mother's words now, even agreed with them.

"Have fun, kids," Jenny called from the doorway. She hastened back indoors, just to reemerge with her car keys in hand.

Maddy had just thrown her belongings into Sean's trunk. She looked at her mother with a frown and called, "Where are you going?"

"Just to Brooke's for a minute," Jenny replied with eager haste.

"You have got to be kidding me. Ugh, Mom! We're going there now!"

"It's just for a minute," Jenny said with a large grin as she climbed behind the wheel of her vehicle.

"Oh my God, Mom!" Maddy protested. "At least wait until we leave his house!"

"Okay, okay," Jenny said. "I'll wait a bit. I promise."

"Oh my God," Maddy said to Piper as she climbed into the car beside her. "She's gonna go and talk about me with Jace's mom. What the hell?"

"She's just happy," Piper said.

"Yeah," Maddy said, annoyed. "Whatever. She's so annoying. And weird sometimes."

Fifty-five minutes later, Sean had a full car, and the friends had arrived at the ocean. Sean parked in the large parking lot, and the kids removed their bags, gear, and games from the trunk. Piper pulled out the cooler and set it on the ground then lugged her backpack over her shoulder —she lacked a bag more suited to the beach—and stretched her arms over her head while letting out a large yawn. She, Maddy, and Princess had stayed up chatting in Maddy's room until well after one o'clock in the morning and then had been woken by Maddy's alarm clock so they could get ready for this trip to the beach. Despite her youth, Piper didn't do well without a good amount of sleep.

Piper slipped her thumb under the thick strap of her backpack, closed her eyes, and tilted her face to the morning sun. She breathed in the salty air and heard the cawing of a seagull in the distance. A slight gust of air blew her brown hair off her shoulders. Piper opened her eyes and threw her hair into a messy knot at the top of her head with an elastic that she had been wearing on her wrist.

"Yay," Maddy said. "We're here. You gonna go in the water with me today, Jace?" She smiled flirtatiously up at Jace, who had settled beside her, bag in tow.

Jace grinned. "Think it's the other way around, yeah? It's you that'll be going in the water with me."

"Is that right?" Maddy placed a hand on her hip.

"Yeah," Jace said. "It's cold. Don't think you can handle it."

"Hmm… I think I've got something to prove here."

"Maybe," Jace said.

"Looks like you've got a job to do."

"What you mean?" Jace asked.

"If I go in the water, it's cold, like you said. You'll have to warm me up."

Piper looked from Maddy to Jace's slightly surprised face then down at the pavement of the parking lot. Her nose scrunched within her grimace. She wanted to throw up. Could Maddy be more forthright? Seriously!

"I brought a blanket," Princess chimed her way into the conversation.

"Beach blanket?" Maddy asked. "I said I'd bring one."

"Not a beach blanket," Princess corrected. "A big, warm blanket. Thought Sean and I might want to use something a bit more comfortable."

"Oh," Maddy said. "Yeah. Good idea. I should have thought about that. But I've got a big towel. It's, like, my mom's favorite. I stole it last night before she could get her hands on it. She's going to the beach, too. Did I tell you all that? She heard we were going, so she decided she wanted to go. She promised she wouldn't come here, though. I don't need my mom here to spy on us."

Princess giggled. "Your mom would so do that!"

Maddy rolled her eyes. "I know it."

Jace flung his arm over Maddy's shoulder. "Let's do this," he said. He grinned down at Maddy, and Piper's heart lurched.

Dustin placed his arm over Jace's free shoulder. "Don't think I like having competition," he said.

"What do you mean?" Jace asked.

"Man, I'm your best friend. We hang out all the time. You've had girlfriends before, but this?" He nodded toward Maddy. "I'm not used to competition. But now Maddy?"

"You're just jealous," Maddy said.

"That's what I'm sayin'!"

Jace laughed. He patted Dustin's chest with an open palm. "There's no competition," he said with a smile. "We're all friends. We hang out together all the time. Nothing will change. Anyway, who said anything about girl-friends? We're all here together today, and Maddy and I are just going out tonight."

"Hey," Maddy said, playfully wriggling out from under Jace's arm and smacking his shoulder. "What's that supposed to mean?"

"Just that we're going out tonight. We haven't—" Jace looked rather embarrassed—"I don't know—"

"I'm kidding," Maddy said, looking up at Jace. "Just teasing. We're going out tonight, but that's"—Maddy

lowered her voice and leaned in a bit closer to Jace's side
—"but that's not all I want. We'll go out again. You'll see."

Jace arched his brows. "Is that right?"

"Like I said," Maddy remarked. "You'll see."

Once again, Piper marveled at Maddy's confidence.

"All right, Greg my man," Dustin said, dropping his
arm from Jace's shoulder and turning to the friend he had
invited along. "Looks like it's you and me today. And Piper.
Got a feeling these two—" He looked at Jace then at
Maddy—"are gonna get a bit cozy and will ignore us. Ah,
man, I'm tellin' ya. This sucks!" But Dustin smiled as he
spoke.

Maddy began to walk toward the beach. Piper grabbed
the handle of her large cooler and began to tug it forward.

Maddy turned to Greg and asked, "You don't say very
much, do you?"

"Nope," Greg replied. "Don't need to with this guy
here." He jerked a thumb toward Dustin. "Or maybe it's
that I can't get a word in."

"He's got a point," Dustin said with a laugh.

The friends found a spot on the sand with a wide berth
between them and other morning beachgoers. Piper knew
it would become more crowded, especially on a beautiful
day like today at the beginning of the season, when New
Englanders from all around were eager to brush the winter
months behind them and soak in the warmer days while
they could.

Maddy reached into her bag and pulled out a large
beach blanket. "Hey, Jace," she said. "Help me with this?"
Jace grabbed the opposite end, and together, they brought it
down to the sand.

Piper then watched as Maddy took out her mother's
favorite beach towel, and when Maddy placed that on top

of the blanket, Piper could tell why it was Jenny's favorite. It was the largest, fluffiest beach towel Piper had ever seen. She eyed her bag and saw the towel she had brought, coiled tightly, small and thin, resting just within. But it would do. Piper removed it from her bag and laid it on the sand beside the beach blanket.

"Damn," Greg said at Piper's side. "I forgot a towel."

"Man, really?" Dustin was laughing. "How can you forget a towel when you're goin' to the beach?"

"Don't know," Greg said with an apathetic shrug. "Just did."

"You can share mine," Piper offered. "I don't think I'll be going in the water. Too cold for me."

"Great," Greg said, plonking himself down. "Thanks."

"There's the blanket, too," Jace suggested. "It's big enough. Maddy brought it for all of us, I think."

"Yep," Maddy concurred.

She wriggled out of her shorts and let them fall to her towel then pulled her sweatshirt up and over her head—mornings were still chilly in New Hampshire—and flung it to land on top of her shorts. She was now in a T-shirt that fell below her hips, revealing just a small portion of her bathing suit. Maddy wrapped her arms around her chest and pressed her knees together.

"It's cold," she said, looking at Jace from under her lashes.

Jace laughed. "Then put your clothes back on."

Maddy walked slowly toward him on the blanket. "Or we can use my mom's towel," she suggested as she nuzzled into his chest.

Jace smiled, but his hands remained at his sides.

"Football!" Dustin said as he leaped toward his bag and

took out a full-sized football. "What do ya say?" He looked from Sean to Greg, then his gaze lingered on Jace.

"What?" Princess said. "Not gonna invite us girls?"

"Girls can't throw," Dustin said with a teasing lilt to his voice.

Princess eyed Dustin, her lip set in a sneer. "Excuse me?" she said. "Oh, hell no, Dustin. You didn't!" She laughed then lunged so quickly for the ball in Dustin's hands that he didn't have time to keep it from her grasp. Princess ran off toward the water, the football cradled under one arm. Sean looked at Dustin with a grin and then followed Princess.

"She got me," Dustin said. "My kinda girl."

Sean turned to shout over his shoulder, "*My* kind of girl."

"Not what I meant, man," Dustin called back as he ran to catch up with the pair. He turned to look behind. "You in, Weatherbee?" Dustin asked.

"Okay." Jace turned to Maddy. "You?"

"Not much for football," Maddy replied.

"And?"

Maddy grinned. "Okay," she said. "Count me in. Pipes?"

Piper shook her head. "Not right now," she said.

"Greg?" Jace asked.

"I'll stay with Piper," Greg said.

Piper watched Jace and Maddy run away, Jace fully clothed and Maddy in her T-shirt. "You don't have to stay," she said to Greg.

"Not really in the mood for football right now," Greg replied. His words were spoken softly and slowly. He leaned back on the towel that Piper had set out, his palms catching the brunt of his weight.

Piper crossed her legs and rested her hands on her knees. "How do you know Dustin, anyway. You don't go to our school, do you?"

"No," Greg said. "We live on the same street. I've known Dustin since I moved here last year. Go to a private school, though."

Piper nodded. "Then that explains why you don't look familiar. Our school is big but not that big. And if you're Dustin's friend, then I would have definitely met you at school."

"Yeah," Greg said. "Imagine so."

"You moved here last year?"

Greg nodded, still leaning back lazily on his hands.

"Where did you move from?"

"Florida."

"That's a big change," Piper said.

"It is."

Piper looked at Greg. She surveyed his profile: sparse lashes, average-sized nose, thick lips, a light amount of brown stubble. Cute. He turned and caught her eye, and she looked down at her hands.

"But do you like it here?" Piper asked.

"So far. Yeah." Greg leaned farther down so his elbows were now resting on the towel and propping his weight.

Piper, still sitting with crossed legs, pivoted so she was facing him. "You were here for winter?"

"Yep," Greg confirmed.

"And what did you think of that?"

"My grandparents live in Maine, so I've been in the cold and snow before. Lots of times. I knew what to expect. Different living in it than just visiting, but it's all right."

"Did you ski or snowboard or tube or ice skate at all? Any of the winter activities?"

"Not so much," Greg said. "Not into all that stuff."

"Then what do you do for fun?"

"I swim. And I row."

"Row as in rowing crew?"

"Yep," Greg said.

"That's different," Piper remarked. "I haven't seen a whole lot of that up here."

"It was hard to find. I did it in Florida, was on a team. There's a team here, but it took my mom some digging to find it. And no, there's not a lot of it up here. Not like there was where I used to live. But I'm doing that this summer."

"Oh, good for you," Piper said.

"Thanks."

"And you swim?"

"Yep."

"Just for fun?" Piper said.

"Mostly. My school doesn't have a team. Last school did."

"Our school doesn't have a swim team either. I don't know of any schools around here that have swim teams, but I also don't know much about other schools."

"I don't either," Greg said. "My school down in Florida was huge, though. Over two thousand students."

"You're kidding!"

"Nope," Greg said.

"That *is* huge."

Greg grinned. "How big is your high school?"

Piper pondered, her eyes traveling to the sky. She brought them back to Greg and said, "I think maybe seven hundred?"

"Sounds about right for town."

"How about yours?"

"Bit bigger. Maybe nine hundred or so."

"But no pool."

Greg grinned. "No, definitely no pool."

"I think the rec department has a swim team," Piper said.

"Not the same," Greg replied. His fingers pulled lightly at the towel.

"Why?"

"Lake swimming versus pool swimming. It's not the same. Pools are much better."

"Why?"

"They just are," Greg said. "You can see where you're going."

"Well," Piper said with a laugh, "that explains it all."

Greg smiled and sat up, crossing his legs and turning so he was eye to eye with Piper.

"You're kind of cool," he said.

"I think you are too. Easy to talk to."

A football came careening toward them, bouncing off Maddy's beach blanket and bonking Piper on the thigh. "Ow!" she said. She picked the ball up and rubbed her thigh with her free hand. "What the heck?"

"Sorry, Piper." It was Jace that had run after the ball.

Piper shielded her eyes from the sun as she looked up. He seemed to loom over her, his head haloed by the sun's rays.

"It's okay," Piper said softly.

Jace retreated, and Piper and Greg chatted for a bit longer, their conversation superficial but comforting and easy.

After a time, Piper noticed her friends making their way back to their spot on the beach. More people had arrived and staked their claims nearby, but the friends still had a good amount of space without the disruption of others in close proximity.

Maddy plonked herself, with exaggeration, belly first onto her towel, and Jace sat beside her. Princess and Sean curled up inside Princess's large blanket, and Dustin laid his towel beside Piper's on the sand and sat down. He immediately stood back up.

"Food," he announced as he opened the lid of Piper's cooler and pulled out a family-sized bag of Doritos and a can of Sprite.

"Nice snack," Maddy remarked.

"You know it," Dustin said. "Want some?"

"You don't know sarcasm, do you, Dustin?" Maddy asked.

"Huh?" Dustin replied, though his voice was teasing.

Maddy rolled onto her back. "I'm all set."

"Over here," Jace said. He held a hand out for the Doritos bag, and when Dustin offered it, Jace reached within and grabbed a handful of chips. He popped one into his mouth and crunched down.

"Now I don't want to kiss that mouth," Maddy said.

Jace stopped chewing, and with his mouth full of chip but a slight grin on his face, remarked, "Who said anything about kissing?"

"Just saying," Maddy replied. She rolled onto her side and looked at Jace.

Jace slowly finished chewing, swallowed his mouthful, and, with a grin, popped another chip into his mouth, biting down with exaggeration.

Maddy laughed. She sat up and lifted her T-shirt over her torso. Piper noticed that Jace was surreptitiously looking at her figure as Maddy's face was obstructed by her shirt, and he looked away as soon as she pulled it over her head. Piper's stomach dropped. Again.

Maddy placed her T-shirt next to her on the towel and lay down on her back, crossing one ankle over the other. She laced her fingers together and rested them on her stomach. She was wearing an orange bikini that Piper thought looked rather fetching with her friend's skin tone and brunette hair. Just as when they had been young kids, Maddy was still petite. Piper didn't think she reached five foot three, or maybe she did, just barely. Although she had developed since they were kids, her breasts were on the smaller side. Her hips were narrow and her legs thin. Piper thought she was beautiful.

Piper watched as Maddy scooted closer to Jace. "Lie down," she instructed as she patted the space between them.

Jace discarded the chips to the blanket easily and lay down on his back, turning his head to face Maddy. She slithered closer, closer, and then her body was pressed against his. She wrapped her arm over his stomach and propped her chin on his chest. She smiled. Then Piper watched as Maddy grazed Jace's cheek with her lips, and he, in turn, lifted his head slightly and initiated a quick kiss.

"Ooh!" Dustin sang. "Man, that was quick!"

*Yes,* Piper thought. *That was quick. Too quick.*

Piper looked away. She had to. Her stomach was roiling, and she didn't think she could witness any other acts of intimacy between Maddy and Jace.

Maddy smirked at Dustin and then rolled onto her stomach. "Pipes, I put some of that banana bread my mom made in your cooler, right?"

Piper opened her mouth, but no sound emerged. With

difficulty, she tried again, eventually emitting a mumble in a voice that didn't sound like her own. "Mmm."

"Cool. Can you grab me some?"

Piper had plonked the cooler on the sand directly at her side, so she merely had to lift her arm and open the large, white top to extract a container of the sliced banana bread that Jenny had made fresh for the kids that morning. Piper had already tasted some back at Maddy's house, and true to Jenny's skill, the bread had been delicious. Piper leaned over and handed Maddy the container.

"Thanks, Pipes."

Piper nodded. She didn't trust her voice at that moment.

"Want some?" Maddy asked Jace.

"I do," Dustin interjected as he stood, walked to the blanket, and held out his hand eagerly.

"Of course you do," Maddy said with a chuckle.

Dustin wriggled his brows.

The friends snacked and chatted for a while longer, and then Dustin suggested a game of spikeball.

"Hell yeah," Greg agreed.

Jace leaped from the blanket. "I'm in," he said.

"All right," Maddy said. "Looks like I am too."

"Don't sound so excited," Dustin said with a grin.

Maddy fixed her bikini bottom and said, "No, I'm good. But I haven't played. You'll have to teach me."

"Deal," Dustin said. "Piper? Princess? Sean? You in?"

"I'm in," Sean said, languidly standing and stretching his arms over his head. He grabbed Princess by the waist. P is too."

"Oh yeah?" Princess said, leaning into his pull and palming his arms.

"Piper?" Dustin asked.

Piper shook her head.

"Come on, Pipes," Maddy urged. "You don't want to sit here alone, do you? It'll be tight, but we can all play. Or even take turns."

"That's okay," Piper managed to say. "I'm comfortable. Maybe I'll play later."

"Suit yourself," Maddy said. "You okay, though? You've been quiet."

Piper nodded. "I'm fine."

Maddy frowned, lines forming on her forehead. "Okay," she said.

She turned to Jace, grasped his arm, and pulled him off the blanket and onto the sand. Dustin grabbed the spikeball game and ran off into the distance, placing it in an open area on the beach.

Piper watched as her friends jostled each other to be the first to the ball and watched as they began to play, faces filled with youthful joy, postures relaxed and comfortable. Why had she come? Piper had known this day was going to be difficult for her. She wished just then that she had formulated some sort of excuse to skip this outing with her friends. But what would she have said? Maddy could already sense that something was up with Piper. If Piper had canceled, then Maddy would definitely have been skeptical. Piper always jumped at a chance to hang out with her best friend. It had been that way for years.

Despite the sun beating down on her, and despite the fact that she was still fully clothed, Piper felt chilled. She tucked her feet under her thighs and crossed her arms as she continued to watch her friends play. Piper's gaze set on Maddy's hair as it flowed in a breeze and she flicked it behind her shoulder. Jace had taken his shirt off, and Piper eyed him now, admiring the way the muscles of his shoulders rippled as he lifted his arms. And his hair: the blond was more pronounced in the sun's rays, and Piper noticed a golden tint in the tresses. Piper watched as Maddy laid a palm gently on Jace's chest, and she had to look away. The day was proving even harder than Piper had anticipated.

Hours passed. The friends threw the football, played another game of spikeball, and snacked leisurely. Maddy and Princess lay on the blanket in an attempt to soak in the sun, and the boys flung themselves under the waves of the ocean, joined by Princess, while Maddy and Piper held back and waded in up to their knees.

At one point, Jace came barreling toward them, water rocketing up with the force of his steps, the droplets glistening in the sun as they plummeted back into the ocean. He flung his arms around Maddy, wet and cold, and Maddy screamed gleefully in protest. When Jace turned to Piper and did the same, Piper was left momentarily baffled and speechless, as she hadn't expected the maneuver, but she soon found herself laughing with appreciation at Jace's antics. Despite Maddy's teasing banter with Jace earlier that morning, she refused to go any farther into the frigid water.

The sun rose to its apex and then began to wane. The friends enjoyed their time at the beach for a while longer, and then Princess suggested they pack up their belongings and head back home. "Me and Sean are going out tonight."

"Us, too," Maddy said, as she looked momentarily over at Jace, her lips curving into a smile.

Princess responded with a conspiratorial grin.

Back in the car, Piper took out her phone and began tapping on the screen. Maddy turned to look at her. "Who you texting?"

"My mom," Piper replied. "To tell her when I'll be at your house so she can pick me up."

"I'll take you home," Sean offered.

"You don't need to do that. I don't live close to Maddy."

"I'm dropping Dustin and Greg off before Maddy's anyway. What's one more?"

"Okay, then," Piper said softly. "Well, thank you."

"Welcome."

At Piper's house, Sean popped the trunk of his car, and she lugged out the large cooler and the backpack she had used at the beach. "Thanks, guys," she said with a wave. She watched as Sean backed his car out of her driveway. Maddy looked at Piper through the rolled-down window, the smile on her face radiating outward, her pleasure of anticipation fully evident.

The following morning, it was official: Maddy Crawford and Jace Weatherbee were a couple.

# Chapter 10

## *Now*

Piper was still upset with her best friend. Upset and hurt that Maddy hadn't told her the entire truth about that fateful night. At least, she didn't think Maddy had. She hadn't had the chance to finish reading Maddy's journal entry, after all. But based on Maddy's reaction after she had found Piper with her journal in hand, Piper thought she had it right. Her mind wouldn't stop reeling, her thoughts incoherent.

She had been sleeping more. Attempting to, at least. She didn't want to think about that night, she didn't want to think about Maddy under those circumstances, and she most definitely didn't want to think about Jace with her. She wanted this all to go away, but she knew, deep down, that it never would. It was a stain in their lives, a mark to set the trajectory of the following days. What had been done could never be undone.

Never.

Despite her misgivings, Piper had agreed to spend time at Maddy's house after school Friday night, one week and one day since her best friend's allegations against Jace. Piper still hadn't spoken to Jace. Honestly, she didn't know how.

Today had been Maddy's first day back in school since the entire debacle with Jace, and she'd stirred up the scene. Voices whispered, and eyes surreptitiously looked her way, searching her out. Fingers were typing out texts. She held her head up high, Piper had to give Maddy that. Piper hadn't thought that Maddy would be able to do so, not after everything that had been said, whispered, spread throughout the school and the community.

Jace wasn't allowed to be near Maddy—the school had ordered this despite Maddy retracting her accusations—because of demands made by Jenny. Piper thought this would prove difficult in a school setting, but luckily, Maddy and Jace didn't share any classes this year. And Jace and Dustin had recently been occupying a table in the far corner of the cafeteria during lunchtime, well away from Maddy and the rest of their friends. Piper had even spied a few teachers looking upon Jace with loathing, lips pursed, foreheads creased.

She wondered what was running through Jace's mind. She also wondered, for that matter, what Maddy had been thinking this entire day at school. She didn't want to pry, though. And she was desperately attempting to keep her own thoughts at bay as a protective measure.

And yet she remained utterly confused and distraught.

In Maddy's driveway now, Piper and Maddy lingered in the car as Jenny exited and headed indoors. "I'm glad you're here," Maddy said.

"Me too." And she meant it. She *was* glad to be at Maddy's. Still hurt, conflicted, and discombobulated. But glad.

Piper pushed the car door open, stepped outside, and

slung her school bag over her shoulder before closing the door behind her. After a moment, Maddy sidled up beside her. "Hey, Pipes—"

But Maddy didn't get the chance to finish her statement. Piper watched as Jace barreled up the driveway, his cross country legs sprinting as fast as Piper had ever seen them. He halted directly in front of Maddy and looked down at her, fuming. Piper swore she could see steam permeating out of his ears. His face was red with rage, his fists clenched at his sides. He was leaning forward, hovering.

Maddy arched her neck and took a step back, but the car impeded her progress.

"Jace, you're scaring me," she cried. Her lower lip was trembling, and her petite frame cowered. She looked diminutive next to an enraged Jace.

"I'm scaring you?" Jace seethed. "Me? What the hell, Maddy? Why'd you do it, huh? What were you thinking? You've ruined my life! They kicked me off the team, no one is talking to me... This is bullshit!" A small gob of spittle fell from his lip. He leaned forward even farther so his face was just inches from Maddy's. When she didn't speak, he yelled, "Answer me!"

"I—I—"

"You what?" Jace asked, his voice no longer screaming, but low and simmering.

Piper clutched the strap of her school bag, her body quaking. She stood immobile, rooted to the ground, as the scene played out before her.

"I don't get you," Jace said, his lips still lined and his brows creased. "You wanted to. Wanted to! And now this? What kind of future do I have now, huh, Maddy? Answer me that. What kind of future do I have? No scouts, everybody thinking I'm some kind of monster. You've ruined everything for me."

Maddy continued to cower, but she found her voice. "I ruined things for *you*?" she asked. "What about me?"

Jace's eyes widened, and his voice rose again. "What about you?"

"Look what you took from me!"

"Are you fuckin' joking with me right now, Maddy? Seriously?"

"You're a piece of shit, Jace," Maddy said. Her back was still pressed against the car, but Piper could tell she had regained a minute portion of her confidence.

Then Jace screamed, the sound low instead of shrill. He rammed the heel of his palm onto the side of Jenny's car, right beside Maddy's shoulder.

"What the hell is going on?"

Piper turned to see Jenny rushing into the driveway, her feet bare, her expression one of shocked outrage.

Jace stepped back and away from Maddy. "Your daughter—"

"Oh, no you don't! Jenny exclaimed. "No you right well don't. Don't you ever come here again, Jace, you got that?" She paused for a moment, staring Jace down, fuming. "Get off my property." She spoke slowly and clearly. To Piper, it sounded as if an entirely different being had inhabited Maddy's mom at that moment.

Jace opened his mouth to speak.

Jenny cut in, her voice now shrill. She lifted a finger. "I said get off my property!"

Jace slowly turned, and Piper watched as he retreated down the driveway. When he neared the end, he suddenly broke into a sprint, which took him out of sight.

Jenny hastened over to her daughter. She placed her

palms on Maddy's hunched shoulders and caught her eye. "Holy crap. Are you okay, baby?"

Maddy nodded.

"You're shaking. I can feel you. Come on." Jenny wrapped an arm around Maddy's shoulder and led her toward the garage door from which she had come. "Piper, you're welcome to stay, but I don't know if Maddy's up for company right now."

"I—I—" Maddy attempted.

"Okay," Jenny said, patting Maddy's back. "It's going to be okay. I'll call the police. He wasn't supposed to be here."

Maddy shook her head. "Don't call." Her voice wasn't much more than a croaked whisper.

"What? Why the hell not?"

"Just... don't call, okay?"

Jenny stopped walking and looked at Maddy, searching her face for an explanation. "I really think we need to call."

"Don't, Mom," Maddy begged. " I just want this to be over with. Promise me you won't call."

"Maddy, I think—"

Maddy looked at her mother and said vehemently, "Promise me!"

"Okay, okay." Jenny capitulated. "I won't call. But if he pulls something like that again, I'm doing something about it."

Maddy sank into her mother's arms, deflated.

"I... I'll call my mom to pick me up," Piper suggested.

"I think that's for the best, Piper," Jenny replied.

Maddy said nothing, merely rested her head on her mother's shoulder and let Jenny lead her into the garage.

Piper remained outside, standing in the driveway. She dialed her mother's cell phone number, put her phone to her ear. When her mother answered, her voice lined with concern, Piper said, "Mom? Can you come pick me up? Something's happened."

---

News of the incident had spread throughout the school by Monday morning, though Piper didn't know how it had happened, and so quickly. Piper hadn't told anyone except her mother, and she trusted that her mom would not have relayed the tale. Piper couldn't imagine Maddy would have told a lot of people, but then again, as she pondered the thought, perhaps she had. Maddy had certainly been shaken by the incident, and it was easy to type out a text to friends, wasn't it? Perhaps those friends had spread the word.

Or maybe Jenny was responsible for the whispered words at school, the bent heads, the eyes that followed even Piper down the hallways. Jenny, as far as Piper knew, had a lot of friends in town. And she was an outgoing personality and a talker. Perhaps she had relayed the incident between her daughter and Jace to those friends, and those friends had then spoken to their kids, and, just like that, word spread.

However it had happened, here she was, in school on Monday morning. And it appeared that everyone had been apprised of the news. Kids that Piper had never seen Maddy speak to approached her best friend and offered their sympathy. One girl handed her a pamphlet from a local nonprofit that specialized in partner abuse. A girl in their grade had even asked Maddy if she'd speak at her sister's college campus during their next Take Back the Night parade and rally. Piper had heard of the organization, a movement to spread awareness of sexual violence.

Maddy accepted her classmates' sympathies and thanked the girl with the flier. She told the girl who asked her to participate in the rally that she'd think about it, but Piper knew her best friend's facial expressions well, and her countenance indicated that Maddy would not, in fact, participate. As much as Maddy had relished the attention of others prior to that fateful night with Jace, Piper could clearly see that now, she did not. It was in the heaviness of her eyes, the downward tilt of her lips, and the slight rounding of her shoulders.

By lunchtime, Piper just wanted to go home. She had a headache, and her stomach was feeling a bit nauseated. She hadn't slept well the previous night, so she blamed her current state on lack of sleep, though she wasn't sure she was being entirely honest with herself.

She found a vacant seat beside Princess and opened her lunch sack. She pulled out a container containing a turkey sandwich and laid it on the table, but she didn't bother to open the lid. She wasn't hungry.

Maddy arrived and sat across from Princess. Princess leaned over the table conspiratorially and whispered, "Okay, you need to dish. Thanks for the text, Mads, but I want more."

Maddy looked down at the table. "I don't want to talk about it. Like, so many people have been coming up to me today. I just don't want to talk about it."

"Yeah," Princess said, "but those are those people. Forget them. This is me. I want to know more about Friday night. I mean, what the hell, yeah?" She tucked her straight black hair behind an ear, the tips of her tresses grazing her chin. "Do you see him over there with Dustin? Acting all... I don't know what. Just acting some sort of way. I mean, hell no, you don't. I'm surprised he's even still in school.

"And what's up with Dustin, right? Why's he still talking to Jace? I mean, I love you and all, but if you were the one that... you know... I'm not so sure I'd be talking to you, and we're like, the best of friends, the three of us, right?"

"I don't know," Maddy said, picking at an oat bar.

"What do you mean, you don't know?" Princess asked. She tucked strands of hair behind her opposite ear. "You okay, though? For real okay?"

"I'm okay," Maddy said.

"What's gonna happen to him, anyway?"

"I don't know," Maddy said.

"Why'd you drop the charges?"

"We've been over this," Maddy said, her voice almost pleading.

"I know, but I still don't get it," Princess remarked. "Guy does what he does to you, and you're just gonna let it go?"

"It's not as simple as that," Maddy said, her voice soft.

"Then explain it to me."

Maddy lifted her gaze, and Piper could see her chest inflate with a large breath. "I don't want to talk about it, Princess," Maddy said. "Leave me alone. Like, really, I don't want to talk about it."

"But, Mads—"

Maddy leaped from her seat. "I said I don't want to talk about it!" She turned and made her way to the cafeteria exit, leaving her discarded lunch on the table.

"What's her problem?" Princess asked Piper. "I just want to know what's going on. Jeez."

Princess didn't seem to want a response, and Piper was thankful, as she had nothing to say. Instead, she watched Maddy's retreating figure. Maddy's steps were long, even for her petite frame, as she hastened toward the exit, appar-

228

ently eager to put as much space between her and Princess as was physically possible at the moment.

Maddy had to pass Jace in order to exit the cafeteria, and as she did so, Piper watched Jace stop talking to Dustin and lift his gaze to Maddy. He followed her movements with a daggerlike squint. Even from this distance, Piper could tell that Jace was clenching his jaw, and his posture was rigid. He raised a fisted hand and uncurled his fingers, running them fiercely through his hair.

He said something to Dustin from across the table, and Dustin leaned in. Jace lowered his hand, leaving his hair a disheveled mess. Piper noticed then that Jace hadn't showered. His hair was greasy. His clothes were wrinkled and in disarray. Piper couldn't remember the last time Jace hadn't appeared put together, if there ever had been a time.

She looked back at Princess, who was stuffing her mouth with a cookie, clearly incensed.

Piper sighed. She lifted her sandwich, took a small bite, and attempted to swallow it down, despite her stomach's protestations.

---

Brooke walked into an empty house on Monday afternoon. She was surprised at the silence. She had been obliged to work an extra hour at the office that day, so she had expected Jace to be home by the time she arrived. She removed her cell from her purse. She looked at the screen, but there was no text from her son. Weird. She sent off a text asking where he was. She waited, but there was no immediate reply.

She was determined not to worry. He had probably just stayed after school for a bit, maybe talking to friends or asking a teacher a question on a homework assignment or some such thing.

Right?

Then she remembered the Find My app that connected her phone to her son's. She swiped at her home screen and found the icon. She clicked on it, then on Jace's name. But it didn't work. She had forgotten that Jace had disconnected his phone from hers.

Brooke walked to her bedroom and changed into a pair of jeans and a comfortable long-sleeved T-shirt. When she reemerged onto the first floor, she decided to start on an early dinner. Perhaps Jace would be home when it was done cooking.

She rummaged through her refrigerator. Brooke had never been one for lists or week-long dinner menus. Nothing appealed to her, so she shut the door and poked around in the freezer. Nothing there either. Brooke walked to the pantry and surveyed its contents: pasta, oatmeal, pancake mix, lentils, rice, cereal, bread. She sighed. She didn't know why she was being so indecisive. She settled on a box of penne pasta and a glass jar of marinara sauce. Dinner would be an easy one tonight, but she knew there would be no complaints from Jace. He liked pasta.

She set some water to boil and opened the top of the pasta box. She set it aside then twisted the lid off the jar of sauce. She emptied half the contents into a stainless steel pot and set the pot on a burner, turning it on medium low to slowly warm the sauce. She lifted her phone, which had been lying on the counter, and looked at the screen. Still no sign of Jace.

To break the unsettling silence, Brooke turned the television set on. She scrolled through YouTube and selected a compilation of instrumental music. The melody seeped through the speakers and to her ears.

Better.

So as not to stand idle, Brooke began to clean the kitchen counters. When the water was boiling, she dumped half of the penne pasta into the pot and stirred it with a large stainless steel spoon.

Where was Jace?

Brooke picked up her phone once again, but this time, she clicked on her son's number, calling his cell. One ring, two. Three, then four. Then she heard Jace's voice on the other end, but just as Brooke opened her mouth to ask him where he was, she realized it was just his voicemail.

When it beeped to indicate that Brooke could leave a message, she said, "Jace, where in the world are you? I'm starting to worry. This isn't like you. Not at all. Call me, please." She hung up and stared down at her phone, imploring it to ring or to ping, at the very least, with a text from Jace. It did neither.

Jace still wasn't home when the pasta had cooked and Brooke had strained the water from it. She ladled large portions onto two plates, spooned sauce over the tops, then sprinkled some shredded mozzarella cheese over the mounds. She slipped forks under the pasta and brought the two plates to the table. She sat down.

Jace was still nowhere to be found.

Brooke called his cell again, but he didn't answer. Panic had begun to rise, but she willed it down. He was okay. He had to be okay!

She ran the tines of her fork along the side of her plate, fiddled the fingers of her opposite hand against the material of her jeans. She pierced a piece of penne and brought it to her mouth. She bit down but didn't relish the taste. Her mind was too preoccupied. Brooke dropped her fork, and it clanked against the plate. She stood from the table and paced the room.

And then—

Brooke rushed to the garage door when she heard the unmistakable sound of an engine in her driveway. Jace had recently acquired his license, and he had the use of an old used car that she had been fortunate enough to find a handful of months prior. She opened the door and rushed into the garage and then outside. But it wasn't Jace's car she saw.

It was Jenny's.

Jenny slammed her car door and stomped over to Brooke. She waggled a finger in Brooke's face and shouted, "You tell that son of yours to leave my daughter the hell alone!"

Brooke's eyes widened, and she craned her neck back. "What are you talking about?"

"I've tried, Brooke. I've really tried. But I've had enough. Maddy told me that Jace tried to talk to her in the hall at school today. That's ridiculous, especially after he showed up on our property after school on Friday. He's supposed to stay away from her. Why won't he leave her alone? Haven't you talked to him?"

"Of course I've talked to him," Brooke said, aghast at her friend's outburst.

"Then he's not listening."

Brooke shook her head, baffled at the situation she suddenly found herself in. "I really don't understand this," she said. "I don't know anything about this."

"Where is he, huh? I want to talk to him."

"He's not here," Brooke said, for the first time feeling relieved that she wasn't cognizant of her son's whereabouts.

"I thought I knew him," Jenny said. "I thought he was a good kid. But I was wrong. If Michael ever did anything…" She let her voice trail off, pressing her lids closed forcefully before opening them again.

Brooke watched her dark pupils shrink in size, the gray-blue of her irises prevailing, the same exact shade that her daughter had inherited and that Brooke had looked into numerous times over the past six years.

"I don't know," Jenny said again. She was no longer shouting. Her voice was low and steady. Lethal. "We had so much fun together, Brooke. I got to know you. Or at least, I thought I had. But recently, I'm not so sure anymore. I know I've said this before, but If I really knew you, if I knew who you were… And Jace. I thought I knew him." Her eyes began to well with tears. "But I didn't, did I? Not really. I hope you never have to go through something like this, Brooke. Your son has hurt my daughter so much. And he's hurt us. Me.

"And you're his mother. His mother! What kind of kid does something like this? How could you… how could he do this? What's gone on in his life for him to do this to my daughter? She'll never be the same. Think about that."

She turned on a heel and stormed back to her car. When she put it in drive and took off, her tires squealed on the pavement.

*She'll never be the same. Think about that.*

She didn't have to. Brooke knew all too well what it was like to be assaulted. Knew, too, how it affected someone long afterward.

———

Jace arrived home later that night, well past the time in which the sun had set and the sky had grown dark, the moon no more than a sliver peeking from behind the clouds. The pasta sat untouched on the kitchen table, the lingering scent of sauce long gone. Brooke heard his car in the driveway even from her position on her favorite chair in the living room. She had been sitting in silence, worrying over her son for the past few hours.

Jace slowly came into sight, halting between the kitchen and living room. He looked at his mother. "Why are the lights off?"

Brooke turned her head so she was looking directly at her son. She couldn't decipher his facial expression, only the shadow of his figure. "Do you know how long I've been waiting for you? Do you know how much I've been worrying?"

"Sorry," Jace said. "I needed time."

"You needed time?" Brooke's voice was low. She attempted to keep it level, though every part of her was screaming inside.

"Yeah." Jace flipped the light switch.

Brooke squinted when the room was illuminated. Her eyes soon adjusted. She stared at her son, challenging him to continue. When he didn't, she asked "Where were you?"

Jace averted his eyes ever so slightly but enough for Brooke to know that he was uncomfortable. Good.

"Just around."

"That's not enough, Jace. Where were you?"

"I'm sixteen. You don't always have to know where I am."

"You're damn right I do!" The fragment of control that Brooke was desperately clinging to was tenuous. She felt it slipping away, and she knew she might regret the words that would exit her mouth in the next few minutes.

"Calm down."

Brooke stood and walked toward her son. "You do not get to tell me to calm down. Not now. Not after all that's happened. And when did you start disrespecting me?"

"What the hell, Mom?"

"Don't!" Brooke shouted. "Just don't, Jace. I'm going to ask you again: Where were you?"

Jace shrugged. "Just around. I needed time to think, and I wanted to be alone. Dustin hung for a bit, we just went to a park. Then I got something to eat and just sat in my car for a bit. Like I said, I just needed time."

"And you didn't think to let me know?"

Jace shrugged again.

"Answer me."

"I guess not."

"You guess not?" Brooke retorted. She tilted her head, her eyes beginning to well. "Who are you? Who is this kid standing before me?"

Jace frowned.

"Who is this kid who doesn't seem to care? Where is the Jace that confided in me, that told me things? Where is my son?"

"What's that supposed to mean?"

"You've never done this before," Brooke replied. "Never. No, I take that back. You did this the day after the police showed up. That morning, you were gone. But not for long. Before then, you'd always check in with me. I know your schedule, and I expect you to stick to it, and if you want to go out with friends, you always ask. If you're going to be late, you always text. Always.

"I've been sitting here, worrying that something

happened to you, wondering if you were okay, wondering if you were in a car accident, wondering if the cops were going to knock on the door—" Brooke caught herself.

"What? Oh, you mean like last time? Maybe they'd tell you I was in jail? They'd spew some bullshit story about me raping another girl?"

"Jace!" Brooke admonished.

"Admit it, though," Jace said. "That's what you were thinking."

"That was not what I was thinking," Brooke replied honestly. "I was afraid you were hurt, and I worry…"

"About what?"

"I worry about your mental state."

"My mental state," Jace scoffed. "And what about my mental state, Mom? Huh? You think this is too much for me? Think I'm gonna off myself?"

"Jace Weatherbee!"

"Well, you're right, Mom, okay? Happy now? You're right. This *is* too much for me. Maddy goes and lies and everyone believes her, not me, even though I didn't do anything wrong! Friends aren't talking to me. I'm off the team. Everything I was hoping for—college scholarship, a good end to high school—all of it is gone now. Gone. Maddy dropped the charges, and still, everyone blames me. You should see the way people look at me, Mom. They look at me like I'm a piece of shit. Kids at school—"

"Kids at school what?"

"Never mind. It doesn't matter."

"It matters to me," Brooke said.

Jace cocked his head. "But does it?"

"What does that mean?"

"Does it really matter to you, Mom? Do you really care?"

"Of course it does. How could you say that? How could you even think that?"

"Because I don't think it does matter to you. Even when I tell you that I didn't do anything, you still look at me like…"

When he didn't continue, Brooke asked, "Like what?"

"You look at me sometimes like you can't figure me out. You get this weird look, like… I can't explain it. But it's not you. And it looks like… like the look you give spiders in the house before you squash them. Like you can't stand them. Like they're in your space and you just want to kick them out." Jace paused then said, "Like they don't belong."

"You really think that?"

"Hell yeah," Jace said more vehemently. "You do it all the time."

"I didn't know you were feeling that way."

"Well, I am," Jace said. "And then I think that maybe, even though you're my mom, I think that maybe you believe her, believe Maddy. Instead of me."

Brooke made no reply.

Jace's lips formed a thin line, and his brow creased. He clenched his jaw. "So it's true," he said. "You think I raped her."

Tears dripped from Brooke's eyes, and her body trembled. She closed her eyes, and behind her lids she saw a room, a boy, a bed. She opened her eyes, more tears dribbling down her cheeks. She reached for her son's arm. "Jace, you need to understand—"

Jace tugged his arm back. "I don't need to understand shit," he said. "What I understand is that my own mother is against me."

"Jace, that's not true." She reached for him again.

Jace leaped back. "Don't touch me," he seethed.

"Jace, please…"

"No," Jace said. "I can't believe this is happening. I can't believe my life right now. What the hell? Thanks a lot, Mom. Just… thanks a lot." He turned his back on Brooke and ran.

Brooke heard him stomping through the mudroom, heard the garage door slam, and heard him peel out of the driveway.

Brooke placed a hand over her roiling stomach and bent over, heaving. She dropped to the cold, hard floor and gave into her torment. She wept until she felt spent of all energy, until her face was thoroughly wet, her skin was puffy, and heat radiated from her pores.

She worried for her son. Where had he gone? Would he be all right, especially in his current condition? What had she done? Had she caused this to happen? What was wrong with her? A mother was supposed to believe her son. A mother was supposed to be there, was supposed to be supportive and nurturing. Instead, she had caused Jace to flee.

She sat there on the floor, her head lolling with exhaustion against the side of the couch. She thought about Jace in the dark, driving erratically. She thought about him stopping the car and exiting, walking aimlessly to an unknown destination. She thought of him wading dazedly in the water of the lake.

And then her mind turned to Brian, the boy in a stuffy college dorm room. She felt his hands on her skin. She felt his lips pressed to hers, the taste of beer. And she felt—

*No, please stop. Please, please stop.*

It had been so long ago, but the memories hadn't faded. The scars hadn't healed.

She remembered the way Jace and Maddy had been

together before that portentous knock on her door, the way Maddy had looked up at her son with unadulterated adoration. The way Jace would slip his hand into hers. The way they'd cuddle on the couch, Jace's arm around Maddy's shoulder, Maddy's head resting on her son's chest.

Had there been signs that she had missed? Had there been signs that she had refused to see because of her biased opinion of her son that, until now, hadn't been questioned? She recalled a time, just last month, when Maddy and Jace were in Jace's room. Despite the door being closed, she had heard Maddy's shouts seep down the stairs. She had heard the door slam. And she had heard Maddy exit their home in a huff.

Brooke hadn't knocked on Jace's door then to ensure he was all right. She knew her son needed time on his own when he was angry. She had known this even before his father had left them, but once Dan had moved out, and especially when he had relocated to Maryland, Jace had become a different person in a way. He had begun using profanity, had curled more into himself, and she had let him. He'd always talk hours later or even the next day, but he wasn't one who could be confronted immediately and asked to voice his feelings. He needed to sort matters out in his head first.

And Brooke had respected this. But in doing so, had she done the right thing? Should she have pushed Jace more to seek out emotional help after his father's abandonment? Sure, Jace and Dan still spoke, but those instances were few and far between. Jace and Dan did not have a good relationship, and Brooke knew that each time Jace spoke to Dan, he spent the following days either wallowing or visibly irritated. Should she have insisted that Jace see a therapist?

*What's gone on in his life for him to do this to my daughter?*

Jenny's words stung. Had she been right? Were they in their current situation in part due to Brooke's faulty parenting?

Jace still wasn't home by midnight. Brooke certainly wasn't going to call the police for their help. What would they do, anyway? He had left of his own volition after a fight with his mother. They'd brush his departure aside, certainly. And honestly, Brooke didn't want to have any further dealings with the local police station. She had had enough already.

She extricated herself from the floor. Her legs creaked, and her neck was stiff. She listlessly walked up the stairs, leaving that night's dinner on the kitchen table. She didn't bother changing out of her clothes before she climbed into bed and sat against the headboard. She pulled her blankets to her chest in the dark room and waited.

And waited.

And waited.

At two o'clock in the morning, she heard the garage door open. A few minutes later, she heard footsteps in the upstairs hallway.

Her son was home.

Exhausted, Brooke let herself slip farther under the blankets, her head hitting the soft pillow. She closed her eyes, but not before a single tear dripped to mark the material cradling her cheek. Four hours later, she awoke, enervated, an execrable feeling inside.

She took the day off.

And she didn't hear when Jace left the house again.

# Chapter 11

## *Two Months Earlier*

Mid-August arrived, and Piper found herself at Maddy's house the week before school was set to begin. This would be the girls' sophomore year, and Piper was looking forward to it. Although most people she knew didn't like school, she did. With the exception of a few teachers and a few past classes, she had enjoyed learning. And with Maddy and Princess and Jace by her side, she had friends, felt like she fit in, and felt a sort of comfortable ease, for the most part, during the school day.

"Mom, these are awesome," Maddy told Jenny after she swallowed a bite of pumpkin muffin in the Crawfords' kitchen. "You sure they're healthy?"

"Mmm-hmm," Jenny replied. "Made them with honey and coconut flour, eggs, almond butter, pumpkin, spices…"

"They are really good," Piper agreed.

"Thank you, Piper," Jenny said, clearly pleased.

"Everyone thinks you're the best baker," Maddy told her mother.

"That makes me happy," Jenny replied. "Would you girls like something to drink with those?"

"I'll get myself some water later," Maddy said.

When Jenny set her gaze on Piper, Piper said, "I'm all set, thank you."

"Mom, we're taking these to my room." Maddy held up the remainder of her muffin.

"Fine with me," Jenny said.

"Coming, Pipes?" Maddy asked after she had started for the stairs.

"Yeah," Piper said. "Thanks again, Jenny."

"You're welcome, Piper."

Piper followed Maddy up the stairs and to her room. Maddy shut the door behind them, and the girls leaped onto the bed, smiles wide. Maddy bit into the top of her muffin. "Seriously, though," she said with her mouth full, "She's the best baker. Like, the best. These better be healthy."

"She said they were."

"Yeah, but, like, maybe she's lying to get me to eat them?"

"I don't think your mom would do that," Piper said.

"No," Maddy said. "I guess not." She took another bite. Piper followed suit, and before long, the girls had both finished. Maddy grabbed Piper's wrapper and deposited both of them in the small trash can at the side of her bed.

Maddy tucked her legs under her and said, "I can't believe we have school next week."

"Me too. But I'm glad."

"I'm not," Maddy said with a frown. "This summer has been way too fun. So much, right? Me and Jace are together all the time, and me and you too. And you and Jace are friends, and that makes everything so much easier, right? I mean, like, so we can all see each other. I'm not picking between you or Jace most of the time." Maddy frowned. "You don't think I'm picking Jace over you, do you?"

"No, I don't think that," Piper replied.

And it was the truth. Sure, she had seen a bit less of Maddy this summer, especially when it came to alone time, but she still saw her often, and despite her emotional difficulties when she witnessed Maddy's physical displays of affection toward Jace, she enjoyed her time with the two of them. She had even seen Dustin's friend, Greg, a few times throughout the summer after their initial meeting at the beach in June. Maddy said that Greg was interested in her, but Piper found she was just too shy to do anything about it. If Greg asked her out, she'd probably say yes, though. She needed to move on. Jace was with Maddy now, and it appeared that they were doing well.

"Okay, good," Maddy said. She leaped from the bed, walked to her dresser, and grabbed a small journal. She opened it and began writing inside. In less than a minute, Maddy had discarded the journal and was back on the bed, facing Piper. She placed her palms on either side of her and leaned forward.

"What was that?"

Maddy shook her head. "Nothing. Just needed to write something quick." And then, smirking, she said, "So, I think it might happen." The expression on Maddy's face pointed to the conspiratorial nature of the explanation that would follow.

"What might happen?" Piper swallowed, her mouth suddenly feeling dry. She should have taken Jenny up on her drink offer.

"I think me and Jace might have sex."

Piper's eyes widened.

Maddy laughed. "Don't look at me like that," she said. "I swear, you look like you're gonna burst. But that's kinda like how I feel."

"Like?"

"Like I'm gonna burst," Maddy clarified. "I mean, like, so on the one hand, I really want this to happen, right? I've never done it before, but Jace has."

"He has?" Piper asked incredulously. She hadn't been aware.

"Yep, he has," Maddy confirmed. "He told me. With his last girlfriend. She was the only one. So he's done it before, but we haven't done it together, right? And I want to. So I think it's gonna happen, but…"

"But what?" Piper felt as if she was hanging over a precipice, only a single foot grounding her, preventing her from plummeting.

"Umm… I'm nervous."

"Are you?"

"Yeah," Maddy said. "I mean, what will it be like?" She smoothed a tendril of soft brunette hair behind an ear. "My first time. And if he's done it before, he's more experienced. I have no experience. So, like, when it happens, will I be good? And will it hurt? And how will he treat me? And… I don't know. Just, everything."

Piper inhaled deeply. She let the breath out slowly and then said, "I don't know what it would be like because it's never happened to me."

"You'd tell me, right? If you had sex?"

"Of course I'd tell you," Piper said, surprised that Maddy even had to ask.

"Okay," Maddy said, clearly pleased.

Piper smiled softly. "I don't know what he'd expect

because… I guess that's just weird for me to think about. You're with him, not me. And I'm sure everything will be fine."

"You can say it'll be fine because, like you said, you're not with him, so it's not happening to you," Maddy remarked. Her words stung, but Piper knew that Maddy hadn't said them to be cruel. "But whatever. I guess I've just been thinking about it a lot. But I know it'll be Jace and not someone else."

Piper nodded. She understood. Jace Weatherbee would definitely be a boy that wouldn't make Maddy—or any girl, for that matter—feel pressured or bad about anything they were or were not doing. She couldn't see Jace doing that to someone. But then again, she also wasn't in a relationship with him or left alone with Jace behind closed doors.

"And what if I suck?" Maddy asked.

"I don't think you'll suck," Piper assured her.

"You don't know that," Maddy said. And then she smirked. "You've never had sex with me."

Piper spit out a laugh. "No," she said. "You've got a point there."

Maddy laughed, and then her laugh trailed off. Her smile faltered, and she looked at Piper. "But seriously, Pipes," she said. "What if I'm bad? What if we have sex and I suck and he's disappointed?"

"Are you kidding?" Piper asked, truly shocked. "How can you say that?"

"It's just been on my mind," Maddy said. "Like, I know *how* to do it, but… that's not the same as actually doing it."

"I'm surprised right now, Maddy," Piper admitted. "You've never been the type of person to think badly of yourself. You've always been confident. Ever since we were really little girls. I know you, Maddy."

245

"Maybe…" Maddy said, her eyes trailing to the window. Her voice lowered, and Piper had to strain to hear her next words. "Maybe it's all been a show… maybe I think bad things just like everyone else. Maybe I'm scared too."

Piper didn't know what to say, so she sat there in silence. Eventually, she slowly reached over and placed the palm of her hand on Maddy's arm. Maddy turned her head and looked back at Piper. Her smile returned.

"It'll be fine," she said. "Me and Jace have known each other forever. It'll be totally fine."

"Are you sure you're ready?" Piper asked.

"Yep," Maddy said, her voice a sing-song. "Totally ready. One hundred percent ready. Super ready. Colossally—"

"I get it," Piper said with a chuckle. "You're ready."

"Yep."

"This is a big step," Piper said.

"Yep," Maddy repeated.

"I can't believe this."

"Yep," Maddy said.

"Holy crap!"

"Yep," Maddy said, and the girls burst out laughing.

Piper grabbed a pillow and used it to swat Maddy on the head.

"Hey!" Maddy protested. With both hands, she lifted another pillow from her bed and knocked Piper on the shoulder.

Piper giggled and then threw herself on Maddy, flinging her arms around her best friend's neck. Maddy tumbled backward, and the girls lay side by side, Piper holding her stomach as it constricted with her laughter. After a time,

Piper was staring at the ceiling when she said, "I love you, Maddy," she said.

"Love you too, Pipes."

"I can't believe this," Piper said.

"Yep."

And Piper could hear her best friend's apprehensive sigh.

---

The first week of school went well for Piper. She met her teachers and classmates, most of whom she already knew, at least by sight, since the high school wasn't all that large. She had one class with Maddy, which thrilled her completely. She also had a class with Dustin and two with Jace. She and Princess didn't share any classes this semester, unfortunately, and she learned that neither did Maddy and Jace.

The bell rang, dismissing students at the end of the school day on Friday, and Piper met Maddy, Jace, and Dustin in the student parking lot.

"Hey, Pipes," Maddy greeted her.

"Hi." Piper watched as Maddy leaned into Jace, running her fingers along his stomach. Today, Jace was wearing a cobalt-blue long-sleeved T-shirt that emphasized the hue of his eyes. He was looking directly at Piper with a smile. Piper averted her gaze.

"You ready?" Maddy asked.

Jace and Dustin had some sort of race the following day, and instead of having them practice after school today, their coach had given them the day off to rest and ensure they were ready to go, spirits high, by the next morning. Maddy had suggested the friends get together at a local pizza place that students frequented and that happened to be within walking distance and then attend their school's Friday-night football game. Piper didn't enjoy football. Not at all, really. But she did enjoy the company of her friends, so she had agreed, as had both Jace and Dustin. So here they were. The game didn't start until six o'clock, and it was only just three, but Piper knew the time would pass quickly.

They set off and arrived at the pizza place a mere twelve minutes later, entering the facility with smiles and jaunty movements, a bell announcing their presence to those already within.

They ordered at the counter, settling on two large pizzas, one plain cheese, the other with pepperoni and sausage. Jace and Dustin offered to pay for everyone, but Piper declined. "I've got money," she said.

"And I'm the one that worked all summer," Jace countered. "Why'd I work then? My treat. And it's just pizza."

It was true. Jace had worked that past summer, accruing a nice stack of extra money that he otherwise would not have had, while Piper hadn't found a job. She wouldn't have her license for many months still, and her parents worked full-time, necessitating the use of their cars. There were no places of employment less than a few miles from Piper, so she had held off with the agreement that she'd obtain her license and find a job the following summer. Maybe something a couple of times a week to get her some extra spending cash for occasions such as the current one. For now, her mother had offered her ten dollars for the pizza.

"I've got me some cash too," Dustin said. "Gotta step up, yeah? Treat the ladies." He winked with exaggerated playfulness at Piper.

"Seriously, Dustin," Maddy said. "Super dork."

"I know," Dustin replied with a chuckle. "But I know

you're gonna take us up on it."

"Yep," Maddy said, sidling into Jace but with her eyes on Dustin. "I'm taking you up on it."

They found an open booth and sat, Maddy beside Jace and Piper next to Dustin, who had made himself comfortable closest to the aisle. They chatted amiably for a while, and then Dustin leaped out of his seat when their number was called. "That's what I'm talkin' about!" he exclaimed. Piper laughed at an image her mind conjured of Dustin salivating, eyes wide, as he peered down at a pizza. Total Dustin move.

He returned, a pizza in either hand, and plonked them both down on the table. Paper plates had been nestled beneath a pizza, and the friends each grabbed one then a slice of their choosing, although Dustin took two with a single swipe. He brought the large portion to his mouth and took an enormous bite.

"Umm… Dustin?" Maddy said. "You've got two pieces there."

"I know," Dustin mumbled through a mouthful, his cheeks extended like a foraging critter.

Maddy rolled her eyes, but Piper detected a grin playing on her lips.

"You really like pepperoni," Piper remarked to Jace.

"Uh huh," Jace said with a nod as he took a bite. "Have since I was a kid."

"You're still a kid, man," Dustin teased.

"I guess," Jace agreed. "But you know what I mean."

After a time, Dustin reached over and took the last slice of cheese off its platter.

"I swear, Dustin," Maddy said. "You ate a whole pizza by yourself."

"Wouldn't be surprised," Dustin said, leaning back in the booth and bringing the slice to his mouth.

"Don't you feel sick?"

"Nope," Dustin said. He tore a bite off with his teeth, a glob of cheese slithering off the crust and adhering to his chin. He lifted it, stuffed it into his mouth, then wiped his chin with his sleeve.

"You are such a slob," Maddy chastised.

"Yep," Dustin said, chewing with a lopsided grin. "But you love me."

"I don't know why," Maddy retorted playfully.

"'Cause I'm loveable."

"Whatever," Maddy said with another roll of her eyes.

They spent a full hour at the pizza place, and then Maddy decided she'd like a coffee. "Dunks, anyone?"

"Yes for me," Dustin said.

"I wasn't asking you," Maddy said. "I knew you'd say yes." She smiled. "Jace? Pipes?"

"Fine with me," Jace said.

"I don't want anything," Piper said. "But I'm good with going."

Recently, Maddy had been on a coffee kick, and although Piper had tried it, even prepared the way Maddy liked it, she found that she abhorred the stuff. She'd be happy to do without.

Piper brought the platters to the front counter, and the friends deposited their trash in the receptacle. They walked outdoors and set off. Because they lived in New England, there was a Dunkin' Donuts at what seemed like every corner. They only had to walk a few minutes down the road to the closest one.

"Hey," Maddy said. "When we get our stuff, let's go to Porter's."

Porter's was a local recreational area that the friends had frequented lately and happened to be across the street from the high school. There were swings that Maddy enjoyed—she loved it when Jace pushed her—and a skate-board area. Piper didn't skateboard, and neither did her friends, but they'd watch people, and Piper did find it interesting, though she grew bored rather quickly. There was also a separate playground for the younger crowd, which Piper and her friends stayed clear of, as well as a gazebo with a picnic table and an expansive grassy area where recreational sports and activities often took place. When the field wasn't being utilized, the friends often sat out in the middle to chat and fool around.

When there were no complaints, Piper soon found herself at Porter's. There was a tot soccer program in progress on part of the field, but it was otherwise vacant. Maddy led them to an area lined by trees on one side, and they sat down in the grass. Piper surveyed the area and noticed that the leaves were beginning to change. Though most were still a vivid green, there were sporadic yellow hues, and a few of the leaves had turned a vibrant orange.

"Do you ever get cold when it's the end of your cross country season? You're only wearing shorts and a short-sleeved shirt. Doesn't the season end in late October? That little girl over there looks like she's shivering, and it's a gorgeous day today. But tonight will be chilly at the game. So I wonder…" Piper mused out loud.

"Nope," Dustin said.

Piper turned to him, only then realizing that she had verbalized her thoughts. "No?"

Jace chimed in. "We're active almost the whole time. We're running. We pace ourselves, yeah, but our pace is fast. Our bodies heat up. No time to get cold."

"What about after?" Piper asked. "You're all sweaty, aren't you? Doesn't that make you cold?"

"No," Jace said. "It feels good, actually. By that point, we're hot and tired."

"Even when it's really cold outside? Even when there's rain or it's really windy?"

"Rainy, windy days are the best," Dustin supplied.

"Really? How?"

"It cools us off. When you're running in the rain…" Jace trailed off, and his eyes left hers to search out the horizon. His expression transformed to one of pure bliss. "Your body moves. It takes over. I don't think about anything when I'm running. Just my breathing. Just my body. In the rain, it beats down on you… you feel… exhilaration? Is that the right word? It's like the world is opening up to you, giving you a gift."

Piper's heart leaped. She had known that Jace was passionate about his running, but she had never heard him speak in such a way. She opened her mouth, but before any utterance emerged, Maddy laughed.

Jace looked at her with a frown. "What's that for?"

"You just sound so… I don't know. Like, philosophical."

Jace's brows arched. "I like cross country."

"I know you do," Maddy said. "But… seriously, Jace. I was just kidding."

Jace shook his head and turned away from Maddy.

"Come on, Jace," Maddy said, clutching his shirt sleeve and tugging it toward her. "Look at me."

Jace made no move to turn his body, but he did tilt his head and eye his girlfriend.

"I'm sorry, okay?" Maddy said. "I get it. You like running."

"It's more than that," Jace said, his voice a whisper.

"Okay," Maddy said. "I'm sorry. I won't laugh again."

Dustin caught Piper's gaze, and she narrowed her eyes as if to say *I don't know.* She twiddled her fingers in her lap.

Maddy sighed, lifted her coffee cup, and took a long sip.

"Hey, Maddy?" Piper said in an attempt to diffuse the hostility around her. "Can I have some?"

"What?" Maddy asked, side-eyeing Piper. "You don't like coffee."

"Yeah, I know," Piper said. "I thought maybe I'd try it again. Can I?"

"Whatever," Maddy said then handed her cup to Piper.

Piper tilted it to her lips, took a small sip, and swallowed. The potent sweetness tickled her tongue, and she grimaced. Maddy laughed. Piper handed the cup back to her friend.

"You still don't like it, do you?" Maddy asked.

Piper shook her head with emphatic tiny, rapid movements.

"That's 'cause you don't make it like I do," Dustin said. He offered Piper his cup, a smaller size than Maddy's.

"I don't think so," Piper said.

"Try it," Dustin said. "Promise you'll like it more."

"How can you promise that?" Maddy asked with a chuckle.

"Just try," Dustin said to Piper.

Piper accepted the cup from Dustin and took a small sip. Though the drink was not as repulsively sweet as Maddy's, she still didn't like it. With a frown and a shake of her head, she handed it back to Dustin.

"You're no fun," Dustin said.

"Then I guess I'm not either." Jace interjected himself into the conversation.

"Yeah," Dustin said. "You suck, Weatherbee. Who doesn't like coffee?"

Jace grinned at Dustin and then nodded ever so slightly at Piper. Her stomach flopped, and she knew it wasn't because of the coffee.

They chatted for a while longer then headed across the street to the high school to make it in time for kickoff. The football games at their school were typically well attended by students and parents and even some community members. Piper had only been to a few, but she knew this detail anyhow. The sport was often spoken about during the school day, and she knew, too, that Friday nights were the most well attended.

They entered the stadium area and found a spot in the student section of the bleachers. There were already quite a lot of people there, most of whom were standing. This was just one thing that Piper disliked about football games—why couldn't people just sit down? She'd certainly have been more comfortable doing so. But she supposed that a lot of her classmates would rather stand so they could shout and stomp their feet and otherwise act like fools. And of course, she knew this was her opinion and that she was in the minority.

Piper watched Maddy laced her arm through Jace's as Jace said hello to several people around them. Dustin had found a friend and was goofing around with him a few benches down. Piper stood awkwardly next to Maddy.

The game began, and the crowd got rowdy. At their team's first touchdown, an eruption of cheering accosted Piper's ears. She covered them with her palms and cringed. Way too loud for her liking. But she persevered, and at half-time, she and Maddy chatted.

Maddy suddenly broke the conversation in midsentence and turned to Jace. "I'm cold, babe," she said.

"Okay."

"Don't you have a sweatshirt in your locker?"

"Yeah," Jace said. "But that's my favorite one."

"I'm not gonna steal it from you," Maddy promised. "Just let me borrow it for the night?"

"I don't know, Mads," Jace said.

He had recently begun using this nickname for Maddy, possibly borrowed from Princess, who had been using it for years now. Piper didn't know how she felt about it, though her feelings shouldn't matter in the least. It sounded endearing from Jace's lips. Almost possessive.

"Come on, Jace. I'm cold."

"Shoulda brought a jacket," Dustin remarked, returning to their side from one of the many times he had left to catch up with other friends.

"Umm… wasn't asking you."

"But I'm still telling," Dustin said.

"Jeez, Dustin."

"I'll get it," Jace said. "But you'll give it back?"

"Of course I'll give it back."

Jace left the bleachers and returned a few minutes later, sweatshirt in hand.

"Thanks a ton," Maddy said with a large grin. "Seriously."

"You're welcome."

Maddy pulled it on. It dwarfed her. Piper discerned the faint aroma of soap, which surprised her. If anything, she would have expected the smell of boy: sweat, deodorant, dirt. But soap? Piper found herself surreptitiously breathing it in.

The game started up again, and Piper watched. Soon,

she was aware of something occurring between Maddy and Jace, though the crowd was so large and boisterous that she was having a difficult time making it out. And then—

"Whatever, Jace." It was Maddy that spoke.

"I just need some time to myself," Jace said.

"Like I said, whatever."

"I don't know why you're being like this."

"Because you promised we'd go out after your meet tomorrow."

"I didn't promise," Jace said. "I told you we would, but now I'm telling you that I'd like to be alone."

"But why?"

"I told you, Maddy." Jace's voice was rising with exasperation. "We're together all the time. I'm busy. School, practice, meets. It's only the beginning of school, and I'm already overwhelmed."

"You can be alone on Sunday."

"I want to be alone tomorrow after the meet."

"I was looking forward to the movies."

"Go with someone else," Jace suggested. "Ask Piper. She'll go."

Piper winced at the truth of Jace's statement.

"I don't want to go with Piper," Maddy said, "I want to go with you."

Piper wanted to distance herself from the confrontation but feared she'd appear rude if she did so. Instead, she remained, rooted uncomfortably to the bleachers.

"I'm leaving," Jace said.

"What? Wait… why?" Maddy asked, flummoxed.

"I don't need this," Jace said. "I just want to go home."

"But we've had such a good night," Maddy said.

"Yeah. I know. But I really want to go now."

"Please stay until the end of the game?"

"No."

He said goodbye to Dustin and a few friends around them, then he said goodbye to Piper.

"Bye," she croaked in reply.

"Wait," Maddy said. She reached for Jace's sleeve, but he pulled back. Piper watched as Maddy attempted to grab onto Jace again, but he swatted her hand away forcefully, his face set in a scowl.

"What the hell, Jace?" Maddy said. "That hurt."

"I just want to go. I'll call you later."

"Whatever," Maddy said. She turned away from Jace and crossed her arms, looking out onto the football field.

Although it was still light outside, the sun was making its final descent in the sky, and the stadium lights had been turned on. Piper looked at her friend, saw the angered expression on her face. She noticed that Maddy's hands were hidden by the long sleeves of Jace's sweatshirt.

Piper felt nauseated. She had seen Maddy and Jace argue before, but little squabbles only. Nothing like this. And she had never witnessed Jace slapping Maddy's hand away.

Maddy had assured her that things were going incredibly well with their relationship. That had been her word too—incredible. Piper didn't think they had been intimate yet, not going so far as sex, anyway. Maddy hadn't told her they had, and Piper knew that Maddy would tell her something of such importance, just as she had done before school had begun a couple of weeks ago, stating that she and Jace would probably soon take that momentous step together.

When the game ended, the girls climbed into Maddy's mom's car, and Jenny joined the mass of vehicles setting off down the parking lot and out into the street.

"No Jace or Dustin?" Jenny asked.

"No." Maddy made no move to explain, and though Jenny furrowed her brows, she didn't push further.

They rode in silence.

Piper wondered the entire time what was really going on with Jace and Maddy.

# Chapter 12

## *Now*

The Tuesday following Maddy and Jace's encounter in the Crawfords' driveway, Piper passed Jace in the hallway between first and second periods. He looked bedraggled and haggard, his hair disheveled and greasy. His eyes were puffy and encircled with dark rings as if he had rubbed them raw or pressed his knuckles into them with such force that he had left them marked. Even the pallor of his skin left him looking wan and weary. He looked as if he hadn't slept at all the previous night, and for all Piper knew, maybe he hadn't. She didn't know what was going on with Jace right now. She still hadn't spoken to him.

Piper stepped to the side and watched him pass, his eyes downcast, his mind seemingly elsewhere. She turned, gazing at his retreating figure, and watched as a classmate rammed his shoulder into Jace's and sent him sprawling. Jace's palm slammed into a locker. He righted himself and walked on, his pace slow and languid. A few girls gave Jace a wide berth, looking at him with disgust, eyes narrowed, lips pursed. Dustin emerged from a classroom and approached his friend's side. He said something, but Jace's head was still downcast, and he made no discernible motion to acknowledge his friend.

Piper shut her eyes and sighed heavily. Then she set off to her second-period class.

Lunchtime arrived. Piper sat with Maddy and Princess and a few other friends at their typical table. She glanced to the side where Jace and Dustin had recently been sitting and didn't notice either of them.

"He's gone," Maddy said.

Piper turned to her. "What?"

"He's gone," she repeated. She nudged her chin upward, motioning to the vacant table. "Jace. He's gone. The counselor said that because he wasn't supposed to be near me and because I'm already dealing with so much, he'd be in another lunch or have lunch somewhere else or something like that. Whatever. He's just not gonna be here in the same room right now."

"Oh."

"It's good," Maddy said.

"Yeah," Piper agreed. "I guess."

"What do you mean, you guess?" Maddy asked, her lips forming a soft pout. "I shouldn't be near him, and he shouldn't be near me."

Piper nodded. "I know."

"Then it's good."

"Okay," Piper said.

"Damn right it's good," Princess chimed in. "That boy should have been kicked out of school."

"They can't do that," Maddy said. "Police said because I dropped the charges and all… something about liability and the law and everyone going to school and all that.

Whatever. It's all just stupid. But he's not here, and I pretty much don't ever have to see him now in school."

"I wish I could say the same," Princess said. "I see him a couple of times a day, and every time I do, I want to punch him. But did you hear?"

"Hear what?" Maddy asked.

"No elite team."

Maddy looked down. "Yep."

"Oh," Princess said. "I didn't know you already knew. So I guess because he was kicked off, he's got no elite team, his friends have all left—other than Dustin, and I don't know what's up with that boy, still talking to Jace and all. I mean… how could he? But did you see the way he looked today?"

Maddy shook her head. "I told you, I don't see him anymore. Usually not even in the hall."

"He looks like shit."

"Yeah?"

Princess wrinkled her nose. "Mmm-hmm."

Piper looked at Maddy, trying to decipher her expression, and failed to do so. Was it apathy? Pleasure? Contemplation?

After a time, Maddy spoke. "Whatever. I just don't care anymore."

"You're a better person than me," Princess remarked. "I'd be all over the police to do something."

Maddy's eyes narrowed. "I told you before, I don't want to talk about the police."

"I just—"

"No," Maddy said forcefully. "I swear, Princess… enough."

Princess replied with a dramatic flourish of her hands, but she dropped the subject.

The girls were quiet for a while, eating their lunches. Piper listened to the conversation two of the other girls were having beside her and closed her eyes when one of them giggled. When her eyes reopened, she swallowed the bite she had just chewed and said, "Maddy?"

"Pipes?"

"We need to talk."

"'Kay. About what?" Maddy asked.

"Everything that happened." Maddy opened her mouth to speak, but Piper cut her off before she could do so. "I know you don't want to talk about things anymore, but there's just… we need to. You and me. Alone. I care about you. I just… we need to talk."

Maddy looked at Piper with a blank expression and eventually said, "Okay."

"My house after school?"

"No," Maddy said. "Come home with me. My mom will take you home," Maddy said. "Or just stay over."

"I don't have any clothes," Piper argued. "Or a toothbrush."

"So?" Maddy said. "Borrow my clothes tomorrow. You've done it before."

"I know," Piper said. "But your clothes are too small. Just come to my house?"

"Fine," Maddy said. "Meet me at the flagpole after school?"

"Yeah," Piper said. "I'll meet you there."

"I want in," Princess said. "Why will you talk to Piper but you won't talk to me?"

Maddy shook her head. "Leave it, Princess."

"No," Princess said, clearly perturbed. "That's so not fair, Maddy."

"Pipes was the one that got me to go to the cops in the

first place," Maddy explained. "She knows a little bit more. No offense, Princess, but there's, like, only so much I can talk about this. It hurts when I do. Even with Pipes, I'm not sure I can talk a whole lot. We'll see. But try to understand, okay?"

Princess frowned. "It's hard to understand," she said. "I've been here for you this whole time, and we've been friends forever, all three of us."

"I know," Maddy said. "And I'll talk to you. Really, I will. But not right now. I still need to get past all this. In time, I'm sure I'll be ready to talk more."

Princess glared at Maddy then clenched her jaw before returning to her lunch. "It's a shit move, Mads."

"Ugh!" Maddy thumped a fist on the table. "This happened to *me*, Princess. Not you. Seriously… what the hell? Have some compassion, yeah?"

"I do!" Princess's tone matched Maddy's. "I'm trying to be here for you, but it's like you won't even let me. But you let Piper."

Maddy stood from the table. "Whatever." She hastily packed up her lunch, flung her leg over the bench, and stormed out of the cafeteria.

"Where's she going?" Princess asked Piper.

The few other girls at their table had ceased their chatter to follow Maddy with their eyes.

"I don't know," Piper said in a whisper.

"Sorry, Piper," Princess said. "Nothing against you. You know I love you. It's just… I don't get it."

Piper nodded. "I know."

Princess held Piper's gaze for a moment longer before popping a mini pretzel into her mouth and chewing.

"I got your progress report today," Brooke told her son when she arrived home from work the Friday before Christmas Day. Just over a month and a half had elapsed since Maddy's allegations.

"Okay." He dropped his backpack to the mudroom floor.

"Let's go sit down."

"We don't need to sit," Jace said without a smile. "I know what you're going to say."

"Why?" Brooke asked. "Why did you let your grades drop like this?"

"I've kinda had a lot on my mind," Jace replied. "Or didn't you know?"

"Yes," Brooke said, letting the retort pass. "But this? Jace, you're better than this. You've always been a good student, always. You're a smart kid, and you know, Jace— you know that you can't let your grades drop and have a chance of getting into the college of your choice."

"I lost that chance when I lost cross country."

"That isn't true," Brooke insisted. "Not at all. You've always had it in your head that you needed cross country to get into school, but that's a lie."

Jace eyed her.

"With your grades, Jace, a lot of schools will want you. Cross country was always just something you had a passion for, something that you wanted to pursue outside of high school, and I always thought it was great. But cross country isn't your answer. It never has been. And I know you're nervous about money, about how we'll pay for your schooling, but Jace, you need to understand that that's on me, not you. We can take out loans, you can get academic scholarships. Cross country isn't needed. It never was."

Jace made no reply.

"Jace, look at me. Thank you. Forget about cross country. I know you're hurt. I know you love it like nothing else. I know this. But your grades, Jace—your grades are what are going to get you into school. I can't say that enough. But if you let them continue to drop like they've done, I mean, you're failing math. Math. You've always been good at math. Why are you failing?"

Jace shrugged.

"Do you even care about this anymore?"

Jace shrugged.

Brooke felt her face flush with anger. "Don't do that to me," she said. "Don't lose your drive. Yes, something terrible has happened in your life, maybe a lot of terribles, but don't let it stop you." Brooke paused for a moment and scanned her son's face, his collarbone, his shoulders. "And it's not just your grades. You've lost weight. I can see it in you, your body and your face. You haven't wanted a haircut, and you haven't done laundry in a while. Sometimes, you... you smell."

Jace looked at her, his face devoid of expression.

Brooke's eyes began to well. "Please don't do this," she pleaded. "Please don't give up."

"Why not?" Jace asked. "I've got one friend. One. Nobody believes me, not even you. Dad doesn't give a shit and never will. He hasn't even made a trip up here to see me since... everything."

Brooke knew what her son meant. Since Maddy's allegations.

"He promised he would, but he doesn't care. Nobody cares. Why should I care?""I care," Brooke insisted vehemently. She clutched Jace's sleeve. "I care!"

"Bullshit," Jace said. He yanked his sleeve out of her

grasp and walked past her. Brooke reached out, grabbed his sleeve again, and pulled him toward her.

"Don't you leave," she said. "Don't! And don't you dare give up, Jace Weatherbee! Don't you dare! You have a future, you hear me? You do! A bright one. Just get these grades up. Try hard.

"Run. Run and then run some more. Run like you used to. Not because you're on a team. Not because you're breaking records and winning medals, but run because you love it. Run because it makes you feel good. Run because it makes you euphoric. Run to clear your mind. Jace, just run.

"It won't be like this forever. I promise you it won't. You'll graduate, and then you're out of that school. Hold onto Dustin. He's been a good friend through this all. Don't lose him.

"And as much as you don't believe me, I'm here for you, Jace. I promise. I'm here. No! Do not look away. Look at me. I promise you. I'm here!" She was crying now, the tears cascading down her cheeks and splashing against her chest.

Jace's lower lip quivered, and his eyes welled, emphasizing the blue of his irises. She felt him physically relax— just a little, yes, but she felt it, she saw it.

"I promise," she said again, her voice now just above a whisper. "It gets better. I've been through trauma," her voice croaked, and she held back a sob, pushing aside the fact that the son standing broken before her was the very son that had been accused of the exact same aggression that had altered her life forever, that had made her scared to walk alone at night for years. The fact of the matter was, this was her son.

Jace was her son.

And she loved him. She loved this boy with her entire being. She loved the boy that she had held in the palms of her hands after carrying him for nine months in her womb and the toddler who had cried to her when he had fallen, running into her open arms. She loved the little boy who had started running in their backyard, around and around in circles with his father, running from her in a game of chase. She loved the boy who had thrown himself whole-heartedly into a new school in a new town and had made friends and embraced the changes in his life. And she loved the teenager that Jace was now. Loved him to her core. She'd never fully understand what had happened that night with Maddy, but she'd have to be okay with that.

He was her son.

She swiped the tears from under her eyes and blinked away the bleariness. She looked up at Jace, reached a finger up, and brushed a tendril of greasy blond hair from his forehead. He let her.

Then Brooke lunged. She flung her arms around her son's back and pressed her cheek against his chest. She squeezed hard. She felt his body melt within her grasp. She felt him tremble. And then her son fell to the hard mudroom floor, Brooke's arms preventing him from injury. Together, they sat on the floor, mother and son. She wept. She wept for the past, and she wept for the present. She wept, too, for the unknown future, though she had to believe there was beauty waiting for her son there. Some-where. Sometime.

Jace's body convulsed as the tears poured forth. He grasped with his fingers, pinching Brooke's skin. She let him. He grasped some more, finding purchase, desperate and wanting. His mouth was open in an expression of agony, his sobs echoed throughout the room. His tears stained her sweater, and saliva dripped from his lips.

Brooke held him until her arms ached. She soothed

him, this son of hers. She brushed back his hair, wiped the tears from his cheeks. She kissed his forehead.

Jace's head dropped into his mother's lap, exhausted. His tears subsided, his eyes closed. And Brooke found herself emitting soothing, shushing sounds, just as she had done when her little boy had flung himself into her arms after a fall.

This boy who had masked his anger, masked how much it had hurt him when his father left. This boy who had held it in. This boy of hers whom she had seen decline both physically and emotionally for the past month and a half. He needed her.

And she was here.

For her son.

# Chapter 13

## *Maddy*

I've heard it said that you never forget your first time, and for me, that's seriously true. I met Jace when I was nine. I even remember the day. I remember that we walked down to the Weatherbees' house from our own, a short walk. I remember that it was fall time because the leaves in their backyard were so yellow and orange and... just so bright. I remember the way he looked, Jace. I remember that blond hair, so light that you almost had to squint your eyes when the sun hit it just right. It was kind of messy but, like, in a good way, and it hung over one eye, even back then. Sure, he got it cut plenty of times from then until now, but when it'd hit that eye—yeah, that's not something a girl can forget. Not even at nine.

I didn't have a crush on him then or anything. I was too young and not into boys that way. But even then, I knew there was something special about Jace Weatherbee. Even that first day. Even the next day when he came to my house with Piper and Princess and he fit right in, at just barely ten years old, knowing just what to say and when to say it. Jace wasn't your typical kid. I knew this. And that thought only got stronger as we grew older.

We were good friends for a long time, but then one day, it just kind of hit me. I swear… just like that.

Pipes had told me back in the eighth grade that she had a crush on him, and I was totally into that. I even tried to help her at the semiformal, telling Jace that he should dance with her and all, right? And I saw them dancing, but nothing came of it. Pipes is shy, I get that. But Jace isn't. And if he was interested, don't you think something would have happened? I sure do. But whatever. Pipes didn't really bring him up after that. Not much, anyway. And not to tell me that she still liked him, so I kinda just figured, well, that she didn't anymore.

Then, at the end of freshmen year, I remember I was talking to Jace like I always did, but then—*bam*! I don't know what happened, and I can't explain it, but now that I've had time to think about it, maybe it was always there, like, just lying dormant until the time was right? I don't know, but things changed for me that day. I looked at those eyes of his, so blue. And that hair that still fell down and the way he'd brush it away sometimes. And for the first time, I looked at his lips in a different way. Like, I wanted to kiss him.

I'd dated before Jace, sure. But nothing really came of any of those relationships. I kind of felt like they were practice for the real thing, and then I thought that maybe the real thing was Jace Weatherbee.

Boy, was I wrong!

I remember the day I asked him out. I swear, I even surprised myself. On the outside, I think I came across as really bold, but let me tell you: on the inside, I was crumbling up. What if he said no? What if he just wanted to stay friends, and then our friendship changed because I had gone and acted like a fool?

I mean, I get it. People at school definitely think of me as this confident girl who knows what she wants and goes for it. But I'm not. Not really. Pipes knows the most about me, and not even she really knows how I feel deep down inside. I don't know why I can't tell her, why I can't tell anyone. It's just how I feel. I've got this sort of persona, and I've fooled everybody, and they like me like that. They like that girl. So if I go ahead and show them the real me, the insecure me, will anyone like me then? I think people are drawn to others that have confidence. At least, I mean… don't you think that's true? So I fake it. I've always faked it. And I fake it well.

Things started out good with Jace and me. I remember when we went to the beach after I asked him out. We were with Pipes and Princess and the boyfriend Princess had at the time, a guy named Sean who didn't last long. Too bad. I liked Sean. But whatever. We were with them and with Dustin and Dustin's friend, Greg, who I saw flirting with Pipes. She was even blushing a little bit. It was so cute. And he kind of showed an interest in her after that, too, but Pipes is just too shy, like I said. So I don't think anything really happened with them.

We went out that night, me and Jace. Alone. Our first real date. And it was awesome. He kissed me. Did I tell you that? He sure did. And it was unlike any other kiss any other boy had ever given me. Maybe it's because it was Jace and I was, like, already comfortable with him? I don't know. All I know is the way I felt when he kissed me. Like I wanted to do it more and more and more and never stop.

Things were good for a while. We started seeing each other in early June, right before the end of freshman year.

And we saw a bunch of each other that summer. He worked, and he was busy, and I was busy too, but we always made time for each other. We just wanted to be together. At least, I know that I wanted to be with him. All the time. And I figured he wanted to be with me too.

But I think I was wrong.

I swear, I don't know what happened or when things went downhill with Jace and me, but there were a few times he told me I was too needy, that he needed his space to be with his friends and do his cross country and stuff. I thought I was giving him space, right? I mean, we had the summer when he hung out without me a lot, but he also hung out with his friends or just did his thing. And we had the beginning of school. But I didn't see him a lot at school. We sat together at lunch, but lunch is only half an hour. That's like, nothing. And then back to classes we went. And after school was cross country for him. So I wanted to hang out after practice, and at first, I thought he was into that, but then he just started, I don't know, pulling away? But not really. Ugh. I can't even explain it. We were still good. I swear. Just… maybe things weren't exactly the same.

But I still wanted to be with him. All the time. I held back because I knew he wanted his friend time, and I get that. Really, I do. I love being with my friends. But maybe I didn't hold back enough…

It hit me when the summer was almost over and we were ready to start sophomore year that I wanted to take the next step with Jace. Maybe I thought—I don't know—maybe I thought it would bring us closer? We had done a lot of stuff but hadn't gone that far together. I never had with anyone else, either. Jace did, so I knew he had the experience, and that kind of made me nervous. I mean, what if we had sex and then I wasn't any good and he could tell because he had already done it? What if he had these expectations and I didn't fill them like his other girlfriend did? But then I kept telling myself to calm down. He'd still be with his other girlfriend if everything was so good with the two of them, right? And he wasn't with her. He was with me.

He wanted to be with me.

I told him that I wanted to take that step right after me and Pipes talked, so right before school started. I don't know what he thought about it. Sometimes, he's hard to read. Sometimes, he doesn't talk so much about his feelings. You'd think he'd jump at it, right? I mean, I always thought boys wanted that. And all the times we'd fooled around, I could tell, you know? I could tell he was into me, into it. The night I told him we should have sex, he made me nervous with the way he was acting. But I couldn't get it out of my head. Like, that's just not something you forget about. I knew that I wanted my first time to be with Jace. I just knew it.

We were together one day in October. We were in my room. My mom and dad were out on some sort of date— they do that sometimes. I think like once a month or so. Mom says that it keeps their relationship alive, whatever that means. They always seem pretty alive to me. Because Mom and Dad were out and Michael was back in college, me and Jace were alone. We were kissing. Then his hand was on me, and then—

I stopped, pulled back. And I just couldn't hold it in anymore. I asked him why he didn't want to be with me, like, you know… Like *that*.

"What do you mean?" he asked me.

So I told him that I knew he didn't want to be with me because of the way he acted when I first brought it up. His face scrunched right up, and he looked at me with this weird expression, so I asked him again: why didn't he want to be with me, especially because I knew he had been with his last girlfriend that way.

He didn't say anything for a long time, and then he told me, real slow like, that things were different with me. He must have seen my hurt expression, because his voice sped up. He told me that things were different with me because he really liked me, that we had known each other for such a long time, and that other girlfriend he had, they didn't really know each other, not really. Not the way he knew me. He said if we took that step, then things changed even more and he just wanted to be careful. Then, he said something really weird, something like, "Because my mom…"

"What does your mom have to do with this?" I asked.

But he shut right up, like someone had smacked him in the face, which I just didn't get. He shook his head and ignored my question, saying instead that things would just be really different if we took that step, and he wanted to be sure that we did everything right. Because it was me. And him. Us together.

I thought I got it then, how he was feeling. I didn't think it was me that was holding him back, and it actually made me feel really good about myself and about us as a couple. But I still couldn't get it out of my head. So I brought it up again. And again.

I mean, we were alone a lot. We could always find the time to let things go further, right? At my house or at his house or on a date.

We fought a little bit. Usually over stupid things. But we'd always make up after, and things would go back to normal. And every couple fights, right? That's just normal.

But then it happened.

We were alone in my room that day. Early November this time. I will never forget it. How could I?

We had the house to ourselves.

We kissed first. Then his hands moved. Then my hands moved. Then... I knew. This was it.

I looked at Jace and he looked at me, his arms wrapped around my bare waist.

We were so close. And I was nervous. I swear I could feel my heart beating through my chest.

And that look in his eye. I can't even explain it.

I put my forehead against his. "I don't have anything. I didn't think..."

I didn't have to say anything else. He knew what I meant. "I do."

I could hardly think! I was shaking a little bit. But this was Jace, so I knew everything would be okay.

And then Jace smiled. This little smile, but it spread all the way to his eyes, like he was amused or something. And then he leaned in and kissed me again.

Things just kind of progressed from there. Lips, hands... I was lying down on my bed, my head on my pillow, and before I knew it, he was on top of me, looking down. My heart raced, my mind was in a hundred different places at one time.

I didn't say anything. I couldn't. No matter how much I had thought I was ready for this moment, I never could have known how I'd feel when it actually came. Never. I just looked at him. I don't think I could even blink, I was so nervous.

And then it happened. And he was moving. And it felt... not like I expected. It was different somehow. And I wasn't sure how to feel.

Until I did.

I didn't want to do this. Not yet. No matter how much I thought I did. I didn't want this. Not even with Jace. Maybe especially because it was Jace. Maybe he was right all this time and we should have waited longer? Or maybe…

I don't really know all of what I was thinking. I was just… it wasn't me there. I wanted to say something, really, I did. I wanted to tell him to stop, even if it was just for a moment, you know? Even if we started up again. I just needed to look at him. Really look at him. Make sure we were okay. Make sure we were really *us*.

But before I knew it, it was over, and Jace was lying next to me. I pulled my blanket up to cover my chest, something I had never been shy of with Jace before. But for some reason, I was now. I was shy all over. I didn't even feel like myself. I felt like someone else had taken over my body, and the feeling I had inside was… it wasn't right.

I turned my head away so he didn't notice my tears.

Jace didn't say anything. I rolled over and swiped at my eyes, trying not to let him see what I was doing. Then I sat up and looked at him, and it seemed like he was unhappy. No, maybe that's not the right word. Uncomfortable, then. Not the Jace I was used to, anyway. He touched my cheek. And he brushed my hair off my lip. I felt so much like this weighted stone that I couldn't even lift my finger to do that for myself! I'm not sure I even noticed it was there in the first place.

I don't remember much after that, really. My mind was going in so many crazy different directions. We got dressed, and we talked about stupid things. Things that didn't matter. Things that seemed so dumb after what we had just done. It was almost like… like we weren't ourselves together anymore. Like he didn't know what to say to me and I didn't know what to say to him.

And I didn't like it. Not one bit.

Eventually, he went home.

And I was alone.

With my thoughts. With my still-racing heart. And with an ache in a place I had never ached before.

When I went to bed that night, earlier than I usually did, even before my parents got home, I went to the bathroom and saw a few dots of blood on my underwear. And that did it for me. I sat on the edge of the bed and just cried and cried until I didn't think I had any tears left in me. I had hyped everything up in my head for what felt like such a long time, and things had been so, so different than I thought they'd be. And now, things were weird between me and Jace. And I felt weird, and we were weird, and the world was weird.

Jace texted me the next day and said he wanted to talk. I didn't go to school. I just couldn't. I wasn't feeling too good, and I just… I just needed to stay home. And when he texted, instead of being super happy like I always was when Jace wanted to get together, I was nervous. After what we had done the night before, what was he going to say? Now we had this huge thing looming above us all the time, right? Maybe if we talked about it, things would be better.

He came over after school. Mom was home. We went to my room, me wearing the sweatshirt he let me borrow at that football game that I promised to return but never did.

Jace looked all weird. Like he was uncomfortable again. He was fidgeting, and he kept running his fingers through his hair. He didn't hug or kiss me when he came into the house. We just went upstairs, all awkward-like.

And that's when it happened.

He broke up with me.

I had no clue what in the world he was babbling on

about, because that's what he was doing—babbling. Like, going on and on. I didn't hear or understand half of what he was saying, something like we weren't ready, and we shouldn't have done that, and things hadn't been going so good between us, and we should be friends instead, weren't we just such great friends? Maybe we should just be friends.

Friends.

Friends.

Friends.

I didn't say anything. I *couldn't* say anything. I was too shocked.

*Friends?*

Was he joking?

I swear… he had to be joking!

Right?

But no. It wasn't a joke. I cried, and he looked, well, weird. I don't have any other word for it. He lingered for a while and kept asking me if I was okay.

Was I okay? Hell no, I wasn't okay! What was he thinking?

Eventually, I think he just wanted to get as far away from me and the sobbing mess I was, because he walked downstairs and out the door, and that was that.

I locked myself in my room. I didn't tell my mom what happened. I couldn't. She'd look at me with that look she gets sometimes, and she'd definitely want to talk to Jace's mom. I know they're like, best friends or something. And that's the last thing I needed. So I kept everything from her then.

I tried texting Jace about an hour later, but he didn't write back. I texted again. And again. And again. Like, within minutes. Eventually, he texted back.

> Maddy I know ur hurt. sorry. for now, we
> need to b apart. we can talk more. plz
> understand.

Understand what? That you agreed to have sex with me and then dumped me the next day? That maybe you never really cared for me, not this entire time? That maybe you were telling me we shouldn't do anything just to get me to want to do it with you so you got what you wanted and then could push me aside. Manipulate me like that?

I didn't know what to think, but I went from a crying mess, hurt and sad and depressed, to outright anger. I was so, so angry at Jace for doing that to me! And then my mind went in a hundred different directions again. Did he love me? Did he even like me anymore? What had he been thinking the entire time? He had sex with that other girl. How had things ended with her? Did he dump her right afterward too? Did I not measure up? Had I done things wrong? What were things going to be like between us now? What about school? What about our friend group?

What had he done?

What had *I* done?

And then all I could think about was how I was feeling when we were having sex, how I had gone from wanting so badly to be with Jace to feeling uncomfortable. Shouldn't he have asked me, while we were in the middle of everything, if I was okay? Shouldn't he have felt that something was up with me, that I was scared, that I wanted to stop?

I don't know. And I get it, okay? I should have said something. I've had time to think by now, but you need to understand, I was so, so, SO mad. And hurt. So desperately hurt. And humiliated. And confused. Boy, was I confused.

And then the anger won out. I texted Pipes right after

Jace texted me and asked if she could come over because something happened and I really needed my best friend. Of course she got back to me right away and said okay. Leave it to Pipes. She's always been a great friend.

She was super worried when she saw me. My mom opened the door, and I just called to her from my bedroom to come up. My mom hadn't even seen me. I just texted her to ask if Pipes could come over. It was almost dinnertime, and I was scared to go down. When Pipes came in, I shut the door, and that was when I told her that me and Jace had… and she looked at me… and the look on her face—excitement? Shock? Disbelief? Curiosity?—sent me over the edge. I started to cry and her eyes went all wide and she asked me what was wrong.

What was wrong?

What *wasn't* wrong?

So I told her I was sorry I didn't tell her yesterday when it happened, but that it wasn't like I had thought it would be. I told her that we started, but that I wanted him to stop and he didn't, he just kept going and going, and then it was over, and, and… and I told her it hurt and it was all weird, and that he broke up with me… and that was when she just looked at me, like, with this expression on her face that I don't think I'll ever forget. And she asked me to say it all again, and when I did, her face was all scrunched up, and she looked hurt and confused, and then she asked me again, did I really want it to stop? I told her that yeah, I wanted him to stop. And then Pipes looked at me again, her face all sad, like she was going to cry, and she used the word "rape." Rape, because I had asked him to stop. But, like, a question. And I guess I just… oh my God! I just rolled with it. I was so caught up in the moment! I told her that yeah, I asked him to stop. Oh my God!

I thought it was just a little white lie at the time. Honestly, I did. Just a little white lie to my best friend to maybe make myself not feel so hurt, to lift some of the pain? I didn't think anything would come of it, but boy, was I wrong! Pipes jumped at me, I swear! She told me she couldn't believe that happened, and with Jace of all people. She was shocked. And she was angry. And I was still so hurt by everything, and she could see it in my face, I'm sure. So she probably thought I was being one hundred percent truthful. Faithful friend that she is. She thought Jace raped me!

See, Piper was the one that told me I needed to do something about it. At the very least, I needed to tell my mom. And then she scared the crap out of me. She told me that if I didn't tell my mom, then she would. I begged her not to. Begged. And I don't beg!

But she put her foot down. Pipes, the girl that is always so super shy, the girl that has been by my side for years and doesn't speak up in crowds, the girl that never shows a whole ton of emotion, that girl was gone in the blink of an eye. And I knew she'd do it too.

So after she left, I told my mom. I told her what I told Pipes. Mom was livid. All the good thoughts she had about Jace died in that very moment. I could see it on her face. She told me she was going to call the cops and press charges, and I cried and begged her not to. She said I was being ridiculous, and she talked to me, and her words, her words… She's just got this way about her. She convinced me. I swear, by the end of our conversation, through all the tears and heartache, I grew to believe that Jace might have actually raped me.

I know it's nuts now. I know what I did was wrong. But once that step was made, I couldn't go back. I didn't know

281

how to go back. I had accused Jace of raping me. The cops had become involved. What would happen if I told them I made it up? That things might not have happened *exactly* like I told them they did?

So I believed the lie. I know it's all messed up, that *I'm* messed up, but I believed the lie.

And then I saw Jace. I saw his face. His beautiful face. No longer the face of the boy I loved. I watched as his friends ditched him. I watched as girls shunned him in the hallway. I knew Michael stood up for me, drove from college and beat the crap out of my ex. My ex-friend. My ex-boyfriend.

I cried myself to sleep that night, knowing I was the cause of all his pain. But I didn't know what to do.

I was so scared.

Just so incredibly scared.

Of everything.

I dropped the charges. I had to. Mom was beside herself. She said she didn't understand. Didn't I want something to happen to Jace after what he had done to me?

Enough had happened to Jace. I couldn't take it anymore.

But I saw the way people looked at him, treated him. And I was petrified that if I told them all I had embellished the truth, they'd look at me that way instead. And "petrified" isn't even the right word. It's not strong enough.

I just wanted it all to go away. Everything. I wanted to run away. I wanted to hide.

But I couldn't show that face to the world, and instead of just feeling super bad—and I did feel bad, I really did—I also felt angry. Angry about it all. Angry that we had done that in the first place. Angry that he didn't stop, even though I didn't say anything, which is stupid, I know. How was he supposed to know if I didn't speak up, right? I get it. But that's not where my mind was at the time.

Piper saw my journal. I'm so glad I hadn't written much at that time, but there was enough there for her to know that I wasn't telling the whole truth. I'm not sure how much she read, but I think she could tell that I didn't speak up. Maybe she knew or at least guessed that I didn't actually tell him to stop, not with words or with actions. And because of that, I think she was left to question what really went on. Maybe she imagined other scenarios. I don't know. I think she still believed that Jace had hurt me.

But I wasn't about to admit my lie to her. No way! Not even when she told me we needed to talk that day in school, almost two weeks after the night me and Jace were together, the night that started all this. I went to her house, but I couldn't tell her the whole truth. I just couldn't. What would she think of me? What would happen? But she looked at me differently then. Pipes just… I was pretty sure she knew.

I had let everything go so far.

Too far!

But Pipes is Pipes. She's a good person. I could tell she was struggling with what to do. But she's always been a loyal friend. And because she wasn't one hundred percent sure of all that went on, well…

We went back to school after Christmas break, and I saw her talking to Jace in the parking lot. I still didn't see Jace during the school day, he wasn't supposed to be near me at all.

After that, everything changed.

Pipes still hangs out with me, but things are different, and we don't hang out a lot. We don't talk like we used to. She's back to hanging with Dustin and Jace, and I see some other kids with them too. I'm glad. Really, I am. But I'm also conflicted. And hurt. And still confused. I'm sad, and I'm… ashamed.

I hate that things aren't the same with me and Pipes. Sometimes… sometimes, I see the way she looks at me, and I wonder what she's thinking. Like, maybe she's thinking I'm this terrible person. And she'd have a right to think that. I know this now. Most days, even I think I'm a monster. I think I've known it all along but was just too… I just wasn't all there. In my head.

I miss my best friend.

It's February now. Jace looks a little better. For a time there, I thought he just looked sick, like gaunt, really. Like he had these circles around his eyes, and his hair was gross, and he just… he wasn't Jace. He wasn't taking care of himself. And I felt guilty. Truly, I did. This is all because of me.

It's all because of me.

I know that now.

But how do I turn back time? How do I reverse what I've done?

I think I'm gonna tell. I think I'll tell Mom what really happened. She'll be pissed beyond belief, but I have to tell, don't I?

I don't know…

I just don't know.

I don't know what to do.

I know what I *should* do. But I'm so scared.

I'm just so, so scared.

Jace, I'm sorry.

I'm so sorry.

Please forgive me.

Please, please forgive me…

I picked up one of our kitchen knives last night, the big one that mom only uses when she's cutting up a full turkey or something. I held it in my hands. I ran my finger down the edge of the blade, almost like I was teasing with it. I let my finger slip and felt mesmerized as the blood dribbled onto the knife, the red so stark against the silver of the blade. It hurt. But I almost didn't mind. It was kind of like I welcomed it, this distraction.

Then I moved the tip of the blade to my chest, then slowly, slowly, I moved it to my chin, my lips, then held it against my neck.

Nobody saw me.

I've gotten good at hiding.

I think I've been good at hiding my entire life.

Sometimes, I think… I think that maybe it would be better if…

No. I won't go there.

I can't go there.

I just feel so much guilt.

I feel so much… accountability.

And even with all those feelings inside of me, I'm still scared to death to tell the truth.

And what does that say about me?

What kind of person am I?

Jace, I'm sorry.

I'm sorry.

I'm so, so sorry.

Please forgive me.

Please.

Please.

Please…

# Thank You

I am thrilled that you have chosen to read *The Marks You Made*. With so many books out there, I am truly honored that you have selected one of mine. My sincerest thanks to you!

I do hope this novel has touched you. If so, then I have done my job as an author. Please consider reviewing this book on the social media platform of your choice. Each and every review made is appreciated immensely and helps get *The Marks You Made* into the hands of new readers.

# About the Author

An author of both adult and children's fiction, Amy Fillion graduated from the University of New Hampshire with a degree in psychology. She worked in the field of early intervention before making the decision to leave and stay home with her growing children. Amy has an insatiable appetite for reading, and you can easily find her juggling between three books at any given time (paperback, ebook, audiobook.) When she's not reading or writing, she loves to walk and cycle outdoors. She lives in New Hampshire with her husband, three boys, one rescue dog (best office companion ever!), and two crazy rescue cats.

Never miss a book release or important news! Sign up here to stay informed and get a free copy of Amy's short story *Hold On* : http://eepurl.com/gPCU1X